# *Highland Fling*

'Charlotte,' whispered Andrew Alexander. 'If I were to place the Highland Ruby around your neck right now, I could have you stripping naked in front of this fire. I could have you, legs apart, begging to claw my trousers off and suck my cock.'

'Stop it!' cried Charlotte. 'I don't have to listen to this filth. I'm a writer, Mr Alexander, not a whore you can talk to like this to get your kicks.' But, inside, his words had inflamed her. He was devastatingly attractive – even though he had no idea of how to behave at an interview.

# Highland Fling

## JANE JUSTINE

BLACK
*lace*

Black Lace novels are sexual fantasies.
In real life, make sure you practise safe sex.

First published in 2001 by
Black Lace
Thames Wharf Studios
Rainville Road, London W6 9HT

Reprinted 2001

The right of Jane Justine to be identified as the Author
of this Work has been asserted by her in accordance
with the Copyright, Designs and Patents Act 1988.

Typeset by SetSystems Ltd, Saffron Walden, Essex
Printed and bound by Mackays of Chatham PLC

ISBN 0 352 33616 1

# Chapter One

$T$he hefty leather-bound tome, *Scottish Heirlooms and Antiquities*, lay strewn on the carpet. It was still open at the page Charlotte Harvey had been looking at before Paul had wandered in from the bathroom to stand before her trouserless, waggling his cock in front of her nose and telling her to get her knickers off.

'I'm reading.' Charlotte had ignored him. She was fascinated by the faded old picture of the ancient pendant and its legend which she'd been researching.

'You're always reading. Get your knickers off, girl and bend over.'

'In a minute,' she had murmured, intrigued by the folklore surrounding the pendant – or Highland Ruby as it was known. It had captured her imagination more than any other antique she'd had to research in her four years as subeditor of the glossy magazine, *Antiques and Legends*.

Paul wasn't prepared to wait a minute, however. He got down on his knees, lifted Charlotte's legs up over her head, reached under her bottom and pulled her panties down. With them still round her ankles, he placed her lace-shackled feet around his neck and buried his face into her warm silken pussy.

1

*Scottish Heirlooms and Antiquities* had slid to the floor, still open at the page showing the Highland Ruby while Paul's tongue got to work on Charlotte's clit.

'Paul, you're not fair!' Charlotte moaned, arching her back and parting her thighs as far as she could without her pants ripping. 'You know I've got to write about this pendant.'

He tapped her outer thigh with his fingers, which Charlotte took as an indication to stop complaining. She gave in, and her head lolled back, her long auburn hair spreading over the sofa cushions like a dark-red halo. Paul was right, she told herself, as his warm tongue lapped eagerly between her splayed legs. Plenty of time to learn about the Highland Ruby. Tomorrow she was off to the Outer Hebrides to meet the pendant's owner, Andrew Alexander – and hopefully to get to the bottom of the pendant's supposed mysterious qualities. Although legends were legends and it was probably nothing but a lot of superstitious nonsense. Yet Charlotte couldn't quite ignore the tingle of excitement that raced through her at the thought that the legend might be true.

Her excitement mingled with the sensations being aroused deep within her at that moment. Paul had the knack of knowing just the right spot to concentrate on, and he licked and nibbled mercilessly at the hard nub of her clit, sending thoughts of some cobweb-strewn Scotsman and his magical pendant sailing out the window.

Paul inched forward, so that Charlotte's knees were almost on her shoulders and her thighs were spread wide open for him. He looked up briefly from her neatly trimmed triangle of auburn pubic hair and growled at her, his face glistening from her juices. Then he buried himself into her again, his tongue lapping at the lips of her pussy before tracing a line down to her anus.

Charlotte's muscles contracted instantly as she felt the soft brush of his tongue on her tight little opening. 'Don't Paul. Not there.'

'I won't go in,' he murmured against her flesh, his tongue nevertheless probing deeper.

Charlotte squirmed. Despite being with Paul for two years there was still this no-go area. Perhaps one of his psychologist colleagues could trace her inhibitions back to potty training or some such thing. But whatever caused the mental block, she just couldn't bring herself to think of her arsehole as an area of pleasure.

'Paul, please, don't . . .'

He moved back, lifting her legs from over his head, his face glistening and wet. He pulled her panties half off, leaving them dangling from one foot. Then, taking her hands, he raised her up from the settee, swopping places so he sat on the edge of the cushions, legs apart, his rampant cock red and shiny.

'Turn round, babe, on your knees.'

'Paul, I have to be up early. I've a train to catch.'

His voice was husky. 'This won't take long, believe me. Now turn around. I want to fuck you.'

Charlotte went down on her knees and shuffled backwards so that she was kneeling between his splayed legs. She felt his cock tickling the cheeks of her bottom, before he took himself in hand and rubbed himself up and down her crack. He stopped and held his cock against her.

'Paul, no! I don't like it there.'

'You've never tried it. It won't hurt, I promise.'

She was on the verge of scuttling away across the carpet. 'I don't care about it not hurting; I just don't fancy it.'

He clutched her hips, holding her and his voice softened. 'OK, babe, I won't. Here, this is where you like my dick, isn't it? Up your fanny.'

Charlotte moaned as he entered her. He was still sitting on the settee, it being just the right height for him to slide easily into her. His hands remained on her hips and he

3

rocked her back and forth while he stayed still, sliding her up and down his long hard length.

Through half-shut eyes, Charlotte glimpsed the open book and its faded picture of the Highland Ruby as she was moved back and forth, sliding up and down Paul's cock like a piston on a steam engine. She'd once watched an old traction engine's piston thumping in and out of a shaft at a steam rally and she'd got seriously damp between the legs.

Her thoughts switched back to the Highland Ruby – truth or fantasy? Myth and magic or a load of baloney? Her questions swayed in time with the sliding piston. Was it really possible that a necklace could have the power to rob women of their free will? That once the Highland Ruby was put around a woman's neck, she had no choice but to obey the man's every command?

Ha! She'd like to see someone telling her she *had* to be fucked in the arse. Magic necklace or no magic necklace. That was something she would *never* do in a million years.

Paul's movements quickened. His fingers bit into the flesh on her hips, then he slid off the settee on to his knees so that he could get more force behind each push of his pelvis. He began pumping into her hard, grunting slightly with each thrust.

Charlotte gasped, bracing her arms against the carpet to stop herself from sliding headfirst into the TV. The open book became a blur but even so – even with Paul banging away at her rear like a rampant bull – she couldn't stop her thoughts from switching back to the Highland Ruby. Tracking down its owner had been a nightmare. She had practically given up hope of Andrew Alexander ever replying to her letters when the note had arrived at the magazine offices. In bold black writing Andrew Alexander had invited Miss Charlotte Harvey to visit the following week if she so wished. She did wish!

4

In fact, she could hardly wait. And tomorrow was the day she was setting off.

She would miss this, though, she realised as Paul continued to fuck her and her arousal began to grow. She would miss Paul badly.

Paul stayed the night, like he often did, despite having his own flat not a ten-minute walk away, and they made love again before Charlotte left to catch her train. This time it was more loving, more romantic. Just a gentle merging of their bodies in the early light of dawn. Paul had kissed her tenderly afterwards, before they had both fallen asleep again, entwined in each other's arms.

The rush of morning and the knowledge that she had a train to catch came as a harsh reality. Racing around her flat, snatching gulps of strong coffee, Charlotte checked she had everything for her trip north. 'Let's see. Camera, film, batteries, notebooks, mobile. What else?'

Paul glanced up from his bowl of muesli. 'Have you any idea what this Andrew Alexander fellow is like?'

'Nope! Ah, Dictaphone. I'm bound to need this; you know what my shorthand is like,' Charlotte said, throwing it into her holdall. 'I reckon he must be still living in the Dark Ages, though. I couldn't reach him by phone, fax or email.'

'Not *the* Andrew Alexander then?'

'Who?'

'You must remember, about five years back. Andrew Alexander, the owner of The Candlelight restaurant chain was accused of causing the death of his new and very wealthy bride. It was in all the papers.'

'Mmm, I vaguely remember something,' Charlotte said, as she made a hasty attempt at her make-up. 'They'd only been married a couple of months. Suicide, wasn't it?'

'Misadventure was the official verdict, if I remember correctly,' Paul said as he sipped his coffee. 'She'd overdosed, but her family brought the police in because they thought her new husband had bumped her off to inherit all her wealth.'

'I doubt it's the same person. My Andrew Alexander sounds like a fusty old Scot as ancient as this relic I'm going to write about.' The sound of a horn interrupted her, and she grabbed her bags. 'Sounds like my taxi. Oh, Paul, I'm going to miss you.'

'Me too, darling,' Paul murmured and kissed her, his hands sliding inside her unbuttoned coat to caress her breasts. 'How long do you think you'll be gone?'

'No idea; a few days I expect. I'll call you,' Charlotte murmured, reluctant to leave him, yet eager to get going. 'Paul, I'm really going to miss you.'

'And I'll miss you – like crazy. Now go, you don't want to miss that train,' he ordered, pushing her towards the door. 'And don't worry about the flat. I'll lock up when I leave.'

'You're an angel,' Charlotte called as she dashed down the steps to the waiting black cab. She knew she wouldn't have to worry. Paul was utterly conscientious over security. The flat would be locked and bolted. The cooker double-checked that it was off, and the burglar alarm double-checked that it was on.

'Where to, miss?' the taxi driver asked as they pulled away.

'Euston station,' Charlotte said, giving Paul a final rueful wave before settling back into the cold leather of the seat. And as the car moved off, thoughts of Paul ebbed away and Charlotte turned her attention eagerly to the legend of the Highland Ruby.

Back at Charlotte's flat, Paul washed and dried the breakfast dishes. Dutifully he hung the clean mugs on the mug tree, stacked the bowls in the cupboard and placed the gleaming cutlery in the drawer.

He double-checked that the cooker was off and collected his overnight bag from the bedroom. Heading for the front door, he hesitated by the telephone. Better if he rang from here; there was never a moment's privacy at the college.

He knew the number by heart, and as he listened to the shrill tone on the other end of the line, he felt his arousal growing. The ringing went on and on. He knew it would ring at least a dozen times before it was answered, but that was half the fun. Desperate to get this arranged and having trouble getting past the first hurdle only made the need all the more urgent.

Eventually his persistence was rewarded. The woman on the end of the line was abrupt and businesslike. At the sound of her voice, Paul felt his erection strain against the zip of his trousers and he congratulated himself for not leaving the phonecall until he got to work.

'Dominique speaking.'

'Hello, Dominique. It's Paul here.' He heard the quiver in his voice, felt the surge of hot blood race to his loins. He was hardening, straining against the fabric of his trousers.

There was a moment's silence and he found himself holding his breath. Then huskily she murmured, 'Hello Paul, I was wondering when you'd call again. It's been two weeks; that's a very long time. I don't think I can let that go without punishing you for leaving it so long.'

Clutching the receiver in his left hand, Paul swiftly unzipped himself and eased out his penis. As Dominique checked her diary in between chastising him, Paul let his hand go to work. This was a freebie.

Dominique wasn't to know. God, what would she do to him if she realised he was wanking himself off while they arranged a time and date.

The thought made his fingers sticky.

*Modest maidens and virgins beware*
*Before accepting this stone so rare.*

*For he who placeth it on thy breast*
*Thy slaveth to him, his every request,*
*Tho' detestable or loathsome he may be*
*Thy will dissolves, thy belongeth to he.*

Charlotte knew the verse by heart now as the train sped northwards, covering mile upon mile of open countryside, passing through endless towns and cities.

Of course the legend couldn't possibly be true. As if by placing the Highland Ruby around a woman's neck she would become a sex slave to some man. It was ludicrous.

Ludicrous – but a great story. So long as she could get some good photos the whole feature should look brilliant when it was published. She only hoped Andrew Alexander knew about the legend and how it got its so-called powers. Of course he might not know anything. He could simply have picked the Ruby up from an antique shop and know nothing of its history. She would just have to wait and see.

She closed her eyes. The monotonous rhythm of the train's wheels along the track mesmerised her. The words from the old book echoed round and round in her head.

*Thy will dissolves, thy belongeth to he ... belongeth to he ...*

By the time Charlotte finally reached the port of Oban where she was to catch the ferry to the island, the air was cooling. The autumn sunshine was turning weak and a northerly chill had her buttoning her coat and turning up the collar.

Once aboard, the ferry began its laborious journey, stopping off at a number of the islands before heading towards her destination. She spent the hours reading, making notes and listing questions for Andrew Alexander regarding his precious gem. That, and sipping endless cups of coffee as the ferry bore on through the choppy sea.

Standing up on deck as she finally neared the end of her journey, she stared wearily down into the frothy grey water churned up by the relentless engines. The day seemed endless. What she longed for now was a hot shower and bed.

The twinkling of a light in the distance caught her eye, and she peered out through the blackness to the murky landmass looming into view. Gradually a few more lights shone out from along the island's rocky coastline and she heaved a sigh of relief that at last her journey was over.

As the droning ferry engines slowed and the boat chugged determinedly into the quay, she could see the outlines of a few cottages against a backcloth of black hills. There was little else. Gathering her luggage, Charlotte finally made her way a little unsteadily down the walkway and on to dry land. But her heart sank. It was nothing like the bustling docks of Dover or Calais. No rows of articulated lorries waiting to board, no streams of cars and passengers. Nothing except a handful of fishing boats, a spattering of cottages and a few street lights.

She felt cold and exhausted. Her need for a proper meal and a soft bed made her feel quite light-headed. But as she looked inland she began to wonder if she would even get a roof over her head that night.

Only three other people got off the ferry with her: a ferryman, who joked with his oilskinned workmates before stepping ashore, and an elderly couple, who disappeared almost instantly into the night. Charlotte was left to wander inland alone, realising horribly that her expectation of finding a taxi to take her to the pub she had booked into was fanciful thinking.

She stood a moment, trying to get her bearings. Along the sea front were a few ancient stone cottages that stood sturdily and defiantly, facing out to sea. But beyond them, only the pitch-blackness of a remote Scottish island.

'Hello, is there no one meeting you, lass?' came a broad Scottish voice. Charlotte swung round to find the boatman peering at her from beneath his woolly hat.

Feeling foolish for not having made better arrangements, she grimaced. 'I thought there would be a taxi service,' she said.

He chuckled and his weather-beaten face crinkled. 'A taxi service! Aye, well there's no' much call for taxis here. Where is it you're going then, hen? It's rare we get visitors.'

Trying hard not to dwell on the vulnerability of her situation, Charlotte explained: 'I have some business here on the island. I've booked a room at the Captain's Table, but to be honest, I haven't a clue how to get there. Do you know it?'

'Aye, I do, hen. I'm away there now,' he said, his eyes raking over her like she was the catch of the day. 'You'd better walk with me. You'll no' find yer way in the dark on yer own.'

Going off with strange men wasn't something she was accustomed to doing. However, under the circumstances she hadn't much choice. Hoping for the best, she smiled. 'Thank you. Is it far?'

'No,' a five-minute walk,' he answered. 'Here, let me carry them bags for ye.'

'Thank you,' Charlotte murmured, managing a smile as she fell into step beside him.

He ambled along, seeming in no hurry, which was just as well, as in the dark Charlotte had difficulty manoeuvring around the fishing pots that littered the cobbled quayside. Once or twice her feet became entangled with the netting draped over the low harbour wall and she had to stop to unravel herself.

'You're a London lass?' he remarked, casting her a sideways glance. 'What kind of business brings ye' here?'

'I write for an antiques magazine,' Charlotte told him as she stopped yet again to untangle her heel and flick away a strand of seaweed that stuck to her fingers. 'I'm researching a necklace owned by one of the islanders – Andrew Alexander. Do you know him?'

'Mr Alexander? Aye, I know him. Everyone knows everyone here,' he said, casting her a curious glance. 'You're a writer you say. A journalist?'

'A feature writer.'

'Is that no' the same thing?'

'Not in my case,' Charlotte smiled. 'I'll be writing a general interest feature on an antique pendant which he owns.'

'And he knows you're coming?' he asked doubtfully.

'Oh yes, I'm here on his invitation,' Charlotte assured him. 'Mind you, I had such a job contacting him. Talk about elusive!'

'Aye well, you're the press. Ye canna blame the man. Anyway, hen, here we are, the Captain's Table.'

Charlotte would liked to have questioned her companion further about Andrew Alexander, but the opportunity was gone. For the moment, however, she was just relieved that they hadn't had to wander out into the black abyss of countryside to reach the pub. The glow of light through the tiny pebble windows was a welcome sight. No doubt she would learn all about Mr Alexander in due course.

'Mind the step,' her companion said as he lifted the latch on the gnarled wooden door.

They stepped down into a narrow tiled foyer which led into a quaint bar with an uneven cobble-stoned floor and rough chunky chairs and tables. The room was cluttered with seafaring objects that were undoubtedly the real thing. Lobster pots, fishing nets, floats, old pictures, stuffed giant fish in ancient glass cases and, almost like stuffed prize specimens themselves, a dozen or so

11

men of varying ages who instantly stopped their chattering to turn and stare suspiciously at her.

Charlotte gave a nervous little smile. 'Good evening,' she murmured.

They were mostly dressed in polo-necked sweaters and old baggy trousers. One or two had seafaring white whiskers, and one was smoking a clay pipe which had Charlotte itching for her camera.

She knew she would have to bide her time, however. She was the newcomer. An intruder. Someone to be wary and suspicious of judging by the way they were staring at her. She guessed she would have to gain their trust before they would pose for her camera.

Not all of them were ancient mariners, however. There was one who looked barely in his twenties, with the most angelic of faces – smooth, clear skin, baby-blue eyes, tousled sandy hair, not to mention having shoulders like an ox and wearing denims that fitted like a second skin.

And another, although he was attractive in an older and wiser kind of way. In his early forties, hard and sinewy from a lifetime of working on the treacherous seas, Charlotte assumed, as she tried not to stare at them. Although *they* were staring. They were all staring, as if they hadn't seen a woman in a long, long time. The thought sent a sudden and unexpected tingling down her legs.

Her throat felt uncomfortably dry as her companion took her elbow and steered her towards the bar. A white-whiskered, stocky little man who was probably nowhere near the age he looked, jumped up from his bar stool and dusted it off with his woolly hat.

'Thank you,' Charlotte smiled, trying not to feel intimidated by their continued oggling as they eyed her up and down with a mixture of suspicion and lust.

'Och! Haven't ye all had an eyeful?' her companion admonished them all. 'Now get back to yer drinking and nattering while the young lady gets her breath. She's had a long journey and I daresay she's ready for a drink and a bite to eat. Where's Nancy?'

'I'm here,' came a broad Scottish female voice from a back room. 'Changing the barrel, again. Keeping you boys well oiled. Where you put it it is beyond me.'

Nancy emerged still complaining. She was a large-bosomy woman in her early forties, pretty in a scrubbed kind of way and with thick black hair that hung in soft waves around her rosy-cheeked face. With her twinkling blue eyes and generous smile, she looked, thought Charlotte, like everyone's favourite auntie.

'Ah, you'll be Miss Charlotte Harvey. We were expecting you,' said Nancy in her broad island accent. 'Your room's all ready and I daresay you could do with a nice hot meal. Did you have a good journey?'

'Exhausting! I'm absolutely whacked,' Charlotte exclaimed, smiling at the landlady. She was relieved to find she wasn't the only female in the vicinity.

Nancy came round to Charlotte's side of the bar. She was shorter than Charlotte, slightly plump, with a face that looked as if it had never seen a dab of make-up in its life and all the better for it. 'Let's be away to your room then. I'll bring your dinner up.' She called back over her shoulder. 'Kenneth, pet, see to the bar; I'll be back in a few minutes.'

Kenneth, Charlotte saw, was the hard, sinewy-looking one. His eyes, like all the others, seemed to be mentally undressing her as she followed Nancy through a door at the back of the bar and up a narrow flight of stairs.

Upstairs, Nancy showed her around. 'This is the bathroom – you'll have to share it with myself and Kenneth. We don't run to en suite, I'm afraid. You don't mind sharing do you?'

'No, not at all, that's fine,' Charlotte assured her, glancing round the tiny room with its white enamelled bath, sink and toilet. It was definitely basic, but spotless.

Charlotte ached to get under the shower and wash away the miles of dust and grime.

'And this is your bedroom. I hope you'll be comfortable.'

The bedroom was half the size of Charlotte's bedroom back home. Nevertheless the bed looked feathery soft and extremely welcoming. 'It's lovely,' Charlotte said graciously.

'Not what you're used to, I'll be bound,' Nancy chuckled pleasantly. 'But it's clean and there's some good home cooking on the menu. Is chicken stew all right for you? If you're one of those vegetarians, I'll take the chicken out.'

'No, leave it in, please,' Charlotte replied, trying not to laugh. 'A cup of tea would be nice, too.'

'Sugar?'

'No thanks.'

'Five minutes,' Nancy said and smiled. 'You get yourself settled.'

As the door closed behind her, Charlotte threw off her coat and collapsed on to the bed. Its softness engulfed her, and she had a sudden overwhelming longing for Paul. With a sigh she realised that she would have to wait. For the next few days, her love life was on hold.

The chicken casserole was as delicious as promised and satisfied Charlotte's appetite for food. The hot shower, however, served only to increase her need for her lover.

Standing beneath the hot stinging needles of water, she soaped herself luxuriously, her slippery hands paying extra attention to the area between her legs. The neat bush of auburn hair was soon lathered and dripping suds down her thighs. She lifted the spray nozzle down from its hook and let the water play directly on to her clit.

It was a delicious feeling and her lower belly began to ache with longing. Swiftly her desire for Paul became more of a craving. Parting her legs a little she adjusted

14

the spray to shoot upwards, its tiny jets tickling the lips of her pussy.

Closing her eyes she let the sensations grow, soaping herself generously, fingering herself, slowly, rubbing her mound and teasing herself stopping only when the water began to cool. Whatever form of power there was here, it certainly wasn't the never-ending supply of electricity she was used to. Reluctantly she turned off the spray and wrapped herself snugly into a huge soft bath-towel. Padding barefoot back to her room, she heard some of the locals bidding goodnight.

After drying her hair she snuggled down between the fleecy flannelette sheets. Instinctively her hands slid down between her thighs, where her skin was soft and warm and her pubes still slightly damp and tangled. She ran her fingertip lightly around her hard little nub before pressing the heel of her hand against her mound, rubbing the hard pelvic bone in just the right place for the feelings to grow. Her climax built up quickly and she came almost immediately. A long leisurely come which she revelled in, repeating the delicious self-administered pleasure three or four times more before she felt satisfied enough to curl into the foetal position and close her eyes.

Drifting off to sleep she thought of Paul, wishing he was beside her, tucked up under the blankets, holding her close, moulding himself into her. She sighed and turned over. In three or four days she would be back with him. And in the meantime there was the Highland Ruby to concentrate on.

Minutes later Charlotte was asleep. A deep, delicious, dreamless sleep.

# Chapter Two

$T$he sharp stinging pain across his taut naked buttocks made Paul writhe in a feeble attempt to escape. But he was tethered fast. Naked and spreadeagled, he was standing upright, legs parted, his ankles and wrists shackled by leather straps to the four corners of the steel framework in Dominique's candlelit apartment. Between his knees was a low black leather bench on to which tiny beads of sweat dropped down from his forehead.

Dominique looked striking with her long blonde hair cascading over her bare shoulders and her eyes shielded by a black leather mask. She was dressed in a black PVC basque edged in red lace. It pulled her waist into a tiny twenty-two inches and pushed her breasts up so that her nipples poked over the rim. She wore red lace crotchless panties, black stockings, suspenders and stilettos.

She paced the floor in front of Paul, slapping a leather-tasselled strap across her hand as she continued to admonish him for neglecting her.

Each time he answered back, no matter how politely, or how apologetically, she brought the leather strap down sharply across his buttocks.

'Silence!' she said curtly, returning to her pacing, this

time slapping the strap against her palm with her hands behind her back, a stance which caused her breasts to protrude even further, and Paul's mouth to go dry with longing.

God, how he wanted those hard little nipples in his mouth. He wanted to nibble and suck them, and squeeze his cock between her full breasts. But most of all he wanted his cock up her arse. Fucking her till she couldn't sit down. But that, he knew, would be a long time coming.

'You've been a very bad boy, Paul. You haven't called me in two weeks,' Dominique said with a warning glint in her eyes. She strutted back and forth, occasionally bending down directly in front of him to remove an imaginary speck of dust from the floor, giving him a full view of her pink lips through the slit in her panties.

'I'm sorry, Miss, I deserve to be punished.'

'Indeed you do,' she breathed, straddling the leather couch so that her face was inches from his. Her nipples brushed against his chest. 'Now I can tell by that look in your eye that you're wanting to do some very naughty things to me. Am I right?'

'I do. I don't deserve it but . . .'

Her heavily mascara-ed eyes widened. 'You admit it? The nerve of the man! That deserves another slap.'

As she walked around to his rear, Paul clenched his buttocks, his cock twitching in anticipation for the moment the leather strap would came down hard across his backside. He wasn't disappointed but it wasn't the strap this time, but a slender cane.

'Did that hurt?' Dominique murmured, her voice softening as she gently stroked the faint red mark the cane had left across his flesh.

'Yes,' he lied. It wasn't pain. It was pleasure. Wonderful pleasure. Pleasure in a form that Charlotte could never possibly understand.

'And this?'

17

Another slap, but this time it was her hand that administered a loud smack. His cock hardened. He needed Dominique now. Since arriving, he hadn't been allowed to touch her. And now he wanted her. Every inch of her.

'Miss, please . . .'

'Please, what?' she teased, standing directly behind him. And although he twisted and turned, he couldn't quite make out what she was doing.

'Miss?'

'I know, I know,' she crooned, her cool hands stroking his buttocks. 'Miss knows what Paul wants.'

Her hand moved down between the cheeks of his bottom, her finger tickling his anus. Paul's body reacted instantly, his muscles contracting, sucking the tip of her finger inside him. She continued her stroking, moving around the rim in tiny circles.

Then, stroking lower, her hand slid between his legs and cupped his balls, tickling them, gently squeezing and pulling them before concentrating on his long angry cock, stroking her fingers up and down its silky length.

'Are you aching for me, sweetie?' she breathed.

'God, yes, Dominique, you're driving me wild.'

'What do you want to do to me, darling?'

Tiny beads of perspiration were beginning to fall like rain on to the leather bench. 'Untie me and I'll show you.'

'I think you should tell me. Tell me or I shall have to slap your bottom again.'

He'd had enough of that now. What he wanted was to bend *her* over this contraption and give her arse a good seeing to.

'I want to fuck your arse. Untie me, will you, before I burst.'

'Now, now, Paul. I don't take kindly to being spoken to in that tone of voice. That really does deserve some severe punishment.' She stood right behind him so he couldn't see her properly but he heard her unscrewing a jar. He smelled its perfume. A mild flowery scent.

'That smells nice,' he murmured.

Her finger was at his anus once more. This time it felt cold and soft after being smothered with the perfumed cream. His muscles contracted as her creamed finger slid up inside him.

The sensation was electric and he threw back his head and groaned. A second finger followed her first, sliding in and out, causing the most acute sensations.

Then she pulled out.

'Don't stop. Please don't stop. That was wonderful.'

'Let's see how you like this then, sweetie,' Dominique said huskily, moving to his side so that he could see.

She had strapped on a dildo. It was thick and pink, with imitation swollen veins. Paul's eyes almost popped. 'Dominique, no! You've got to be joking.'

She smiled wickedly as she manoeuvred herself directly behind him. 'Paul, sweetie, you've been a very naughty boy. I'm going to have to punish you.'

'Yes, but maybe not like this . . .' But he was breathing fast and his cock was rock-hard with anticipation. He nodded.

She stood up on the bench behind him and delicately parted his buttocks to position the bulbous tip of the dildo into his tight little opening, at the same time lathering it with some type of lubricant. Very slowly she began moving her hips backwards and forwards. The hard rubber cock eased its way further inside him.

The pain at first was excruciating. Burning. And then as his muscles relaxed Paul began moving in time with her, pushing back against her thrusts, feeling the imitation cock filling him. The pain quickly became pleasure – such exquisite pleasure.

As Dominique continued fucking him, her hands reached around to his front. Her right hand closed around his erection and slid up and down its length in time with her pelvic thrusts. Her left hand cradled his balls, occasionally giving them a gentle squeeze.

Paul was on the verge of coming. 'Oh yes, babe. Yes . . .'

Cruelly, Dominique released him, withdrawing the dildo from his arse. Stepping down off the bench, she slipped the contraption down over her hips and stepped out of it. 'Did you like that, sweetie?'

Paul's cheeks were flushed and there was a glazed look in his eyes. He still wanted to come, but he needed her to touch him, or to be able to wank himself off, which was impossible, seeing as he was still shackled to this contraption.

'Well? Did you like being fucked up the bum? I'm sure you've done it enough times to your girlfriends, now you know how it feels yourself.'

He wasn't quite sure what to answer. The truth was he'd loved it. It wasn't the first time, but it had certainly been a long while since he'd had it that way. Years ago he'd gone out with a girl who was up for anything and she'd used her vibrator on him. But as for Charlotte, she'd run a mile if he was to even suggest it.

Dominique was still waiting for his answer and the last thing he wanted was to let her know how much he'd enjoyed it in case she withheld from doing it again just to punish him. Slapping on a sad little-boy-lost look, he murmured, 'I suppose I deserved it.'

Her red lips pouted as she looked down at his cock sticking out like a baseball bat. 'And just look at him. He wants my pussy, doesn't he, sweetie? Is that what you want now, Paul, a good hard fuck?'

'Oh yes. God, yes. Untie me, Dominique.'

The glint in her eyes was wicked. 'You do like giving me orders don't you, sweetie? And you know I don't like being told what to do. I might have to punish you again, and just when I was starting to think that I might be nice to you.'

She was so close he could almost taste her. He wriggled as near as his tethers would allow and tilted his pelvis so his cock pressed hard against the shiny fabric of her basque.

'Naughty,' she warned, tapping his erection with her fingers. Then, slowly she lowered herself on to the bench until she was sitting at eye level to his cock. She raised her eyes briefly and wickedly to his, before lowering her head and taking him fully into her mouth.

Paul's eyes squeezed shut as the sensations rocketed through him. Her mouth was hot and moist, her tongue like a snake coiling around his hard penis, licking, sucking, drawing him further and further down her throat. Her fingers scratched at his balls, so, so softly.

She was an expert. She knew just how far she could take him. Knew just when he was close to coming and so pulled away in time. Smiling seductively, she got to her feet and untied the straps holding him, his feet first. This was a shame because if she'd released his hands first he would have fingered her good and hard as she bent down to undo his feet.

But she was in charge, and he loved it. It drove him wild. Mostly he liked to be in the driving seat, but occasionally, every couple of weeks or so, he had the urge to be dominated, humiliated even. And now, as she took his hand, he allowed her to lead him like a lamb over to the bed. As he went to follow her on to it, she pushed against his chest.

'Oh no, you're not fucking me yet, sweetie. Oh don't look so disappointed, it will happen, I promise. Only first you've got work to do.'

It was obvious a moment later what this work was. Dominique crawled on to the silky red sheets and kneeled on hands and knees with her bottom upturned towards him.

'Lick me, Paul,' she murmured. 'Lick me and finger me, and if you do it nicely enough I might let you fuck me.'

Paul dropped to his knees at the end of the bed and

pulled the slit in her panties wider to reveal her shaven pussy and anus. Eagerly he began licking, his tongue softly probing, his fingers stroking. His hand curled around to the front of her mound, slipping down the front of her panties, loving the feel of her smooth pubeless skin.

'Mmm, yes that's nice,' Dominique murmured. 'So nice.' She curled around on the bed to face him. 'I think maybe you deserve your little reward now.'

Paul moved eagerly, wanting to get between her legs and get his cock right up her, but she pushed against his chest again then wagged her finger. 'Not on the bed, sweetie. It's a hard chair for you.'

The chair was in the corner, hard-backed with a thin leather cushion. It was cold against his bottom. He sat, at her instructions, his hard cock erect, red and glistening. Dominique slid out of her panties, giving him a full view of her beautiful shaven mound. Then she straddled him, spearing herself on to him, grinding down into his lap. Slowly she began to gyrate against him, satisfying herself, grinding hard. She came quickly and fiercely, dismounting in time to take his cock into her mouth and suck greedily.

He couldn't stop himself from coming and, with a cry, his hot come filled her mouth. As she swallowed, a few drops trickled from her lips.

Paul closed his eyes. Guiltily, he thought of Charlotte.

Charlotte wasn't sure what woke her. A cry, or voices. But she awoke suddenly, for a second unable to work out where she was. Then she remembered and switched on the bedside lamp to glance at her watch. It was almost three in the morning.

As she turned over, she heard something again. A loud moan, then voices, softly spoken, coming from downstairs in the bar.

She tried to ignore the noise and get back to sleep.

Licensing hours were probably unheard of around here. But sleep refused to come and she lay staring up at the ceiling, thoughts of Paul filling her head. Eventually she realised there was no point lying awake thinking about him. She needed her sleep if she was to conduct a successful interview tomorrow with Andrew Alexander. Perhaps a warm drink would help.

Pulling on her dressing gown, Charlotte tiptoed out on to the landing intending to take a peep in at the bar. If it were just Nancy and her partner, she would have no qualms about asking for a nightcap. If the regulars were still drinking, however, she would make a hasty retreat.

She crept downstairs and inched the bar door open a fraction. For a second she couldn't quite make out what was going on, and then she couldn't believe her eyes. Nancy was there, but not alone. There were two men with her. Three, if you counted the figure peeping around the far door, watching unseen by Nancy and her friends.

But Charlotte's attention wasn't on the voyeur, not then. All she could do was stare at the collection of semi-naked people in the centre of the room. Nancy was lying across a bar table, her blouse hung undone, her bra rucked up around her neck, her skirt pushed up around her waist and her knickers dangling from one ankle. Her large breasts dangled over the front end of the table and her plump bare bottom shone up at the dingy ceiling.

The moans came intermittently – not just from Nancy, but from the two men. Charlotte instantly felt a hot tingling between her legs as she took in the scene.

Kenneth stood at Nancy's head, fondling her large breasts, his eyelids fluttering. His flies were undone and his thick red cock was being grasped firmly by Nancy. Her hand slid up and down its short but stout length in a jerky rhythm – understandable, considering what else was going on.

At Nancy's rear stood the young angelic-looking creature Charlotte had seen earlier; he was hardly behaving angelically now, however. His trousers were around his ankles, his beautiful tight, firm buttocks on view for the world to see as he pumped away at Nancy with such vigour that Charlotte felt herself becoming decidedly moist and aching.

Unable to drag herself away, she remained, peeping around the door. She was no better, she told herself, than the red-bearded voyeur peeping from the far door. She just couldn't believe her eyes. How could a respectable woman like Nancy subject herself to having two men at once? Not only that, they were being observed. She bit her lip, not sure whether to warn them or not.

In the end she did nothing, except to remain watching, out of sight, as the threesome continued their fun. Kenneth now had his cock in Nancy's mouth and stood there rigid, gripping her shoulders, his eyes still tightly shut. He soon began jerking spasmodically as he pumped his load down her throat.

At Nancy's rear, the spunky hunk continued thrusting back and forth into her with increased vigour. His buttock muscles clenched and relaxed and his skin shone with a thin layer of perspiration as he continued to give Nancy what Charlotte would have loved herself – if she was the sort to be unfaithful to her boyfriend.

Her attention switched back to the voyeur. He was a hugely built man, not in height but in girth, with wiry red hair and a bushy red beard. He was wearing the traditional kilt, and a moment later she was left in no doubt as to what Scotsmen wore under them. He lifted it up and took himself in hand.

His enormous cock stuck out from beneath the green and red tartan like a truncheon, the heavy fabric draped over it, and two massive testicles hung down from a forest of red pubic hair. The bulbous shiny red head bobbed expectantly as he worked his thick hand up and down.

Charlotte gasped. Nancy and friends must surely realise they were being watched; he was hardly being particularly secretive. She could hear his grunts from here!

She didn't wait to see more. For all she knew she could be next. Turning away, she ran swiftly and silently back upstairs. Throwing herself down on to her bed she stared wide-eyed up at the ceiling. So this was what went on after the fishing boats were home for the night. This was how the men spent the cold lonely nights. Well it certainly beat monopoly!

She couldn't wait to tell Paul.

Charlotte awoke the next morning to find Nancy bending over her. Expecting to see her voluptuous naked breasts dangling before her eyes, Charlotte was infinitely relieved to see the woman was demurely dressed in a sweater and skirt and not a telltale glow to her cheeks at all.

'Good morning. Did you sleep well, lass?' Nancy greeted her warmly, placing a breakfast tray on her bedside table.

'Like a log,' Charlotte lied, not about to embarrass her hostess by admitting she'd seen her enjoying the lusty attentions of two of the local clientele – plus voyeur.

'There's porridge, bacon and eggs, and a nice pot of tea. That'll set you up for the morning.'

'Wonderful,' murmured Charlotte, dying to know if last night was a regular occurrence or a one-off drunken orgy.

'I believe you're away to see Mr Alexander today,' Nancy remarked, drawing back the curtains to allow the bright autumn sunlight to flood in.

'Yes, I am. I wonder if you could give me directions to his house?'

'Aye, he lives at Stonemoor House, way across the island. But you've no' to worry. I've asked young Jamie to take you and bring you back. You'll no' find it on your own.'

'Are you sure? Only I've no idea how long I'll be.'

'Och! He'll not mind waiting on a pretty lass like yourself.'

'That's very kind of you,' said Charlotte, sipping her tea. 'Who's Jamie, by the way?'

'He's just one of the young fishermen. He was in here last evening; perhaps you didn't notice him. Och, he's a darling. A real sweetheart. Tall laddy, sandy hair, bonny face.'

'Oh yes, I think I do remember him,' Charlotte murmured, picturing him, trousers around his ankles, buttocks clenched, giving Nancy a right good shagging.

The thought caused a fierce burning between her legs and Charlotte found herself writhing under the bedclothes, somehow resisting the urge to quell the tingling feelings with the heel of her hand. 'Er, what time is he coming?' she asked, then almost cursed her choice of words.

'He's downstairs now, enjoying a nice bit of breakfast. Big lads like Jamie need to keep their strength up.'

'I'm sure they do,' Charlotte remarked, wondering enviously whether Nancy had enjoyed another session with young Jamie while the bacon was sizzling.

Charlotte went downstairs somewhat trepidously, making sure her feet rattled the staircase, and that her cough was loud enough to allow anyone to uncouple, should they have to.

In fact, she found Nancy peeling potatoes and Jamie drinking a mug of tea and doing a crossword.

He looked up as she entered and speared her with the most innocent baby-blue eyes. 'Hello, Charlotte, ma name's Jamie.' He got to his feet and shook her hand. 'Did ye sleep well?'

'Yes, thank you,' she replied, trying not to picture him in the throws of passion. 'It's very kind of you to take me to Mr Alexander's.'

26

'Och! It's my pleasure,' he smiled, releasing her hand and folding his newspaper. 'I'm ready when you are.'

Charlotte suddenly realised to her dismay that she hadn't given the Highland Ruby much thought since arriving here. Rather her mind had been dwelling somewhat on sexual matters.

She made a determined effort to concentrate on the job in hand. 'We'll go now then, shall we?'

'Aye, grand,' Jamie said, heading for the door. 'Bye, Nancy.'

'Bye now, be good,' Nancy called after them.

Dressed in her beige slacks, thick sweater and ankle boots, Charlotte went out into the cool morning sunshine. The air smelled wonderfully fresh and she threw back her head and breathed deeply. In daylight, the island no longer looked a black void of desolation. It was rich in colour. Greens of every shade, and purple, pink and lilac heather and thistles, while in the distance the hilly terrain was swathed in white cloud.

'Is this your first visit to these islands?' Jamie asked, setting off inland with long loping strides.

'It is, yes. I never even knew this place existed.'

'It's a grand wee island. Folk here just get on with their lives, no' bothered by anyone else.'

'You do your own thing,' Charlotte mused, smiling to herself. They certainly did that all right. 'How far is it to Andrew Alexander's house?'

'It'll take us a good thirty minutes,' he said, casting a long look at Charlotte suddenly. 'I can get there by myself in fifteen. Here, let me carry your bag. It's too heavy for a wee lassy like you.'

Charlotte had never been described as a 'wee lassy' before. At five feet eight she was one of the tallest women in her office. Nevertheless she willingly handed over her bag. Jamie swung it effortlessly over one broad shoulder and strode on. She smiled to herself. Compared to him, she supposed she was *wee*.

The road to Andrew Alexander's place was simply a narrow footpath that meandered inland. The only other living souls they came into contact with were sheep. Lots of bedraggled-looking sheep with thick matted, woolly coats and startled, suspicious expressions. And cattle. Or rather one steer. An enormous straggly long-haired beast with horns belonging to something from the wild west. It stood, a little way off, staring at them.

Charlotte stopped dead in her tracks. 'Do you see what I see?'

'Och, he's just a wee lamb. Come on, lass, he'll no' bother us.'

Charlotte dug in her heels. 'Sorry Jamie, I can't. I'm not going anywhere near that *thing*.'

'If it's the big horns that bother ye, you'll have to get used to that around here,' he remarked, chuckling to himself.

Ignoring the innuendo she stood her ground. 'No way! I don't like the look of him at all.'

'He'll move aside, don't ye bother yourself about him,' Jamie said, marching towards the beast.

'Are you mad?' Charlotte gasped, catching him up and cowering behind his back.

'You have to let them know you're not afraid.'

'But I'm terrified!' she exclaimed, peering at the cow from under Jamie's arm, although cow just didn't seem an appropriate description for such a monster.

Jamie smiled at her. It was the most disarming smile. She would have to watch herself. 'Here, I'll keep ye safe,' he said, tucking her into his broad back and holding her close with one arm.

Charlotte slid her arms around his waist and buried her head between his shoulder blades. With the fresh male scent of him, and the feel of soft wool against her cheeks, she shuffled along behind him, quite enjoying the close proximity of such a gorgeous-looking companion.

'Hello there, wee fella,' he called out as they

approached the steer and Charlotte suddenly realised his idea of wee wasn't quite the same as hers.

The animal took a step backwards, lowering its head, making Charlotte wonder if it had relations in Spain.

'Jamie, it's going to charge,' she cried, burying her head deeper into the softness of his sweater and squeezing her eyes tightly shut.

'How much?' he joked, as unperturbed he bent down and plucked a handful of grass, almost overbalancing her. 'There ye go, this is nice.' He held out his hand. 'Charlotte, look, he's eating from ma hand.'

She peered out from the safety of Jamie's back. The steer was indeed slobbering all over his outstretched hand. Close too, it was quite a magnificent-looking animal. A dense brown coat, long and tangled through the wild elements, and a huge black snout and the most endearing long-lashed brown eyes. It would make a fantastic picture.

Her fear evaporated. 'Jamie, quick, give me my bag.'

She took out her camera, focused on the animal and photographed it, positive she could use the photo in the article, seeing as the Highland Ruby was located on a remote Scottish island. And this was a remote Scottish cow.

Jamie stood back, watching her work. Every now and then she cast him a little grin, pleased with herself at overcoming her fear. The animal stood there quite unperturbed, not minding all the attention in the least. Eventually, however, it grew bored and plodded off to investigate some heather sprouting from a rock.

Delighted with herself, Charlotte turned her attention to Jamie. He was standing indolently by, thumbs tucked into the pockets of his jeans, one foot raised on a rock. His head was bent slightly to one side so that his hair fell across one blue eye. He looked irresistible.

Impishly, Charlotte then focused her camera on him

and clicked the shutter. He raised one eyebrow. 'You don't mind, do you?' she asked with a smile.

He shrugged, his bright eyes not wavering from her face. 'I've no' had my picture taken since I was a wee bairn. You'll have to give me a print to keep.'

'Yes, of course,' Charlotte agreed, adjusting the settings. 'I'll take some more then shall I? Then you'll have a choice.'

'Aye, help yourself, lass.'

She worked leisurely, photographing him from all different angles: straight on, then from on top of a rock looking down, and stooped down at his feet, shooting upwards.

As she crouched down at his feet, she couldn't help but admire the way his jeans moulded perfectly to his muscular thighs. Her gaze was drawn to the bulge to the right of his zip. The warm tingling sensation between her legs sprang up again.

He was a natural model. No inhibitions, no unnatural poses, no stilted smiles nor over the top sultriness. Plus, he had the most sexy, alluring eyes. Eyes which promised things she didn't dare to dwell on.

'Do ye want me to take ma top off?'

Charlotte felt suddenly like a porn photographer seducing some young thing with promises of fame if he would just take off his clothes. The thought made her giggle. 'You'll freeze!'

'Och no. I'm tough!' he said, peeling the sweater off without another word of argument.

'I can't disagree with that,' she agreed, looking appreciatively at the hard young body. There wasn't an ounce of fat, just hard muscle and sinew. Charlotte couldn't resist positioning him where she wanted him, enjoying the feel of his cool silky skin and hard body beneath her fingertips.

She took picture after picture, knowing that these photographs would never be offered for sale. These were hers – and Jamie's of course. But mostly for her. She had an urge. A naughty urge that wouldn't be silenced. 'You wouldn't mind undoing the belt and top button of your jeans, would you?'

He raised one eyebrow, but she managed not to flinch. Rather she felt the tingling between her legs become more acute as he did what she asked.

Charlotte viewed him through her lens, then took a step towards him. Daringly she gripped the flaps of his jeans and pulled them a little wider so that the zip moved down a few more notches and the top of his sandy-brown pubic hairs brushed against her fingertips.

His blue eyes took on a glazed look. Charlotte captured the mood on film, taking shot after shot. Suddenly he held up his hand, signalling for her to stop. For a second she thought she'd gone too far. He was just a young fisherman after all, not a model. But she couldn't have been more mistaken.

Standing facing her, he unzipped his jeans completely, pushed them down over his hips and stepped out of them.

His semi-erect penis bounced free from the confines of the denim, and stood proudly amid a nest of curly pubic hair. Charlotte almost dropped her camera.

Some professional, she thought, composing herself. There was nothing wrong with nudity, for heaven's sake. It was a basic artform. Artists had been painting the naked body since time immemorial.

She raised her camera again and continued photographing him, but her mouth and throat felt dry, while other parts of her anatomy were decidedly damp.

He, however, seemed completely unperturbed at posing nude, and gladly sat, lay, and stood in whatever way Charlotte suggested.

She took her photographs, her cheeks burning, trying her hardest not to dwell on Jamie's beautiful penis and his neat, pert balls. He was larger than Paul, even at this

31

stage, and she could well imagine how Nancy had felt last night with him fully aroused and fucking her hard as she bent over that table.

When the film automatically rewound in her camera, she wasn't sure whether to be relieved or not. 'That was the last one,' she murmured, removing the film and storing the camera away, avoiding his eyes as he stood closer to her – too close. So close that she could smell his freshly washed scent – as fresh as a sea breeze.

He was too gorgeous by far, and she turned away from him, making sure everything was neatly back in her camera case. 'You'd better get dressed Jamie. This breeze is chilly.'

'Are you sure that's what you want?' he murmured, sounding disappointed.

'Well, I've got enough pictures. I'd better save some film for my real work.' She smiled awkwardly then fixed her gaze far off towards the hills. Listening to the rustle of clothing as Jamie got dressed, she made herself concentrate on Paul. Dear, sweet, unselfish Paul. How could she even look at another man?

A moment later Jamie's hand on her shoulder made her jump. 'It's all right, you can look now. I'm dressed.'

She swallowed hard, avoiding his gaze. 'We'd better get on then. Is it much further to Andrew Alexander's place?'

'Another ten minutes' walk. Here, give me your bag again.'

They walked in silence. An awkward silence which she knew was all her fault. Eventually she couldn't stand it a moment longer. 'Jamie, I hope you didn't mind.'

'I'm flattered you wanted to take ma picture. When I get ma copies I'll be able to give one to ma girlfriend.'

'Your girlfriend!' Charlotte exclaimed. Not for one minute thinking there was a girlfriend on the scene. Particularly after last night – and just now. 'Won't she mind, knowing you've been posing nude for a female

32

photographer?' she asked, deciding not to venture the stupid question of wouldn't she mind you shagging Nancy last night?

'Well, nothing happened,' he remarked with a slight shrug. But it was an open-ended remark, and Charlotte was instantly reminded that there was still the long walk back to come.

Charlotte strode on, hoping and praying her willpower was up to it.

# Chapter Three

$A$t last Stonemoor House came into view. It lived up to its name. Bleak, barren, unfriendly. Not only that, there seemed to be a lonely, desolate aura about it. It seemed so isolated out here on the moors, miles from anywhere, exposed to all the elements. Who on earth would want to live such a solitary existence?

Charlotte shivered. Softly she asked, 'What's he like, Jamie?'

'Our Mr Alexander? Och, I'd say he's a bit of a mystery. Rumours say he came here to escape.'

'Escape?' Charlotte breathed. 'Escape from what?'

Jamie glanced down at her, his blue eyes piercing. 'Some say he murdered his wife.'

'Murdered his wife!' Charlotte exclaimed, shook rigid. So it was *that* Andrew Alexander.

Jamie chuckled and she wondered suddenly if he was just winding her up. 'Would ye like me to come in with ye?'

She gulped against the nervous dryness in her throat. 'He's not . . . unbalanced or anything is he?'

'That's not how he strikes me.'

Charlotte gazed at the house, so remote, so utterly

isolated. Yes, it looked like a place where someone could escape and hide away. A place where no one would think of looking.

*But murdering his wife!*

'Aren't the police after him?' she asked anxiously.

Jamie laughed. 'Och it's no' like that. Anyway, it's just rumour. You know how stories get about.' He looked steadily at her. 'You'll have to ask him yourself, then we can all read the truth in your magazine.'

'Yes, I'll do that,' Charlotte answered through gritted teeth, wondering how on earth she would pose that little question. Now tell me, Mr Alexander, is it true that you murdered your wife or am I mixing you up with another homicidal maniac? She pulled a face at Jamie. 'So what will you do now, Jamie? I don't know how long I'll be. It's not fair you should be hanging around for hours.'

He kicked idly at a clump of thistles. 'Away and do your wee interview. I'll wait here for ye. It's no bother.'

'Are you sure?' she fretted, reluctant to just leave him standing. 'I've got my mobile. I could ring the pub when I'm ready to come back.'

'Och! Away with ye. I've nothin' better to do.'

'OK then,' she sighed, taking her bag from him, feeling suddenly very wary and vulnerable. 'Wish me luck,' she said, grimacing as she turned her feet none too eagerly towards the imposing Stonemoor House.

There was nothing appealing about it at all. It was barren, grey, cold and unwelcoming. Charlotte wondered if the man himself was going to match up to his surroundings.

There was no knocker and no bell on the massive weather-beaten door, so Charlotte rapped her knuckles against it but the sound went nowhere.

She knocked again harder, so hard that it hurt. Still there was no response. Finally she thumped her fist against the thick wood.

She glanced helplessly back to where Jamie was sitting

on a crumbling wall. Surely Andrew Alexander would be home after she'd come all this way.

As she banged on the door once more, she heard a movement from inside and then a bolt being drawn back. Her stomach lurched. If only Jamie hadn't imparted that little snippet of information about Alexander being a wife murderer!

The door creaked open on hinges that had rusted through decades of infrequent use. But the man that stood there was not the whiskered old Scotsman she had imagined, nor some deranged axe-murderer.

Andrew Alexander – if this was Andrew Alexander – was a man of quite startling appearance. Late thirties, well over six feet in height with dark collar-length hair expertly styled and groomed yet with an air of disarray that Charlotte found oddly appealing. His dark-brown eyes were set deep into a face that wouldn't have looked out of place on a celebrity calendar. But despite his undeniably good looks, his expression was fierce, as if he had been wrestling with some problem and she had interrupted his train of thought.

Charlotte resisted the urge to let her gaze travel the length of him, except to note that he was dressed entirely in black. He, however, let his gaze roam freely from the crown of her shiny flame-coloured hair to the toes of her ankle boots. His expression when it returned to her face showed neither approval nor disapproval.

'Miss Harvey?' he said at last. He had an English accent and Charlotte surmised that the Alexanders were far-flung ancestors.

'Mr Alexander?' she responded, extending her hand.

His grip was firm. His fingers long and slender. Well-groomed hands. Not the callused hands of a labourer or fisherman. But the smooth hands of a businessman. Or perhaps the smooth hands of a wife murderer, Charlotte thought morbidly.

He stepped aside and bid her enter.

Charlotte hesitated, glancing back to Jamie.

'Young Jamie walked you over?' Andrew Alexander asked and when she nodded, he called out, 'Go back, Jamie. I'll see Miss Harvey home.'

'No!' Charlotte exclaimed fiercely, startling even herself. She blushed, feeling ridiculous, as if she were a frightened child afraid to be left alone with a stranger. Only wasn't Jamie a stranger too? Not to mention one who might easily lead her astray if her exploits on the way here were anything to go by.

Andrew Alexander glowered at her. 'No? You want the boy to stay out there all day and probably half the night?'

Charlotte felt ridiculously tongue-tied and she clamoured to regain the calm, sophisticated poise she usually adopted for interviewees.

'As long as that? I rather expected us to talk for an hour or two.'

One dark eyebrow arched demonically. 'You have come to talk about the Highland Ruby?'

'Yes, of course.'

'Then let the boy go,' he said, drawing her in and closing the door. As the rough wood slotted home, he drew the top bolt across the door.

'Is that really necessary?' Charlotte demanded accusingly. Was he so insensitive not to realise how alarming such a gesture could be.

Fortunately, with her height, she could, if she stood on tiptoe, reach the bolt and draw it back. But what if she was shorter? She doubted it would have made a difference to him somehow.

A spark of dark amusement flashed briefly into his eyes. 'The wind rattles it if I don't draw the bolt across.'

Charlotte wondered whether that was true or not. But a point was struck in favour of the Highland Ruby *not* living up to its reputation. If he owned a pendant that was supposed to have women at his beck and call, why would he need to bolt them in?

Her confidence returned momentarily and she followed him along a stone passageway to his living room. It was sparsely decorated: a few rugs were scattered on unpolished wooden floorboards, and there were some well-worn armchairs – one with high wings set close to the fireplace. Charlotte wished he had taken the trouble to light the fire and add a little cheer to his dreary home seeing as he had a visitor. There was a brass log bucket piled with cut logs in the hearth, and logs on the fire, but Andrew Alexander hadn't bothered to put a match to them.

She gave a little shiver, partly because of the drop in temperature after the warmth from the October sunlight outside, and partly out of devilment. Letting this man know that considering she had travelled hundreds of miles to speak to him, the least he could have done was to have given her a warm welcome.

He ignored her gesture, or perhaps didn't even notice it, and seated himself in the big armchair. He indicated she take one of the others, leaving a wide expanse of cool air between them.

The prospect of sitting here all day and half the night, as he put it, filled Charlotte with dread. She decided to get swiftly on with the interview and get out as quickly as possible.

She took her Dictaphone from her bag. 'You don't mind if I use this?'

'Feel free,' he replied, entwining his fingers and looking directly at her.

Charlotte forced herself to smile at the man. It wasn't that she disliked him exactly, it was just a feeling of unease. Probably because he had made no effort to make her feel at home. And of course because of what Jamie had said.

'This is quite some house, Mr Alexander,' she began,

forcing herself to make polite conversation and break the ice. 'I don't suppose you suffer from noisy neighbours.'

'And you're wondering why I should live here?' Andrew Alexander said in tones that were deep and rich and well cultivated. 'You're asking yourself if it's a secluded little bolt-hole or solitary confinement as punishment for my sins.'

So much for polite ice-breaking conversation, she thought wryly, fighting back with a few well-chosen words. 'Actually no. Whatever sins you've committed are really of no concern to me.' Nevertheless she couldn't help wondering if his *sin* was the murder of his wife? 'I'm here purely to talk about the Highland Ruby, Mr Alexander. The legend, it can't possibly be true?'

He relaxed back in the big armchair, studying her. 'What have you heard?'

'I've heard the verse. It implies that if a man places the pendant around a woman's neck, she can't resist any request he makes.'

'And do you believe that?'

Charlotte pushed her hair back from her smoky grey eyes and regarded him coolly. 'In a word, no, but I'm fascinated to learn how the myth came to be.'

He leaned forward, a dangerous gleam in his eyes. 'So it's nothing but a fairy story. Would you care to try it?'

She couldn't help but smile.

He looked suddenly very demonic. 'You're looking very sure of yourself, Miss Harvey. Perhaps you'd like to put your money where your mouth is, as the saying goes, and try it for yourself.'

There was something about him. Something dark and dangerous. There was an aura, a certain charisma which made her feel far from comfortable in his presence. Nevertheless, she met his gaze. 'Maybe I will.'

He was attractive, there was no denying that. Any woman would find him so. And she wondered suddenly if he used the Highland Ruby as a ploy, so that he could seduce women to make them feel it wasn't their fault if they abandoned all their inhibitions and morals and slept with him.

She felt amused suddenly. Did it work? Was he successful in seducing his women in this way. Did the women themselves believe it, or did they just go along with the legend for fun? She desperately wanted to know. At this stage in the interview however, it wasn't the sort of question to come out with.

'So, Miss Harvey, or may I call you Charlotte?'

'Charlotte's fine,' she murmured.

'Charlotte. So you'd be prepared to let me put the Highland Ruby around your neck and to hell with the consequences?'

She met his gaze confidently. 'There wouldn't be any consequences.'

'You're sure about that?'

'I don't believe in magic, Mr Alexander, or enchanted necklaces. Are you telling me that you do?'

He suddenly gave the glimmer of a smile and relaxed back. 'Who knows?' he said softly. 'Who knows?'

A silence sprang up. He looked lost in thought for a moment and as she watched him, she saw the faint smile dissolve – only to be replaced by a look of pain.

Frowning, she broke the silence. Broke his train of thought. 'I would very much like to see the Highland Ruby, Mr Alexander.' She began unzipping her camera case.

He got to his feet, but Charlotte soon realised it wasn't to fetch the Ruby. Instead, he lit a taper and put it under the logs in the fireplace. Kneeling on one knee with his back to her, Charlotte found herself involuntarily admiring his physique. She had thought that Jamie had a good body, but compared to Andrew Alexander she could see that Jamie was just a boy.

Like Jamie, Andrew Alexander's shoulders were equally as broad, but there seemed an inner strength about them – about his whole physique. As if he were capable of carrying the weight of the world on those shoulders.

Thinking back to that dark expression she had seen on his face a moment ago, she couldn't help wondering if he did indeed have the weight of the world on his back. As her gaze centred on him kneeling there, coaxing the fire to life, she couldn't resist letting her gaze roam lower, following the curve of his spine, down to his bottom. It was a very nice bottom – taut, well shaped, firm. He obviously didn't spend all his time here. He must work out somewhere. You didn't keep a body in that shape without making a deliberate effort to keep fit. And as far as she knew, there wasn't a gym on the island.

As the fire began to spit and crackle into life, she thought what a striking image he portrayed. Kneeling there, dressed all in black, he was almost like a silhouette against the red flames. She had a sudden urge to photograph him, to capture the moment forever.

She bit her lip. For heaven's sake, she couldn't just snap away merely because he looked good. What was wrong with her? First photographing Jamie in the nude, and now wanting to take pictures of another good-looking bloke! At this rate she'd be ready to get a job on a porn mag.

Her cheeks flamed brightly. Determinedly she shut off her overheated thoughts as to whether Andrew Alexander had a nice bottom or not. And moments later, when he glanced back at her, she was relieved that she was then concentrating on her camera, and not on him. He walked over to a cabinet.

'A small malt whisky, Charlotte?' he suggested, taking a crystal decanter and two chunky crystal glasses.

'It's a bit early for me,' she began but, to her dismay, he simply moved to the window and drew the curtains together. They were thrown suddenly into darkness, except for the firelight. The sensation was claustrophobic and an unnatural heat surged through Charlotte's body.

She felt she ought to protest, but a moment later came the glimmering of a tiny flame as he lit another taper. Wordlessly he went around the room lighting candles that stood in black cast-iron holders in niches around the walls. As each candle flickered into life it gave off a heady, woody scent that was far from unpleasant.

Charlotte's pulse quickened. Her heartbeat fluttered against her ribcage like a tiny bird desperately trying to escape. Breathlessly, she watched his shadowy figure move panther-like around the room. Before long what had been a cold, unfriendly place was as warm and seductive as a lover's boudoir.

And she was captured within it. Alone with a man who could, if Jamie was correct, be a wife murderer. And who could, if legend was correct, have her totally within his power. To enact whatever sexual perversions and fantasies he desired.

All good sense told her to get out now. To rearrange this meeting in a more public place. But, for once, good sense seemed to have sailed out of the window.

Andrew Alexander placed the glass of malt whisky into Charlotte's hand, his eyes as liquid gold as the drink itself. 'Is it still too early?'

'Well, it won't kill me, I suppose,' she murmured, taking a sip, suddenly in need of something to calm her nerves. Perhaps this was how the Highland Ruby gained its reputation. Some good-looking man set the scene for seduction, plied a girl with alcohol and then placed the pendant around her neck before making love to her.

Well, she was ready for him.

He moved another chair closer to the fire, directly opposite his. 'Come over here, Charlotte, it's much warmer.'

To refuse would have been churlish, and so she moved

– camera, camera case, bag and drink across the room, deliberately in as ungainly a fashion as she could muster.

She didn't want to be seduced by this man. He was probably a number-one letch who did this routine to every passing female. Not that there could be that many. The thought made her sweat. If he hadn't had a woman in a while, didn't that make her situation even more dire?

Swallowing the lump in her throat, Charlotte got determinedly back to business. 'The Highland Ruby, Mr Alexander. How did you come by it?'

He turned and stared into the flames. Charlotte waited, not realising she was holding her breath, until she remembered that she really ought to exhale. He finally returned his gaze to her. 'I stole it,' he told her simply.

Charlotte almost choked on her drink. That was hardly the answer she was expecting. She rather hoped the pendant had been unearthed by some farmer digging a lamb out of a snowdrift or some such thing. But to discover the owner of this precious artefact was a thief . . . That would really impress her readers, not to mention her editor.

'You wouldn't care to elaborate on that, would you?' she asked blandly, a glazed look in her eyes.

'Maybe later. It's enough for you to know that I took the Highland Ruby off people who were not responsible owners.'

She stared at him. 'What do you mean, not responsible owners? This is a piece of jewellery we're talking about, not a stray dog.'

Andrew Alexander's face hardened. His words struck out like shafts of steel. 'We're talking about an object that can wreak havoc in the wrong hands, Charlotte. The Highland Ruby has the power to totally destroy lives and relationships. It's a powerful object that should not be handled lightly.'

'Yet you asked me if I'd like to try it out,' she shot back, not caring to be spoken to so harshly.

43

'I have my moments of humour,' he said mirthlessly.

'Meaning?'

'If I *had* placed it around your neck, I assure you I would have used every ounce of willpower to keep our subject of conversation well away from anything sexual.'

Charlotte ran her fingers through her hair and stared at him. 'You're very sure of the power of this pendant. So you do believe it possesses magical abilities?'

'Whether it has or whether it hasn't, The Highland Ruby affects people.'

'In what way? Are you telling me they lose their self control?'

'Self control, inhibitions, call it what you like.'

Charlotte was rapidly becoming fascinated. 'Against their will?'

He regarded her quizzically. 'Ah, now that's another matter.'

She sat forward on the edge of her chair. 'I don't understand. Are you saying that if you placed the Highland Ruby around my neck and asked me for a kiss, for example, then what? I'd have to oblige?'

His dark smile returned as he regarded her for an uncomfortably long moment. Finally he said, 'Yes, I think you probably would.'

For a second she didn't quite know what to say. Deep down she had the strangest sensation that his assumption was less than complimentary. A slight slur on women as a whole rather than anything personal. But it was such a vague feeling she couldn't find a reason to argue. Instead she felt even more determined to experience the Highland Ruby for herself so that she could put him firmly in no doubt that it didn't work for everyone.

'I want to try it. I really do . . . on the one condition that you ask me only for a kiss and nothing more.'

'So you do believe it has the power to make a woman do what she normally would not?'

'No, just the opposite. I want to prove it doesn't work.'

44

'And what if you're wrong?'

She hesitated. The consequences, she suddenly realised, were pretty serious: *Thy slaveth to him, his every request.*

Did she really want to be a slave to Andrew Alexander's every request? The answer that leaped into her head shook her to the core. The thought was far from abhorrent. She took a steadying breath. It was all just folklore and superstition. There couldn't possibly be any truth to it.

'Mr Alexander, I honestly don't think there's an ounce of truth in the legend. In my opinion, I'd say the Highland Ruby is an excuse both for the giver and the receiver to act out their fantasies and put it all down to the legend. It's all a bit of harmless fun. But it really will make a great feature in the magazine.'

'Harmless fun,' he murmured and his eyes fluttered shut. That look was back, the one where he carried the weight of the world on his shoulders. He gulped down some more whisky before turning his attention back to her. 'Perhaps I will permit you to wear the Ruby, Charlotte. Perhaps. But first, I think we should talk more. I should get to know you. And you shall get to know me.'

'That's fine with me,' Charlotte said, setting her glass aside, and checking her Dictaphone was still recording. 'So, Mr Alexander, I'd like a little background on yourself. Let's start off with where you were born?'

'No, my turn first,' he interrupted. 'Tell me about your fiancé.'

'My fiancé?'

He glanced down at the solitaire diamond ring on her finger. 'I'm not clairvoyant, it's just that no one could miss a rock like that. Staked his claim has he?'

'It's not actually an engagement ring, it's more a friendship ring,' Charlotte informed him, slightly irritated that she should have to explain anything about herself when she was supposed to be interviewing him. She raised her right hand so he could see it wasn't even on her third finger. Now and again, she secretly wished it was an engagement ring. Paul was so right for her – well, except for him going on about trying out things she wasn't keen on – like anal sex. She faced Andrew Alexander squarely. 'We are very serious about each other, however.'

'How long have you known him?'

'Two years.'

'And does he make you happy?'

'Of course he does, or I wouldn't be with him, would I?' she answered irritably. Then she bit her lip, remembering times when her refusal to have anal sex or let him tie her up had sent him off into a sulk – or the opposite and he'd made love more aggressively than she'd liked. She took another sip of whisky, avoiding Andrew Alexander's probing gaze.

'So what's the problem?' he asked mildly.

'Problem? There isn't a problem.'

'Do you love him?' the man continued his interrogation.

'Madly,' she answered, looking him squarely in the eye.

'And does he satisfy you sexually?'

'I beg your pardon!' Charlotte spluttered.

He looked vaguely bored for a second. 'I can't think of any clearer way of putting the question, Miss Harvey. Does he give you everything you want in bed?'

A number of smart replies shot through her brain. But when she opened her mouth to let him know it was none of his damn business, she felt tongue-tied and couldn't think of anything that would put him firmly in his place. She settled for, 'Absolutely!' and felt the colour rushing to her cheeks.

'I'm pleased to hear it,' he remarked, continuing to stare at her until Charlotte turned away.

'I can't imagine why,' Charlotte uttered angrily.

He regarded her coolly. 'I needed to know, Charlotte,

so that when you kiss me, we'll both know it's the influence of the Highland Ruby, and not because you actually want to.'

Charlotte burst out laughing. 'Oh my, I do admire your technique. But I have to tell you I wouldn't kiss you even if I had a hundred Highland Rubies around my neck.'

His fingers tapped a rhythm thoughtfully against his bottom lip. 'Charlotte,' he murmured softly. 'If I were to place the Ruby around your neck right now, I could have you stripping naked in front of this fire. I could have you legs apart, begging me to lick and suck your undoubtedly gorgeous pussy. I could have you clawing my trousers off so that you could suck my cock –'

'Stop it!' Charlotte cried, jumping to her feet. 'I don't have to listen to this ... this filth. I'm a writer, Mr Alexander, not a whore who you can talk dirty to and get your kicks. I, I think I'd better go. Perhaps, if you can keep your lewd thoughts to yourself, we could meet up at the pub in the harbour and finish the interview. Right now, I'm leaving.'

He extended an arm towards the door. 'Then leave. I'm not stopping you. You're the one interested in the Highland Ruby. The very reason you're here is because of its legend, its reputed sexual power over women. Yet at the first hint of what its claims are, you're off running like a frightened rabbit. Charlotte, I was merely warning you of what the consequences *might* be. Perhaps now you will begin to understand why it needs to remain in safe hands.'

'And yours are those safe hands?' Charlotte mocked, throwing everything into her bag and hurrying to the door.

'Yes,' he answered simply, following her. 'The Highland Ruby is safe in my keeping. It can't do any more damage to people's lives.'

Heatedly, Charlotte stretched up and tugged at the bolt

securing the door. She might have guessed it would be stiff. She couldn't budge it.

He moved to stand directly behind her, so that she felt the faintest brush of his flat hard torso against her as he slid the bolt across. She hated herself for the tingling sensations it caused within her.

'Allow me,' he uttered.

She cast him an angry glance as she yanked open the door. 'You'll find me at the Captain's Table, Mr Alexander.'

'And you'll find me here,' he replied calmly.

As the heavy wooden door thudded shut behind her, Charlotte stood outside seething. The nerve of the man, talking like that! Like she was some tart.

Furiously, she stormed away from the house, her blood boiling. The cheek of him. The absolute nerve of him. It was just outrageous talking to her like that. He was a pervert. A horrible, dirty old man.

But, as her pace slowed and her anger abated she realised he wasn't old, or dirty, and she had to admit he certainly wasn't horrible. The sensation of being a total abject failure washed over her.

She hated to admit it, but he was right. She was here to talk about an artefact that was supposed to have sexual powers, therefore they had to talk about sexual matters. Why on earth had she exploded like some modest virgin?

She felt stupid. Stupid and childish. She should have handled that differently instead of taking it personally.

She was in two minds whether to turn round and go back. But another more stubborn part of her said, no! Let him come to the pub. He was the one at fault – talking dirty to a woman he had only just met. Had he no idea of decorum?

She stumbled on, in what she hoped was the right direction, unable to find the actual footpath, picking her way through clumps of thistles and around clods of rough earth. Fortunately she guessed right, and finally spotted the chimney tops of the harbour town in the distance and the grey horizon of the sea.

She trudged on, head down, careful not to fall and twist her ankle. When she glanced up next it was to see a man walking directly towards her.

Her stomach contracted. She recognised him instantly. The huge red-haired, red-bearded, mammoth-cocked Scotsman who was in the pub last night. He was still in his kilt and Charlotte blushed as he came nearer, unable to stop herself from picturing the 'thing' that he brandished beneath his sporran.

'Mornin' there, lass, you're a stranger to these parts, aren't ye?'

She swallowed hard, forcing herself to smile at the face that was mostly hidden behind a bush of red hair. 'Yes, I'm interviewing one of the islanders, Andrew Alexander.'

'Aye, Mr Alexander. He's ma neighbour. Ma cottage is just a half a mile from Stonemoor House.'

'Is it really?' she said and smiled awkwardly. 'Well, must get on . . .'

But he extended his big rough hand. 'The name's Angus McDonald. What's yours, little lady? Y'know, you're an awful pretty wee lassie.'

'Charlotte Harvey,' she replied, finding her hand grasped inside his. It was a warm, clammy grip and Charlotte instantly recoiled.

'So where's it you're staying?' he asked in his gruff Scottish brogue.

'At the pub in the harbour,' she answered, wishing he would let go of her. She knew where his hand had been: round that enormous dick of his!

'The Captain's Table?' He nodded, his bulbous eyes widening. 'No doubt I'll see ye later then. We'll have a wee dram together.'

Charlotte extracted her hand from his grasp and forced herself to keep smiling. 'Must fly, loads to do.'

'Don't forget now,' he called after her. 'I'll be lookin' forward to it.'

Not on your Nelly, Charlotte thought to herself as she made her escape. That man gave her the creeps.

Reaching the harbour, she decided a walk along the sea front would be good for her nerves. She glanced at her watch. Paul would be between lectures now; she might be able to reach him. Perching herself on the harbour wall she tapped his number into her mobile. At first it didn't connect and it took two more tries before it eventually began ringing.

Paul sounded breathless. 'Charlotte, darling, how's it going?'

'Oh, Paul, it's so good to hear your voice,' she sighed, gazing out over the choppy grey sea and feeling suddenly very homesick.

'Good to hear you too, darling. Are you okay? You sound a bit anxious.'

She didn't want to tell him about the disastrous interview; she still felt a failure. 'Yes, I'm fine,' she lied. 'It's slow progress but everything's OK.'

'So is it *the* Andrew Alexander?' Paul asked, chuckling slightly.

Charlotte frowned. 'I don't know. The funny thing is, there's a rumour that this Andrew Alexander killed his wife. What do you think, Paul, coincidence?'

'Ask him,' came his suggestion.

'You're the second person to suggest that,' Charlotte answered, thinking of Jamie. 'Only he's not the easiest person to talk to. Oh, anyway, I don't want to talk about him. How are you, Paul? Missing me?'

'Like crazy, darling. Oh, sorry, it's time for my next lecture. When are you coming home?'

'I'm not sure.'

'Well, phone me, OK?' Paul insisted. 'Make sure you phone me and I'll pick you up from the station. Promise?'

'I promise,' Charlotte said, not wanting to break off the

call. She needed a friendly voice. Someone she was sure of. 'Paul –'

'Darling, I have to go. I've got forty students waiting to hear about the theory of relativity.'

'OK, bye.' The line went dead. With a sigh, Charlotte slipped her mobile away and wandered along the shore.

Around the coast a little way she discovered some roughly hewn steps leading down to the shale beach. She clambered down and stamped over the pebbles and shells and half-eaten crabs. Overhead, seagulls circled, screeched and swooped down to scavenge from the seaweed and debris washed ashore by the tide.

Walking on and rounding a small headland, Charlotte found herself in a tiny secluded cove. A young couple had claimed it as their own. At first glance they looked to be enjoying a bit of horseplay, too wrapped up in each other to notice her. As she went to turn back and let them keep their privacy she saw the young man lift his blonde girlfriend up into the air and sit her down on a rock so she was sitting head high to him.

Giggling, the girl wrapped her ankles around her boyfriend's head and clapped his ears. He responded by grabbing her ankles and opening her legs wide apart. It was blatantly clear she was knickerless under her skirt. He held her like that, ignoring her shrieks to let her go, and that he was 'being awful rude'.

A moment later, he was awful ruder. Taking a step towards her, he buried his face into her blonde-pussy and her legs wrapped fiercely around his neck.

Charlotte hurried away. God, what was it about this place? Was everyone sex mad?

Burning inside, she retraced her steps, wishing that Paul was here now. More than anything she needed his long beautiful cock up her.

She threw back her head. Oh, God, how she wanted it!

She walked on, trying not to think about sex and just how badly she wanted fucking right at this moment.

'Think about work,' she muttered under her breath. 'Work, that's what pays the bills.'

Forcing herself to concentrate, she focused on the Highland Ruby. The legend couldn't possibly be true. A piece of old jewellery couldn't really be enchanted. It was all just a fanciful tale, a myth which had grown in reputation through people's own desires to abandon their inhibitions and enjoy whatever sexual pleasures they wished.

Nevertheless, it intrigued her and she knew that before this trip was over she would experience the Ruby for herself so that she could prove the legend was false. Being positive of the truth wouldn't be detrimental to her written feature. On the contrary, it would help her to write about it. There was no point in half-researching an article. She needed to know all the facts.

She headed back to the pub, the verse repeating itself in her head:

> *Modest maidens and virgins beware*
> *Before accepting this stone so rare.*
> *For he who placeth it on thy breast*
> *They slaveth to him, his every request,*
> *Tho' detestable or loathsome he may be*
> *Thy will dissolves, thy belongeth to he.*

# Chapter Four

Charlotte waited all afternoon for Andrew Alexander to show up at the Captain's Table. As darkness fell, she was forced to admit that he wasn't going to come. She would have no choice but to go back to him, cap in hand, if she had any hope of writing this feature on the Highland Ruby.

The prospect of seeing him again in that isolated house caused a nervous fluttering in the pit of her stomach. She was really not looking forward to it one bit.

One by one the regulars came into the Captain's Table for their nightly tipple. To pass the time, Charlotte took the opportunity of photographing some craggy-looking old-timers. Jamie leaned on the bar, watching her, an amused smile playing around his lips. Catching Charlotte's attention he cast his eyes briefly down towards his loins then raised one eyebrow suggestively. Charlotte laughed and shook her head.

She was putting her camera away when Angus McDonald lumbered in and she silently debated whether to include him in her shots. He epitomised the image of the wild Scottish highlander – even though he did give her the creeps. And, she thought, smiling to herself, the

Scottish were famous for tossing the caber – and he was an expert!

She finished putting her equipment away, ignoring Angus's look of disappointment and protests that she should stay and have a 'wee dram' with him. There would be no point in photographing him in this setting anyway. If she wanted shots of Angus, they would have to be outside in the mountains, or by a stream. Not indoors. That wasn't the image she wanted to portray at all. And she had no desire to be out in the heather with Angus and his mighty caber.

Bidding everyone goodnight, Charlotte went up to her room, hoping to get a good night's sleep. In the middle of the night, she was awoken once more by the lusty moaning of her hostess. She buried her head into her pillow, trying not to imagine what was going on down-stairs. But it was impossible to drown out the obvious sounds of love-making.

Throwing herself o ton her back, Charlotte couldn't help wondering whether it was just Kenneth and Nancy tonight, or had Jamie joined in again? Shagging Nancy as he would have done her that afternoon, if she'd let him. Or maybe the huge Angus McDonald was getting to grips with Nancy? Grossly unpleasant though the man was, the size and power of his cock was quite breathtak-ing, and Charlotte could only imagine how it would feel to have *that* rammed up her.

Unable to stop her imagination from working over-time, her hand slid down between her legs. She wasn't really surprised to feel how moist she was.

'Oh Paul, why aren't you here?' she groaned, throwing herself on to her back and rubbing hard against her clit, her middle finger probing deep inside of herself. She came quickly, taking only a moment's breath before bringing herself off again, her thighs parting and squeez-ing, needing much more than her own touch, but know-ing she would have to make do.

Unless . . .

As soon as the thought struck her, she dismissed it as being totally immoral. More like one of Paul's lurid suggestions than anything she would think of herself. Besides, Nancy might not welcome another woman joining in her fun.

Charlotte rolled on to her stomach, her fingers still tangled in her soft pubic hair. She closed her eyes and tried to get back to sleep. Tomorrow she had to face Andrew Alexander again. The thought filled her with dread.

Way across the island, Andrew Alexander paced back and forth across the wooden floorboards of Stonemoor House. The fire crackled and spat as it devoured yet another log while the candles had long since died down. He grasped the Highland Ruby in both hands, a fierce rage inside him flaring as wildly as the flames licking up the chimney.

His desire to throw the Highland Ruby into the embers was pointless. It wouldn't burn. He had dragged it blackened but intact from the ashes of a fire on more than one occasion. It was indestructible.

He gripped it fiercely. Why had she come now, raking up the past? Miss Charlotte Harvey, an innocent – a beautiful innocent he had to concede – with no idea of what she was asking. He should have destroyed her letters asking for an interview instead of giving in. What kind of idiot was he to think he could talk about the Ruby now and imagine it wouldn't affect him?

'Fool!' he shouted in rage, throwing the necklace across the room.

It clattered against the wall and he collapsed into his chair, head in hands. His thoughts tormented him.

No, there was no magic to the Highland Ruby, not in the true sense. If anything, it was cursed. If not for the Ruby, Fay would still be alive.

For once, however, his thoughts didn't linger on his young bride who had died five years ago. Instead they switched to the inquisitive journalist who had banged on his door earlier today.

So the Highland Ruby had no power, she insisted. In a way she was right, it was the women who had the power. The power to forget right from wrong. The power to betray. The Ruby just gave them the excuse they needed.

Would it be the same with her, this Charlotte Harvey? He guessed it would even if she was sceptical. He could see the fires of lust smouldering in her eyes. It only needed a key to unlock her inhibitions, and what greater key than a medieval piece of jewellery that supposedly possessed great sexual powers? She would be no different from all the other women who had met with the Highland Ruby. She'd be no different at all.

The prospect of that sent a sudden raging heat through his loins. He was only human, and there was something about Charlotte Harvey that struck a cord deep inside him. It had been a long time since a woman had meant anything to him. Five years since Fay died. Not that he had been without sex for that long. There were always plenty of willing women: though not so many here on the island. But then this retreat was just a tiny part of his life. His working life was tied up in his chain of restaurants. And there were always plenty of women when you had money.

But women that he could feel something other than lust for, now they were a rare commodity.

He heaved a sigh. It would be better if Charlotte Harvey didn't come back. Better for her if she caught tomorrow's ferry and sailed back to where she came from. Let her write about the Highland Ruby as if it were some fanciful myth. That would satisfy her readers.

He raked his hands through his black hair. But he knew she would return. He'd caught a spark in her eye;

she was curious – more than curious. She was fascinated. He sighed, and closed his eyes.

Yes, tomorrow she would be back. God help her.

'Would you like Jamie to walk with you?' Nancy asked, as Charlotte gathered her things together the following morning.

'No, thank you, Nancy. I know the way,' Charlotte assured her, peering out at the weather. It had changed since yesterday. A blustery wind had sprung up and storm clouds were gathering on the horizon. Charlotte put on her coat. 'I'll need this today, judging by that sky.'

'Aye, the fishermen are predicting heavy rain later.'

Charlotte groaned. 'Wonderful. I'll get off now, then.'

'Mind how ye go.'

Charlotte set off determined that today she would not allow Andrew Alexander to upset her. If he wanted to talk about what the Ruby could make a woman do, then she would listen objectively. Not take it personally as she had done yesterday.

Yet a fierce heat sprung up inside of her as she recalled his words.

*I could have you stripping naked in front of this fire. I could have you legs apart, begging me to lick and suck your undoubtedly gorgeous pussy. I could have you clawing my trousers off so that you could suck my cock . . .'*

That was hardly impersonal!

She marched on, over the moor, spotting the steer in the distance and giving it a wide berth now Jamie wasn't around to protect her.

Halfway across the moor, black storm clouds rolled over the hilltops, billowing and ominous. She groaned at the sight of them and quickened her pace. Minutes later she felt the first drops of cold rain. She hurried on, desperate to reach Stonemoor House before the heavens opened. But the sky blackened swiftly, turning day into night, and long before Andrew Alexander's house came into view, the clouds burst and a torrent of icy, stinging rain fell from the sky.

'Shit!' she muttered as her hair became plastered to her head and her vision blurred from a combination of rainwater and mascara. Within minutes Charlotte was soaked to the skin.

Underfoot, the ground became a quagmire. Dips and holes rapidly filled up becoming deep puddles that overflowed into her ankle boots. She squelched on, rain lashing her face, taking her breath away.

After a further ten minutes of dragging her mud-caked feet through the boggy terrain, she was starting to feel exhausted. When Stonemoor House finally emerged through the misty blanket, a few hot salty tears of relief mingled with the cold rain on her cheeks.

Shivering and bedraggled she thumped on the door, aware that she looked and felt a saturated wreck.

'You're persistent, I'll give you that,' Andrew Alexander remarked when he opened the door. 'And wet.'

She didn't wait to be asked in but stumbled into his house, glad to be out of the storm. 'It wasn't raining when I set off. Oh, God, I'm drowned.'

'Go through, the fire's lit,' he said, drawing the bolt across the door as the wind began to shake it violently. 'I assume you have no objections to me bolting this?'

'Carry on,' she replied, leaving a trail of water and muddy footprints behind her as she squelched along the stone passageway. At that moment she really wouldn't have cared if he had put an iron bar across his door. Anything to keep the storm out. 'Does it always rain this hard?' she asked accusingly, deciding it was his fault that she was in such a state. 'You can't see a hand in front of your face.'

'You shouldn't have come,' he said, following her into

the main room. 'When the rain sets in like this it can go on for days. You could be stranded here.'

'I've work to do, Mr Alexander,' Charlotte replied, heading straight towards his log fire. As she stood in front of its open flames steam immediately began to rise from her wet clothing. 'A bit of rain won't stop me.'

'How professional,' he remarked sarcastically, closing the space between them. To her astonishment, he began unbuttoning her coat. 'Only you won't be doing much work if you remain in those wet clothes.'

The proximity of the man was like a bolt of electricity charging through her. Charlotte caught her breath, as if her heart had suddenly missed a beat. He was so close that she could smell his musky male scent. There was a raw sexuality about it and she breathed it in deeply.

As he lowered his gaze to concentrate on unbuttoning her coat, Charlotte took the opportunity to take a good look at him. He was, without a shadow of a doubt, absolutely gorgeous. He had the longest silky black lashes she had ever seen on a man, and a well-shaped mouth that just begged to be kissed.

She bit her lip. Lord, what was happening to her? Would she never stop thinking about sex? She was here to interview Andrew Alexander, not to kiss him.

His hands brushed against her body as he peeled her coat from her back. And although it was just her coat, the sensation of having him strip off this one garment sent shockwaves through her body. As he stepped away to hang it over a chair, she was trembling.

At a loss as to what to do next, she stood dripping on to his rug. She was far too wet to sit down on his furniture, and she wondered if he intended stripping all her clothes off her. The thought sent little tingles of delight shivering up her inner thighs.

Her jumper was saturated and had moulded itself to her breasts so that her nipples protruded through. Her trousers were like a second skin, the pale-beige colour giving her the appearance of being naked from the waist down.

Briefly, Andrew Alexander cast his dark eyes up and down the length of her. But the sight seemed only to irritate him. 'If you'd had the sense to wear a waterproof coat, you wouldn't be soaked to the skin,' he snapped. 'You'll have to take them all off. I don't want to be responsible for you catching pneumonia.'

Her insides lurched. So he did intend her to strip. She gulped. 'I can't. I've nothing to change into.'

He shook his head in despair and with a groan said, 'I'll get you a shirt or something. Don't move.'

He disappeared to return with a large towel and one of his shirts. He practically threw them at her. 'Shout me when you're decent,' he told her, and disappeared from the room again.

Charlotte was hit with an acute feeling of disappointment. But she pulled herself together sternly. Obviously he wasn't going to physically undress her. She bit down hard on her lip again. There was no denying it. That's what she'd secretly wanted. For him to strip her naked, right here in front of that roaring log fire. And then . . .

She put a halt to her overheated imagination as her cheeks began to burn and the tingling between her thighs turned into an ache of longing. 'Behave yourself, girl!' she murmured under her breath. For heaven's sake, she barely knew the man. She didn't even like him particularly. Yet there was just *something* about him.

Perhaps the power of the Highland Ruby had rubbed off on him, making him irresistible. She smiled wryly to herself. Very unlikely. The truth was, she simply found him attractive. The man had sex appeal. Lots of men did, and certainly not because of some enchanted pendant.

With a sigh, Charlotte set about peeling off her jumper and slacks – she could have wrung them out they were so waterlogged. Instead, she hung them over the chair with her coat. Standing there in just her bra and pants, she began towelling herself dry, but even her knickers and bra were wet. With a reluctant groan she realised they would have to come off too.

Glancing back at the door Andrew had left by, she reached behind her back, unhooked her bra and threw it over the chair.

Her breasts were damp, her nipples dark rosy pink and erect. She ran the palms of her hands over the hard little peaks, wishing they would soften and relax instead of standing to attention. She just prayed they wouldn't be too visible beneath his shirt. Turning her attention then to her wet knickers, she reluctantly slipped them down over her hips and stepped out of them.

As naked as nature had intended, Charlotte stood in front of Andrew's roaring log fire. Its glow felt wonderful on her bare skin and she rotated in front of the flames, letting the heat bring the colour back into her skin. Then mischievously she bent over, toasting her bottom, and the heat from the fire mingled fiercely with her inner warmth. She revelled in the sensation of being stark naked in a stranger's house. There was something very naughty about it.

She straightened and studied her reflection in the huge gilt mirror on the wall. People often complimented her on her figure – especially Paul. Being quite tall and slender gave her a certain elegance that often turned heads. Her breasts were full and rounded; she didn't consider them to be particularly large, but they tended to give that impression because of her slim build.

Looking at herself in the mirror, she began to stroke her left nipple with her middle finger. Gentle, circular strokes that hardened the rosebud peak while her other hand slipped down over her flat stomach. The neat bush of silky damp hairs curled around her fingers as she touched her small hard nub. She tickled it feather-lightly making it, too, stand out. She parted her legs a little, rubbing harder, filled with the sudden urge to masturbate herself to orgasm. That would be even more naughty.

She glanced around the room, looking for somewhere she could perch and quickly bring herself off. It was immoral, she knew. Immoral and very, very wicked. But then who was to know?

Quite suddenly, a thought jumped into Charlotte's head, reminding her of what Andrew Alexander had said yesterday. It shook her to the core.

*I could have you stripping naked in front of this fire. I could have you legs apart . . .*

And here she was, stripped naked, legs apart.

*I could have you begging me to lick and suck your undoubtedly gorgeous pussy . . .*

Charlotte's eyes fluttered shut at that prospect! She perched herself on the arm of the chair, her legs wide so that she could put her hand between her thighs and rub hard at herself.

*I could have you clawing my trousers off so that you could suck my cock . . .*

She wasn't too sure about that part of his prediction although, judging by her behaviour now, perhaps he wasn't that far wrong.

As his words went round and round in her head, Charlotte opened and closed her legs, her hands squeezed between the tops of her thighs, her forearms crushing her breasts. Now she couldn't stop thinking of what Andrew had said. Her fevered imagination worked overtime and she pictured him kneeling between her open legs now, his tongue lapping at her clit, sucking her sex into his mouth, driving her insane as she came with surprising ferocity.

Moaning softly with this self-administered pleasure, Charlotte half opened her eyes. To her utter shock and horror, she saw that she was being spied upon. There was a face at the window. A face streaked with rain. A large, red-bearded face. Angus McDonald's face!

She shrieked, mortified that he'd seen her naked and playing with herself. With a leering grin he turned and quickly lumbered off into the mist.

Two seconds later, Andrew Alexander strolled into the room. He stood, transfixed, his dark eyes feasting on Charlotte's nakedness.

Still rooted to the chair-arm, her legs still spread wide apart, she swiftly leaped to her feet and scrambled for the dry shirt he'd given her.

'Get out!' she screamed at him, tangling herself into knots with the crisp white cotton shirt that was miles too big for her. 'Who the hell said you could come in?'

'I heard you shout. I assumed you were decent,' he remarked, seeming fascinated by her con tortions as she tried to cover up.

'I shouted because there was a pervert peering in through the window,' she snapped, discovering the reason the shirt wouldn't go on was because she had twisted a sleeve inside-out in her panic.

Andrew headed straight for the window. 'Are you sure?'

'Of course I'm sure!' Charlotte retorted, burning with embarrassment. Andrew Alexander must have guessed what she was doing sitting perched on the chair-arm with her legs wide open like that. Oh, God, she wanted to die!

'What did he look like?'

'It was Angus McDonald – your neighbour. He wants locking up.'

'Oh, Angus,' Andrew Alexander nodded, as if that was

perfectly OK. He pulled the curtains shut and began lighting the candles. 'That figures.'

Charlotte gritted her teeth, knowing the only way to overcome this acute embarrassment was to keep on the attack. 'Oh, so he's a well-known pervert, is he? Your resident local weirdo-cum-voyeur. Do you know what he was doing the other –' She stopped. She couldn't tell him what she'd witnessed at the Captain's Table.

He raised one eyebrow curiously.

'Never mind,' Charlotte said moodily. 'I just don't like being spied on.'

A quirky little smile touched his dark eyes as his gaze raked over her once again. 'You can hardly blame a man for looking. I had trouble dragging my eyes off you myself.'

Charlotte glared at him furiously, determined not to let her guard slip, although deep down she warmed to his compliment. Then her own body let her down again, her gaze involuntary, flicked down to his crotch area. She hadn't meant to, it was as if she was on autopilot. She suddenly found herself looking at the bulge of a hardening erection straining the fabric of his trousers. To her horror, she felt a trickle of moisture running down her inner thigh. Mortified, she prayed he wouldn't see it. But when she raised her eyes, she saw that he was watching her closely.

She prayed fervently for the ground to open and swallow her up.

It didn't, and she quickly sat down and wrapped the shirt tightly around her legs.

God, what was happening to her? Was the power of the Highland Ruby reaching out to her even though she wasn't even wearing it?

She took a deep breath. She had to get through this somehow. 'I . . . I'd like to get down to business, Mr Alexander, we've wasted enough time,' she said, in the most brusque voice she could conjure up.

64

'Are you sure, Charlotte?' he asked, regarding her steadily, seeming almost to be able to pierce right through to her soul with those dark searching eyes. 'Are you absolutely sure you want to go ahead with this?'

'Of course. Why ever not?' she retaliated, knowing that he knew she was feeling horny already, without further talk of what the Highland Ruby could or couldn't do. She struggled on with the act. 'I haven't come all this way to go back without my story. I haven't even seen the Ruby yet.'

'Then we had better rectify that, hadn't we,' he said almost kindly, crossing the room to where an oil painting hung. It was of a wild sea crashing over rocks with a painted sky as black as that outside. He slid the master-piece aside and removed a loose brick from the wall.

The Highland Ruby was wrapped in a piece of old red velvet, tucked away inside a niche in the wall. He unfolded the velvet package and held it out for Charlotte to see.

She gasped, getting swiftly to her feet again. The sight of the Highland Ruby was putting everything else in the shade. Her acute embarrassment of moments ago was forgotten. The fact that she was half-naked seemed unimportant.

'It's beautiful!' she breathed. 'It's just so incredibly beautiful.'

The old photo in the book didn't do it justice at all. The ruby was of the deepest, darkest red. And larger than she expected. Around its circumference were spark-ling crystals that glinted in the glow from the fire and candlelight. The chain from which it hung looked as if it weighed a ton.

She reached out to touch it, but Andrew drew back. She shot him a startled look. 'You're not saying its powers are that strong?'

'Is it worth the risk?' he asked, looking steadily at her.

'Don't tell me I'm going to fall under your spell if I so much as touch it?' she mocked.

His mouth curved a little. 'Who knows?'

'I don't think so somehow,' she answered, hoping she sounded convincing. Deep down she knew she was already under his spell. The last thing she wanted was for him to realise it though.

For some moments then, they both gazed down at the Highland Ruby. Charlotte had never seen anything quite so enchanting or so perfect. 'Was this your sin, Mr Alexander?'

He frowned. 'My sin?'

'You asked me yesterday whether I thought you lived here to atone for your sins,' said Charlotte, dragging her gaze reluctantly from the pendant to his face. 'Was it the sin of stealing the Highland Ruby?'

'Ha!' he uttered, throwing his head back a little. 'Nothing so simple, Charlotte. Taking the Highland Ruby wasn't a sin. I'd say I've probably done everyone a favour.'

'Everyone?'

'Perhaps not everyone,' he conceded. 'Let's just say that a few less lives will be wrecked now that this isn't accessible.'

'I can't believe you stole it,' Charlotte persisted. 'It must be worth a fortune. You'd have the police after you.'

He congratulated her with a smile. 'You have me there. Perhaps *stealing* isn't exactly the right expression. The fact is, it belonged to my wife – my late wife – Fay.' His words faltered momentarily. 'Bought at auction by her over-generous father for her twenty-first birthday.' Bitterly he added, 'And the legend came with it.'

'What happened?' Charlotte asked intrigued, realising by the anguish in his voice that catching her masturbating wasn't all he had to think about.

He took a deep breath. 'The Highland Ruby fascinated

everyone who heard about its so-called enchantment. It was passed around like a toy. Women used it as an excuse to screw around. Men used it as a power thing. Marriages crumbled like sandstone.'

'Including yours?'

'Including mine.'

'Why?' Charlotte murmured. 'Did you use the Ruby to enslave her, like the legend says? Did you demand things she didn't want to do?'

He looked at her sharply, startling her with the intensity of his dark eyes. 'I didn't need to use power over Fay; there was nothing she wouldn't have done for me willingly.'

Charlotte looked away, thinking how different that sounded from her and Paul. There were plenty of things she wouldn't do for him.

Andrew Alexander strode across the room and poured himself a drink. 'I may as well tell you. Fay slept with someone else. We'd been married just one month. We were in love, but she slept with someone else.'

'Why?' Charlotte breathed.

He swallowed half of his whisky. 'She got drunk. She'd gone out with a cousin whose marriage had just crumbled because of messing around with the Highland Ruby, and they got drunk. They'd taken the Highland Ruby with them – for a laugh,' he added bitterly. 'And they both ended up having sex with a couple of guys they met in a bar.'

'And her cousin told you?' Charlotte exclaimed.

He shook his head. 'No. Fay told me herself. She was mortified about the whole thing once she'd sobered up. She cried and begged me to forgive her but at the time I couldn't. I was too hurt – male pride, I guess. I couldn't believe she'd sleep with someone else when she'd got me. I was too hurt to forgive her – then. I just turned my back on her.'

'What happened?' Charlotte asked softly.

He downed the last of his whisky. 'Fay believed our marriage was over. It wasn't. I just wanted to hurt her like she'd hurt me. Only I took it too far. She got desperate and swallowed some pills – ' his voice broke. 'The poor angel didn't realise how few she needed.'

'Oh, God. Andrew,' Charlotte gasped, finding his first name slipped easily off her tongue and finding too that her hand was on his arm, wishing she could do something to help.

His anguished expression seemed to ease a little, and he looked steadily at her again. But when he spoke the bitterness and anger was evident in his voice. 'So you see, Charlotte, this blasted Highland Ruby has a lot to answer for. Still want to try it on for size?'

Charlotte realised there was little she could do to console him. The way he was looking at her seemed to imply that all women were the same. Sex mad and unfaithful at the first opportunity. Well, she would show him.

Her hand slipped from his arm and she gazed defiantly into his face. 'Yes, why not? After all I can't write about something that I haven't experienced, can I?'

His forefinger traced the circumference of the ruby as he looked down at her. His gaze centred on her breasts, barely concealed beneath the loose fabric of his shirt. 'Don't tempt me, Charlotte.'

'I need to know, Mr Alexander, otherwise anything I write will be totally ambiguous.'

'I'll tell you its legend, how it came to be. And I can tell you stories of how it was passed down through the centuries. Isn't that enough to satisfy your readers?'

'Perhaps,' she answered, raising her smoky grey eyes to his. 'But it's not enough to satisfy me. Are you afraid that I'll reveal the truth of the Highland Ruby? Afraid I'll tell the world the legend is nothing but a load of medieval hocus-pocus?'

'Charlotte, that would be doing me a great favour. I suggest you go away and write exactly that.'

'I can't,' she murmured reluctantly. 'I need to know the truth.'

He looked momentarily weary. 'Charlotte, you already know the truth. It's just a legend. An old legend that men and women have exploited to act out their sexual pleasures – to do what they please and put the blame on the Highland Ruby.'

'But what if it really is enchanted?' Charlotte insisted, watching him as he poured another whisky for himself and one for her. 'What if they can't help themselves?'

He looked at her with the semblance of a smile on his lips. 'Did you believe in fairies as a child, Charlotte? I'm telling you, the legend is pure fantasy.'

Her hand reached out and touched the pendant, and this time he allowed her to do so. Softly she said, 'But wouldn't it make the most marvellous story if it were true: that a beautiful pendant had some enchanted power that incites uncontrollable passion.'

His eyes softened. 'I can see you're a romantic at heart, Charlotte. Here, drink this, you must be chilled to the bone.'

She took the drink and sat opposite his chair, close to the fire. She sipped her whisky; it was rich and smooth, and warmed her deep inside. The flames from the fire threw out their heat and she saw the glow on her bare legs. Andrew didn't take his seat. He placed his glass on the stone hearth and moved to stand over her, the Highland Ruby in his hands.

Charlotte's heartbeat drummed faster, alarmed at the proximity of the man. 'You ... you're going to let me wear the Ruby?' she asked, hearing the tremor in her voice.

'It's what you want, isn't it, Charlotte? It's what you've been saying all along.'

'Yes,' she uttered, her voice trembling while her

thoughts began to race. Yes, but what if the legend were true? What if it really is enchanted? What if Andrew Alexander had used reverse psychology to get her to wear it?

What if she was to become *enslaveth to him, his every request*?

Her heart thudded wildly. The idea of being enslaveth to his every request suddenly seemed exciting. Her eyes travelled up the length of him, liking what she saw. She didn't need any magical mumbo-jumbo to attract her to him. The truth was, she wanted him.

And the prospect of being enslaveth to his every request sounded very arousing indeed.

Charlotte tilted back her head, looking up at Andrew Alexander holding the Highland Ruby just over her head.

There was no turning back. She would allow him to put the Highland Ruby around her neck, and if she fell under its spell, if she became enslaveth to Andrew Alexander's every request, then she had no one to blame but herself.

Her heart thudded wildly as softly she breathed, 'I'm ready.'

# Chapter Five

*V*ery slowly, Andrew Alexander placed the ancient necklace around Charlotte's neck, lifting her damp hair so that it rested against her skin. The heavy gold chain was warm against her throat and the weight of the pendant nestling between her breasts felt almost vibrant.

A strange tingling sensation quivered through her body as his hands brushed against her flesh. As her own hand went involuntarily to the pendant, she thought of all the women who had worn this over the centuries. Now it was her turn. She was the latest in the long line of, what – victims? Victims of men's lust or of women's desires?

Or was it nothing more than a pretty necklace?

Not taking his eyes off her, Andrew sat back in his chair and picked up his drink. 'I'll tell you of its legend.'

'Yes,' she murmured, unable to stop herself from stroking the glowing orb with her fingertips, loving the feel of the pendant against her skin. Loving too the sound of Andrew's rich velvety tones, now that she was warm and dry and comfortable.

'During the tenth century,' he began, turning to stare deep into the flames of his fire. 'There lived a leader named Cameron the Worthy. He was a powerful warrior feared by the islanders partly because of his strength as a fighter and partly because he was the ugliest-looking swine in the district – or so the legend goes.'

Charlotte smiled as he continued. 'Cameron fell madly in love with the prettiest maiden in the village, Enritha, who unfortunately disliked him intensely. No matter how he tried to woo her, she would have nothing to do with him. In desperation, Cameron prayed to the gods for something to make this maiden love him. When nothing happened, he saw no point in living and threw himself off a mountain top.'

'Poor man,' Charlotte murmured, stretching her long bare legs out before the fire, seeing that her toes rested just an inch from Andrew's leather-clad feet.

His dark eyes glanced briefly at her legs as he continued. 'Cameron made one last passionate plea to the gods before plunging over the precipice. As he fell, however, his belt caught on a branch and he ended up dangling in mid air. And as he hung there, he spotted something glinting in the rock face. A shiny red stone. Using his dirk he managed to dig it out and discovered it to be a ruby. Later, when he was rescued, and no doubt relieved that he hadn't perished at the bottom of the mountain, Cameron looked on the ruby as a lucky charm and made it into a brooch for himself.'

Charlotte sipped her drink as she listened. The smooth malt felt as if it had been distilled purely for her. It was odd, she rarely drank whisky, but this was so unlike anything she had ever tasted before.

'One day the fair maiden Enritha noticed this brooch and admired it so much that the smitten Cameron gave it to her. She was so pleased she asked how she could thank him for the gift. Taking a chance, Cameron asked for a kiss. She responded – and with such passion that Cameron realised things were looking up.'

'So it didn't stop at a kiss,' murmured Charlotte, eager to hear more.

'Indeed it didn't,' agreed Andrew. 'As she didn't object to his first kiss, he asked for another. Once again she obliged. Encouraged, he asked if he could put his arms around her. The girl agreed willingly. Hardly able to believe his luck, Cameron asked if he could touch her breasts. When she didn't refuse this, he knew he was on to a good thing.'

Charlotte did her best to listen objectively and not put herself in the place of Enritha and Andrew in Cameron's shoes. 'What was his next request?' Charlotte asked, her voice soft.

'To make love,' Andrew said, looking directly into her eyes, causing her to quiver inwardly. 'Not just once either. Cameron made the most of this change of heart in Enritha. They made love morning, noon and night. In every way possible. From the front, from the rear. He had her up against the pine trees, he even had her when riding his horse.'

'What!'

Andrew answered without any hint of embarrassment. 'I assume it's possible, though I haven't tried it myself. They sat astride his horse, facing each other. Enritha straddled him, and with him hard up her, she clung to him, bouncing up and down on his penis as the horse galloped along, no doubt getting the ride of a lifetime.'

Charlotte gulped, imagining how that must have felt. She felt her cheeks, and other parts of her anatomy, begin to glow.

'For weeks Cameron kept the lovely Enritha beside him. His every whim and desire granted. She refused him nothing. Eventually her brothers came looking for her. They discovered her in Cameron's house and ordered her home. Cameron ordered her to stay. Of course, she stayed, and as if to rub salt into the wounds

Cameron then told Enritha to make love to him, there and then, in front of her brothers.'

'She didn't!' Charlotte exclaimed.

'She had no choice,' shrugged Andrew. 'Legend has it that Cameron simply stood there, hands on hips, not touching her, while she virtually raped him. She pushed him down on to the floor, lifted up his kilt and her own skirts and straddled him. In front of a whole crowd of family and onlookers, Enritha humped Cameron like there was no tomorrow.'

'Wow. I bet that impressed the family,' murmured Charlotte, wondering what Andrew's reaction would be if she leaped on him like that. The way her pussy was tingling, she felt quite envious of Enritha.

Andrew continued. 'They were outraged and tried to pull Enritha off him. In the tussle they only managed to rip her blouse off her. The ruby came off with it. Without the magic of the ruby to blind her, Enritha was absolutely repulsed by what she'd done – and had Cameron slain by her brothers right there and then.'

'That was a bit drastic,' Charlotte quipped. 'So what happened to the ruby?'

'Realising its potential, Enritha's eldest brother took possession of it. He had it made into a pendant with crystals which supposedly enhance feelings of love and sexual desire. Then he used it to ensnare whatever woman he fancied.'

'And have his wicked way with them just like Cameron,' Charlotte added, feeling deliciously tingly inside.

'Of course,' Andrew agreed, his dark eyes flicking once more over her long naked legs. 'From then on stories abound. True or false, who knows? But men fought for the ownership of this magical pendant – this Highland Ruby as it became known. People died because of it.'

Like your wife, Charlotte thought, determined not to let him dwell on that again. The atmosphere was too convivial to let sadness creep back in. She had to do something, before his thoughts drifted back to his bride. She drained her glass and held it out to him.

'That was really nice. Would I be very cheeky in asking for a refill?'

'It's quote potent – are you sure?'

'Quite sure,' she smiled.

He poured her another drink and sat back down on the edge of his chair. His eyes rested on the pendant between her breasts. 'That looks good on you.'

'It feels good,' she replied, touching it again, her hand brushing over her nipple as she did so. It was still hard and, lowering her eyes, she saw the protruding peaks prominent through the fabric of the shirt. She wondered if Andrew had noticed. He was still looking at her, and the silence between them grew heavy and uncomfortable.

She put an end to it. Hoping to sound flippant, she said: 'At least the Highland Ruby hasn't made me leap uncontrollably on you! I haven't been overcome with sexual desires like Enritha.'

One black eyebrow arched demonically. 'Ah, but I haven't made any requests of you yet.'

A fierce heat raged through her suddenly, forcing her to look away.

'What is it, Charlotte?' Andrew coaxed, amusement in his voice. 'You don't seem quite so confident now. Are you remembering what I said yesterday?'

'Not at all,' Charlotte answered swiftly. The last thing she needed now was to be reminded of him saying he could have her begging him to lick her pussy. The prospect of *that* was nowhere near as abhorrent as it had been.

Think about Paul, she told herself. But for some strange reason Paul seemed an awfully long way away. Feeling Andrew's gaze burning through the fabric of the shirt, she checked her Dictaphone for the want of something better to do.

There was dark amusement in his tone. 'Shall we put the Highland Ruby to the test, Charlotte?'

She felt on fire and suddenly very afraid. 'I, I don't think that's necessary.'

'I thought you had to know the truth.'

She swallowed hard. 'I think I know it. The legend is purely a fairytale, and the pendant has no magical powers at all.'

He leaned towards her, devilment glinting from his eyes. 'So if I was to ask you to kiss me, as Cameron asked Enritha, you'd be able to refuse?'

Just a kiss! For one moment she thought he was going to suggest something far more sexual, such as telling her to suck his cock or something. But just a kiss – that wouldn't be so awful. Her thoughts raced and heatedly she realised that neither would it be so awful to get down on to her knees in front of him, unzip his trousers and fill her mouth with his cock.

Her cheeks burned at the very thought and she answered abruptly, 'I'm sorry, Mr Alexander, I don't want to kiss you, or do anything else to you.'

'You called me Andrew earlier.'

She shrugged. 'Andrew then. And I think I've just proved a point once and for all. The Highland Ruby isn't enchanted. You asked me for a kiss and I've said no.'

'Congratulations, Charlotte. You obviously have more willpower than the lovely Enritha,' he said with a wide smile that seemed to Charlotte as if he was mocking her. She prayed he hadn't read her mind. He settled back in his chair, spreading his thighs wide, his eyes catching hers as her gaze slipped involuntarily lower to glance at the slight bulge at his crotch.

'Obviously,' she agreed, swiftly shifting her gaze to his face. Keeping her expression bland and praying her willpower had staying power. But if Enritha couldn't resist Cameron, who she hated, what chance had she to keep resisting Andrew, who she fancied like crazy?

76

She took a deep breath, remembering that this was pure fantasy. Nothing but legend. There wasn't an ounce of truth in any of it.

Andrew was still smiling to himself. 'Then Charlotte, let me tell you more stories of the Highland Ruby for your magazine. Of times when people were more inclined than you and I to believe in magic.'

'That's fine with me,' she murmured, wishing she felt more relaxed. Perhaps if she were properly dressed she would feel less aroused. She felt practically naked sitting here in his shirt and nothing else. It was large and, despite the buttons being done up, it slipped off her shoulder and rode up her thighs whenever she moved. Another gulp of malt whisky might relax her more. She swallowed hard and felt it burn through to the core.

Relaxing in his big armchair by the blazing fire, Andrew began to recount more stories of lusty warriors and weak-willed females who seemed to need little persuasion to open their legs for anyone who had possession of the Highland Ruby. The images he threw up heightened her own desire: All this talk of lust was doing her no good at all.

She began to writhe in her chair; the weight of the pendant was heavy and the effects of the whisky and the fire were making her feel decidedly odd. Curling one leg beneath her, she slid her hand between her thighs. Her thumb brushed lightly against her silky pubic hair, and she could easily have slid her hand up further to press hard against her pussy lips without Andrew realising.

As he talked, he stared absently into the flames, not watching her at all. His words were lyrical as he continued to embellish the legend. This time it was the tale of a nobleman and a peasant girl in the thirteenth century.

'She was a virgin,' Andrew said. 'But with possession of the Highland Ruby she had no choice but to obey the earl. And his first request – that she open her blouse so

77

that he might suck on her breasts – was obeyed without argument.'

Charlotte felt her own breasts tingle and she wondered what it would be like to have Andrew's lips around her nipples, tugging at them, biting . . .

She could feel the tiny nub of her clit between the silken hairs and she touched it, feeling its soft peak against her fingertips. She writhed deliciously as Andrew stretched out his long legs and continued to recount his tale to the crackling logs in the grate, seemingly oblivious to her.

'Lift up your skirt, woman,' he said then, louder, as if in character and Charlotte stroked the flesh of her inner thigh, her legs parting just a fraction. 'I want to see those intimate parts of you that no man has seen. I want your legs wide apart so that I can finger you. I want to taste you.'

Charlotte moved restlessly in her seat, the moistness between her legs spreading across her fingers. Glancing down she saw the telltale glistening on her hand.

'The maiden had no choice. She lay on her back and raised her legs upwards and wide. He kneeled between her legs, placing her feet on his shoulders. His hands stroked her thighs, parting her, inserting first one finger and then a second into her tight little hole.' As Andrew spoke, his own legs spread wider and Charlotte thought that the bulge in his trousers seemed more pronounced. Was he becoming aroused, too? It looked that way.

'The maiden gasped as his finger slid deep into her,' Andrew continued and Charlotte suddenly had the most desperate need to feel his finger deep inside of *her*. Unable to resist a moment longer, Charlotte slid out of her chair as if to sit closer to the fire – closer to him. She didn't look up at him. She *couldn't* look at him. Instead, she gazed into the fire as he continued talking.

'He was gentle with her, and soon her moans of pain

were moans of pleasure and she arched herself towards him, eager for his hands to explore her more deeply.'

Charlotte knew the feeling. Like the girl in the story, she too ached to be touched. Before she knew it, she found herself resting very lightly against Andrew's knee as he continued his storytelling. He didn't recoil or object; he barely seemed to notice her. As for Charlotte, she refused to think logically, refused to remind herself that this was a man she was interviewing, not a lover. Rational thought was suddenly a long way away.

As his words continued to lull her, she turned, so that she was on her knees, between his legs. She placed her hands on his thighs, her gaze lowered. She was afraid to meet his eyes in case they were harsh and accusing. In case they said no.

He continued recounting the story, but now his words were broken, disjointed, as Charlotte began to slowly stroke his thighs through the smooth fabric of his trousers.

His legs were firm, muscular, and she suddenly wanted to feel more intimate parts of him. She stroked upwards, letting her fingers slide lightly over his crotch. Instantly she felt him harden. The feeling was good beneath her fingertips. She could trace the shape of his manhood, feel the very tip. It throbbed a little beneath her featherlight touch.

He stopped talking and Charlotte glanced up, only to find his eyes were closed. His head was back and his lips were set in a firm line. She continued her stroking, watching him, aware of every flinch and movement in his face.

At any moment she sensed he might grab her hands and stop her from doing what she was doing. But while he still allowed her, she continued, growing more daring by the second.

Under his clothing his cock was now quite rigid. She loved the feel of it straining against his trousers. She knew he would be itching for her to release him, and she had no intention of disappointing him.

She felt for his zip and eased it down, flicking open the top button of his trousers. Her excitement was rising, while he seemed to have become almost rigid. Her hand slid eagerly inside his trousers. She felt his warmth, and the springy coarseness of his pubic hairs as her hand closed around his big hard cock. It felt glorious and stiffened even more.

Without a word, she eased it from the confines of his trousers and heard him catch his breath. Her gaze travelled the length of it, marvelling at its thickness and length. Gently she ran her hand up and down the long shaft, then eased his balls out from his trousers, so they sat perkily at the base of his zip.

She couldn't resist it and her tongue flicked over the shiny purple head. When he didn't protest, she continued to make long slow licks up and down its length, making it wet and slippery so that her hand slid easily up and down.

But she was hungry to taste him properly and, parting her lips, she sucked his cock fully into her mouth. Although already large, once inside her mouth it seemed to erupt, filling her completely, almost making her gag. The sensation was electric and she sucked greedily.

'Oh, Charlotte,' Andrew suddenly moaned, stroking her hair. 'Charlotte, Charlotte, didn't I warn you?' The stroking became more urgent; he began to apply a gentle pressure, holding her head down over him as his hips jerked and he thrust his cock harder and deeper into her mouth.

She held him around his waist, her mouth full of cock while his hands slid down her back, tracing the curve of her spine, teasing her shirt up towards her shoulders, exposing her bare bottom. Charlotte felt the heat from the fire warming her naked buttocks.

She groaned, arching her back and parting her legs,

wishing there were two of him so he could fuck her from behind while she was still sucking his cock.

He sensed her need and reached over her back, easing himself even further down her throat. His finger slid down between the cheeks of her bottom, stroking the tight little opening of her anus. Charlotte groaned and writhed and wriggled, trying to dislodge his finger from that most private part of her body.

In desperation she arched her head back, his erect cock coming out of her mouth, standing rigid, wet and shiny. She clawed upwards to his shoulders, pulling his head down so that she could kiss him. The second their lips touched, hers parted, her tongue flicking swiftly inside his mouth to entwine with his while his finger continued to play around the opening of her pussy and anus.

She writhed again, moving his finger to her pussy and pressing her pelvis downwards, wanting to spear herself on his finger. 'Andrew . . . please . . . do that . . . please.'

She saw his lips curve as he brought his finger up to her mouth for her to suck. Then he returned it between her legs and slipped it into her. First one finger, then two, moving slowly in and out, side to side, gently making circular movements. Charlotte groaned, moving in rhythm with him, then took his throbbing cock back into her mouth while he continued fingering her.

She loved the taste and the scent of the man, loved the feel of his long hard shaft in her mouth. She wanted to stay like this forever. But, eventually, he lifted her from him and turned her around, still on her knees but facing away from him, her little bare bottom gleaming up at him.

On her knees, she felt his hands move in circular movements over the cheeks of her bottom. Then one hand slid down to stroke her anus again, not seeming to care that she wriggled whenever he touched her there, but not exploring deeper. Then he played with her pussy lips, discovering the little nub of her clit. Then back, lingering at the opening to her pussy, his finger darting deftly between its warm moist folds.

Charlotte groaned, arching her back, pushing her bottom upwards. His hand stroked her flesh again and, suddenly, without warning, he smacked her bottom.

There was no pain, but the effect was like a trigger and she wriggled and squirmed, her head going down on to the rug, her pussy longing to feel him inside of her.

'Andrew,' she murmured, tasting the rug on her lips as he kneeled behind her and lowered his head to her rear. Charlotte felt the softness of his hair against her bottom and then, to her delight, felt his tongue licking at her pussy, while his hand reached beneath her to squeeze her breasts. She groaned, wanting him so badly she could die. 'Fuck me, Andrew. Fuck me as hard as you can. I want to feel your cock in me. Now, quickly, Andrew, please.'

She heard him groan.

'Charlotte, this is the Highland Ruby doing this. I warned you.'

'I don't care,' she cried, her whole body aching for his touch. 'I don't care. I just *need* you!'

'No,' he uttered hoarsely. 'This isn't you. It's this damnable enchanted relic.' And he suddenly scrambled to his feet, snatching the pendant from around her neck. 'Curse the thing!' he raged, throwing it fiercely across the room. 'Curse the blasted thing!'

He was on his feet, his eyes blazing. Every muscle in his body looked coiled tight as if he might explode. Charlotte crumpled on to the rug, her head spinning and her body trembling. She stared up at him. His penis remained stiff, standing erect and dark red, towering menacingly over her.

The Highland Ruby lay in the far corner of the room. Charlotte stared at it. Had it enchanted her? She waited for the shame to hit her, as it had Enritha. Waited for the overwhelming feelings of lust to subside. Waited to feel disgusted at her own wanton behaviour.

Those feelings never came. She lay there in agony in her need to have him inside of her. But there was no chance of that happening now. She saw the anger in his eyes and knew he was blaming the Highland Ruby for enchanting her. Or if not enchanting her, then giving her the excuse to behave like a slut. No doubt that was the way he thought all women behaved, given the opportunity.

Tears of frustration stung her eyes but still there were no feelings of shame or disgust in herself. The Highland Ruby had nothing to do with the way she had felt or behaved. She wanted Andrew Alexander to fuck her – Highland Ruby or no Highland Ruby!

Sharp stinging raindrops lashed her face as Charlotte stepped reluctantly outside Andrew Alexander's house. The heavy wax jacket he had given her to wear was about five sizes too big, as were the sweater and old faded jeans. He had dressed for the weather too but, unlike Charlotte, his clothes were his own and fitted him perfectly, while she looked a sight.

She hadn't wanted to leave. She'd wanted to stay and convince Andrew that it wasn't the pendant that had turned her into a raving nymphomaniac – it was him. But Andrew, it seemed, was taking no chances. After zipping himself up and stowing the Highland Ruby back into its wall safe, he had found her some dry clothes and ushered her swiftly out of the door.

Having been so rudely rejected and ejected, Charlotte's passion swiftly turned to hurt and humiliation. He'd managed to turn off so easily, while she was still as horny as hell. That's what hurt the most. The fact that he'd dumped her so easily.

Charlotte was so wound-up about it all that she almost told him where to stick his offer of accompanying her back to the pub. It was only because she was too embarrassed to strike up a conversation of any sort that she allowed him to walk back with her.

Pulling the door shut behind them, Andrew set off. Charlotte followed, squinting against the lashing rain. He strode on ahead, carrying her sodden clothes for her in a holdall. What a gentleman, Charlotte thought wryly, carrying her bag and refusing to fuck her in case she was under some magic spell.

There was no spell and no magic. The Highland Ruby was well and truly back in its hiding place, while she still ached to be fucked.

Paul! His face swam hazily through her mind. But rather than feel guilt, she only felt irritated because he wasn't here to satisfy her. If Paul were here she wouldn't be lusting after someone who clearly wasn't going to touch her ever again.

'Damn him!' Charlotte cursed under her breath as she traipsed along behind Andrew Alexander. She'd never seen a man move so quickly nor react so angrily once he'd made up his mind it was the pendant making her so wanton. Obviously he had strong beliefs when it came to the Highland Ruby. Either he did honestly believe it was enchanted, or he honestly believed that all women, given the chance, would throw away their inhibitions for a quick shag.

Charlotte wondered whether he'd be as quick to reject her if they'd been out on a date or some such thing, where the Highland Ruby didn't come into it. Or just out walking together like they were here on the moors.

The tingling sensation between her legs reared up again. Did she really want sex in the mud?

The answer was simple enough – yes.

Not that she was going to get the chance. Andrew marched on, head bowed against the torrent of rain, barely glancing behind to see if she was following. He was clearly in a desperate hurry to return her to where she belonged and get her out of his hair.

He reached the pub first and went in, leaving Charlotte to trudge wearily and dejectedly in a couple of minutes later, by which time he had already taken off his wet coat and was perched on a bar stool. Nancy was pouring him a drink.

'Och, here she is now, the poor wee lamb,' Nancy wailed, hurrying around from the bar to fuss over Charlotte. 'Just look at you, soaked right through. Away in and have a wee dram, too. You look in need of one.'

'She's had enough,' Andrew stated, downing his drink in one and slapping his glass down on the bar, no doubt for a refill.

Charlotte's blood boiled. 'I'll decide whether or not I've had enough, thank you. And yes, I'll have a Scotch please, Nancy. A large one.'

Nancy's dark eyebrows raised a little as she glanced from Charlotte to Andrew. Then she gave a little knowing smile and poured two more drinks.

'I'll take it upstairs, if you don't mind,' Charlotte said, fixing Andrew with an icy glare. 'I need a hot bath.'

He responded with a look which clearly said, Don't blame me, I did warn you.

Taking her drink, Charlotte swung away and hurried upstairs. Behind her, she heard them talking. Then Nancy started laughing. Charlotte halted on the stairs, listening. What were they saying about her? Was Andrew saying how easily he could have shagged this woman who was supposed to be here on business?

Nancy giggled again. A girlish giggle, and Charlotte had another thought. Perhaps they weren't discussing her at all. Nancy and Andrew were all alone down there in the bar ... Charlotte strained to hear what they were talking about. Eavesdropping wasn't usually her thing, only in this case she made an exception.

What if Andrew was still feeling horny? After all, he

was pretty well aroused. Had the rain cooled his ardour, or was he ready for a fuck? And if anyone was able and ready for shagging it was randy Nancy.

Downstairs, she heard the distinctive sound of a piece of furniture scraping along the stone floor. Charlotte slumped against the stair-wall feeling utterly miserable. It could, she knew, be Andrew scraping his stool back to leave. Or it could be them adjusting the table so he could lay Nancy across it and fuck her.

'Shit!' she swore, slamming into her room and throwing off her clothes – or rather *his* clothes. Naked, she went into the bathroom and turned on the taps. Hot water gushed into the enamel bath, drowning out any sounds of passion from below.

She hated him. Absolutely hated the man. No, she didn't, damn him, she fancied him rotten.

With a groan she eased herself into the steaming bath and lay there, eyes closed, sipping her whisky and trying not to picture him with Nancy. Oh, it wasn't fair. That woman had more sex than she knew what to do with, and here was Charlotte absolutely aching for it.

The bathroom door opened suddenly. Wide-eyed, Charlotte brought her knees up, protecting her modesty as Kenneth, Nancy's partner, strolled in.

'Och, I didn't realise you were havin' a bath, hen. D'yer mind if I take a piss, I'm bursting.'

Charlotte was so astonished she shook her head and stared in surprise as, unabashed, he unzipped his flies and took out his cock.

'Nasty day,' he politely chatted as he peed into the toilet.

'Awful,' Charlotte answered, her throat dry and her head starting to spin. She took another gulp of whisky.

'You've no' been out in this, have ye, hen?' he asked, giving his dick a little shake before putting it back into his cords.

'Yes, I got soaked,' she muttered, hugging her knees to

her chest, hardly able to believe she was having this conversation.

He washed his hands. 'Were ye doing your interview with our Mr Alexander?'

She nodded. Her face felt as hot as the bath water. Nancy's words leaped back into her mind. *This is the bathroom, you'll not mind sharing?* She hadn't realised when Nancy said sharing, she really meant sharing!

'And how did it go?'

Charlotte lowered her eyes. 'Not brilliant.'

'Och, now why's that, ma hen?' Kenneth asked kindly, putting down the loo seat and sitting on it. 'Did ye no' get what ye wanted?'

Charlotte uttered a humourless little laugh. 'You could say that.' Then to her dismay, tears began to prick her eyes.

Kenneth was quick to notice. He came over and kneeled down at the side of the bath. He looked concerned, although his eyes quickly shifted from her face down to her breasts, half hidden though they were behind her knees and arms. He stroked the back of her hand. 'Do ye want to tell me what happened? I might be able to help.'

Charlotte shook her head. The effects of the whisky and the combination of cold and heat were beginning to make her feel woozy. She felt tired suddenly, tired and weary.

'You're looking awful tense, hen. Why don't ye relax and let the water help you unwind. It's a canny big bath this; you've no need to be all huddled up like that.'

Charlotte opened her eyes. The room looked misty. Steam haze or a drunken haze, she wasn't sure. The whisky was certainly taking its toll. She drained her glass.

'Stretch out your legs, hen,' Kenneth said softly. 'You've no' to be worried about me. I've seen ma share of females wi' no clothes on, you'll no' embarrass me.'

Charlotte sniffed. He was being awfully nice. And nice

was just what she needed at the moment. She unfurled herself, lowering her legs back into the hot water although she still held her arms stiffly in front of her, hiding her nipples, and clasping her hands over her neat bush of auburn pubic hair beneath the water.

The sound of the bathroom door opening once more made them both glance guiltily towards it. Nancy stood there. Her cheeks were pink and her hair seemed more tousled than Charlotte remembered it being. Whether she'd been shagging Andrew Alexander, however, didn't seem too important at that moment. Charlotte was more concerned about Nancy finding her like this: sitting naked in the bath, chatting to her man.

Kenneth seemed none too perturbed. He nodded his head in Charlotte's direction. 'Our guest's had an awful difficult morning, so it seems.'

'Did it no' go well with our Mr Alexander?' Nancy asked, closing the bathroom door and joining Kenneth at the side of the bath.

'Didn't he tell you?' Charlotte asked, feeling decidedly odd having such a public bathtime. She half expected Andrew to walk in next. Her fingers pressed harder against her mound. Oh, if only!

Nancy shrugged her plump shoulders. 'He said very little to me. He's away home again now. He only stopped for a quickie.'

Charlotte eyed her suspiciously. A quick drink or a quick shag? She desperately wanted to know. Oh, damn him. What did it matter?

Nancy smiled. 'Och, ye poor wee lamb, you're awful tense. Move aside Ken, let me help the lass relax.'

She rolled back her sleeves, then, lathering her hands, began to gently massage around the base of Charlotte's throat and across her shoulders.

Charlotte's initial instincts were to push her off. It had been years since a woman had helped her bathe. Not since she was a child. Men, yes. Or rather one or two –

Paul. Although he wouldn't have bothered with soaping her shoulders. He would be straight to her breasts and from there down to her fanny.

Nancy seemed perfectly happy to gently massage the upper half of her body, however, and once Charlotte had got accustomed to the strange feel of a woman's hands on her skin, she had to admit that it was quite pleasant. Certainly softer and lighter than a man's touch.

Slowly she began to unwind. She allowed her eyes to close and relaxed down into the hot water. Her arms drifted at her sides, leaving her breasts bobbing half in, half out of the water. A cluster of foamy bubbles gathered around her pink nipples, pure white against the dark pink of her hardening peaks.

'You're getting your blouse wet, Nancy pet,' Ken murmured, and when Charlotte opened her eyes a little, she saw him unbuttoning Nancy's flowery blouse.

It didn't really surprise Charlotte to see that Nancy didn't wear a bra. It did surprise her – if only briefly and vaguely – to see that Ken was also concerned that Nancy didn't wet her skirt. As the older woman continued to lather and soap Charlotte's neck and shoulders, with her huge white breasts swaying in front of Charlotte's blurred vision, Ken unzipped his partner's skirt and let it drop on to the bathroom floor. Her knickers followed.

In a way Charlotte was quite glad that Nancy was naked too. She felt less vulnerable now, as if the odds had shifted in her favour. Two naked ladies and one fully dressed man.

'That water looks lovely and warm, hen,' Nancy crooned, 'And it's awful chilly all of a sudden.'

That wasn't surprising, Charlotte thought, trying to get used to the sight of such a plump naked woman in front of her eyes, whose goose pimples were beginning to erupt all over her skin.

Charlotte felt awful suddenly. It really was impolite to leave her host standing out in the cold when the bath was big enough to accommodate two. So, sliding her bottom further towards the taps, Charlotte parted her legs and smiled invitingly at Nancy to join her. The water slopped over the sides of the bath as Nancy clambered in.

Charlotte resisted the urge to giggle. It was so odd, sharing a bath with another woman.

*You'll no' mind sharing?*

No, she didn't mind. Not this once anyway, and especially with the lovely warm glow of the whisky running through her veins. In fact, at that moment she couldn't think of anything nicer than sharing her bath with Nancy.

Kenneth stood looking down at the pair of them. His smile reached from ear to ear. 'Just look at the pair of ye. I think I'd better give ye both a good latherin'. Now, where's the soap.'

It suddenly seemed a wonderful idea not to tell him. Glancing at her new-found bathing companion, Charlotte mischievously said, 'Find it!'

Kenneth needed no persuasion. Rolling up his sleeves, he plunged his arms between the four naked legs. Giggling like schoolgirls, Charlotte and Nancy splashed and writhed to avoid his exploring hands.

There was no hiding place, however. With Nancy's heavy thighs clamped down over her spread-eagled legs, Charlotte couldn't avoid Ken's probing hands for long. She gasped as he touched her between the legs.

He looked like the cat that got the cream. He was practically purring as he explored deeper, stroking Charlotte's inner thighs, then higher, teasing at her silken wet pubic hairs, his finger coiling beneath her, entering her.

She tried to escape, to wriggle backwards, but the taps were hard against her spine and Nancy's legs felt like great weights on her slender thighs. Charlotte clutched the sides of the bath as Ken slid his finger in and out of her hot wet sex.

'Here, Kenny,' Nancy breathed, taking his other hand and guiding it between her legs. 'Maybe you'll find the soap here. There's certainly something nice and slithery to play with, anyway.'

Ken kneeled there, a mixture of ecstasy and concentration on his face as he finger-fucked them both. Once over the initial shock of having him touch her, Charlotte found herself moving her pelvis against him, enjoying the sensations coursing through her and feeling her climax rising. She parted her legs wider, as wide as the limited space would allow, and Nancy smiled at her.

Ken bent over the bath to kiss Nancy and as he did, so his hand up Charlotte's fanny increased its pressure. He probed deeper and harder, penetrating her with three fingers, then four and making her cry out. He switched his attentions then, shifting position to kiss Charlotte. As their mouths touched, she felt him upping the pressure on Nancy. Fingering her hard as he had done her.

Nancy began groaning then, with a lot more splashing, she got up on to her knees in the bath and unzipped Kenneth's fly. He stopped kissing Charlotte and crouched at the side of the bath as Nancy took out his cock.

It bounced out, stocky and red and Charlotte watched fascinated as Nancy gripped it and swiftly began to run her hand up and down its thick length, pulling back the foreskin to reveal the bulbous red knob. Kenneth remained crouched, knees trembling against the bath, with a hand on both of the women's shoulders as Nancy gave him a good hard wanking.

Feeling a little left out, Charlotte reached out and cupped Ken's balls in her hand, moulding and manipulating them, enjoying the feel of their hairy softness. At her touch, Kenneth's fingernails dug deeper into her shoulder blades and he uttered a groan of pleasure.

Nancy relinquished her hold on Kenneth's dick, took Charlotte's hand and placed it around Kenneth's penis, giving it an encouraging little jerk as if to get her moving.

Charlotte obliged, running her slippery hand up and down his length, finding that she had a tremendous urge to feel it up her.

A moment later, she realised someone was fingering her pussy again. It wasn't Ken – he was gripping their shoulders, his eyes screwed tightly shut. No, this was a much softer feel, and Charlotte flashed a startled if bleary look at Nancy.

The other woman smiled at her and continued stroking Charlotte's clit with slow, velvet strokes, asserting just the right pressure in just the right spot. Charlotte felt her climax rising quickly and unexpectedly. There was nothing she could do to stop it. She came with a cry of pleasure and astonishment that a woman could do this to her. Nancy kept up the pressure and Charlotte's body jerked spasmodically against Nancy's hand, startling her by the intensity of the sensations flooding through her.

The moment was exquisite and acute and left Charlotte trembling as she collapsed back in the water. Only then did she realise that she had been gripping Ken's cock so hard it had turned purple. She released it guiltily, although he obviously had no objections. Nancy eagerly took her turn. Slopping bath water everywhere, she took his cock into her mouth and sucked greedily.

Getting over the shock of a woman bringing her off, Charlotte watched Nancy as she continued to give her man a blow job. Up on her knees, her curly black bush was only inches from Charlotte's face. She didn't quite know what to do. She had the feeling she ought to reciprocate in some way, only she had never touched another woman. She really didn't know if she fancied it or not. What she did want was a big, hard cock right up her fanny.

However, sitting and watching was going to get her nowhere. She got up on to her knees and pressed her warm wet body against Nancy's. Her slippery breasts crushed against the side of Nancy's left breast. The other woman's plump arm went around Charlotte instantly, her hand coiling around her buttocks, holding her close. After a few moments more Nancy relinquished her sucking and Kenneth's swollen dick stood proud and throbbing.

Charlotte knew it was hers for the taking and she slipped her lips around the bulbous knob, while Nancy's hand slid down between the cheeks of her bottom. She began tickling Charlotte's anus, making her writhe, and then exploring the swollen lips of her sex.

Charlotte desperately wanted to come again but from this angle it was impossible and she moaned in frustration. Releasing Ken she looked up at him. Her vision made him appear bleary. The only thing she was sure of was that she wanted fucking. Right now. Right this minute.

Holding on to Ken's shoulders to keep her balance, she clambered out of the bath and stood up, pressing her dripping bare body against him. She wrapped her arms around his neck and ground her hips sexily against his erection. She gyrated slowly, leaving him in no doubt as to what she wanted.

'I think the lassy is after a wee shag, Kenny,' said Nancy, her voice drifting like a haze. 'I think ye had better oblige before she passes out. She's looking awful queasy.'

Charlotte's eyes were growing heavy and it was only the fierce need to have sex that was keeping her awake.

'Och, I think I can see to that,' Ken said huskily, putting one hand behind Charlotte's backside, his fingers sliding between her pussy lips. He bent his knees so that he could reach up into her further and he fingered her hard, making her gasp.

His free hand was on her breast, squeezing it, pulling at her nipple before lowering his mouth to it, nibbling until she cried out. Still his fingering continued relentlessly.

Finally he turned her around and walked her over to the little enamel sink on the wall. He bent her over it. Charlotte caught sight of herself in the mirror. He was standing behind her and she felt the hot tip of his cock against her bum cheeks. He parted her legs, then parted the pink lips of her sex and pushed his cock up inside her hot wet pussy.

Charlotte cried out at the initial thrust. In the mirror her eyes widened. He rammed himself up into her again, harder, grunting slightly. The enamel was cold against her stomach and uncomfortable against her bones. But there was no going back – no asking him to let her lie on her nice soft bed while he fucked her. He was shagging her doggy fashion and loving every minute of it.

But she couldn't come this way, and she desperately wanted to come. Her whole body cried out for release as he continued pumping his cock in and out of her. She almost wept when Nancy came between them. But instead of offering her own eager pussy to her partner, she took Charlotte's hand and led her back into her bedroom.

Puzzled, Charlotte allowed the older woman to lay her back against her pillows and then, to her astonishment, Nancy kneeled between her legs and buried her rosy face deep into Charlotte's swollen sex.

Too shocked to cry out, Charlotte allowed the woman to lap at her and delicately nibble her clit. Within seconds Charlotte felt herself starting to come. The sensation rose, until there was no stopping it and she arched herself against Nancy's face, dragging at the woman's hair as she pulled her into herself, hoping vaguely that she didn't do Nancy an injury.

When at last Charlotte was satisfied, when she had come over Nancy's mouth in one long exquisite climax, she collapsed back into her pillows, exhausted and ready to sleep.

She didn't hear either Nancy or Kenneth leave.

# Chapter Six

Charlotte awoke to find herself tucked up in bed, naked. She lay there, trying to work out whether it was morning or night. Her watch showed just after six and, judging by the light, it looked more like six in the evening than six in the morning. Slowly, her muzzy head cleared and she recalled with growing horror and embarrassment, the events that had happened before she fell asleep – or passed out.

She groaned into her pillow as it all came excruciatingly back to her: her steamy romp in the bath with Nancy and Kenneth; how she'd practically begged Kenneth to fuck her – and he had; then, to top it all, how Nancy had gone down on her, making her come.

And then of course, before all that, was Andrew Alexander and the Highland Ruby.

Lying in bed, Charlotte's cheeks burned crimson with embarrassment. How could she have done all that? She was normally such a nice, respectable, faithful girl!

She couldn't even put it down to the effects of the Highland Ruby. She was attracted to Andrew Alexander before he'd even got the Ruby out of his wall safe. And as for Kenneth and Nancy, that was pure wantonness on her part. Her only excuse for that was Andrew Alexander's extremely potent malt whisky.

Well, she wasn't going to touch that ever again. That was for sure.

She crawled out of bed, thankful that she hadn't got a headache. Holding on to the dresser to keep her balance as the room swam, she pulled on jeans and a sweater, and applied a little make-up to hide the pasty pallor caused by the alcohol.

She eyed herself in the mirror, her thoughts dwelling on the events with Andrew when she was at Stonemoor House earlier that day.

She recalled the way he'd spoken of the legend, and remembered how badly she had wanted him. It had been virtually impossible to keep her distance and keep her hands off him. He'd been irresistible.

Charlotte chewed her bottom lip, remembering the cool silkiness of his skin and how it felt when he had touched her. The scent of the man, the taste of him . . .

She had to see him again. There was still a lot of work to be done on the article. She hadn't even photographed the Ruby yet. Plus of course, she still needed to know the truth about it. Was its legend pure fantasy or was there just a little bit of magic about it?

Logic told her it was fantasy but, at the same time, it intrigued her to think there might be something enchanted about it. How else could the story of Enritha and Cameron have come about?

She laughed at her own gullibility. It happened hundreds of years ago – if it happened at all. The story had probably been embellished out of all recognition over the years. Nevertheless, she wanted to know for certain, for her sake, and for her readers.

The problem was, it was going to be difficult discovering the truth. Her own experience of feeling as horny as hell when Andrew had placed it on her was nothing to go by. She wanted him fiercely. She hadn't needed an enchanted pendant to make her open her legs to him. No, what she needed was some obnoxious male to place the Highland Ruby around her neck and try to make love to her. That would do the trick and prove it one way or the other.

There was a knock on her bedroom door and a cheerful female voice called from the landing. 'Hello, hen, are ye awake yet?'

Charlotte's eyes widened. Nancy! Oh God, how on earth could she face her after what they'd done together?

'Hello, Charlotte,' Nancy called again. 'Yer dinner's ready, if ye'd like to come doon.'

Charlotte inched open the door. She had to face the woman sometime. The sooner the better, she supposed. She peered around the half-opened door at her hostess standing on the landing. 'Yes, I'm awake. Er, thank you for putting me to bed.'

'Och, think nothin' of it, hen. Now away doon and have yer dinner.'

Charlotte blinked as Nancy trotted back downstairs without another word. She felt like pinching herself. Had she dreamed the steamy session she'd shared with Nancy and Ken? No, the puffiness around her sex told her she'd definitely been having fun recently.

Closing the door, Charlotte realised Nancy would guess she'd be feeling embarrassed. Not mentioning it was her way of helping Charlotte handle it. Charlotte smiled to herself. That was nice of Nancy.

Downstairs, a few of the locals were already having their nightly tipple, including Ken, who winked as she sat down at a table.

'What'll ye have to drink, Charlotte?' he asked, going around to the bar. Like Nancy, he made no reference to what had gone on earlier.

'Just a soft drink, please. Lemonade would be nice,' she replied, as Nancy brought her meal out: a big plateful of beef stew and dumplings. Charlotte did her best to eat it.

She was down to the last dumpling when the big red-haired Scot, Angus, lumbered in. His bulging eyes widened as they settled on Charlotte sitting on her own.

He pulled up a stool and seated himself next to her, his hairy knee brushing roughly against her leg as he adjusted his kilt to sit down. Charlotte automatically shuffled her stool a little further away. Not that he took the hint; he inched closer and his big freckled hand came down on her knee, giving it a squeeze.

'You've nearly finished your drink, lass. I'll buy ye another. What are ye having?'

Charlotte cursed under her breath. She didn't want to be stuck with Angus. She had been quite looking forward to chatting to the locals. Not this local, however.

Good breeding, though, forced her to smile politely. 'No, I'm fine, thank you.'

'Och, you've only a wee drop left,' he cajoled, giving her a nudge and almost sending her flying.

She gritted her teeth as she regained her balance. 'I'll have another lemonade then, thank you.'

He guffawed – a loud snort of a laugh – and little drops of saliva shot from his mouth and landed on her plate. Charlotte put her knife and fork down. 'Lemonade is for bairns. Have a drop o' Scotch with me. It'll put hairs on your chest.' His eyes flicked downwards, oggling her breasts, and Charlotte would liked to have slapped him.

'Lemonade is fine,' she said tightly, hoping he at least would go to the bar so she could manoeuvre her stool further away from his. But he just shouted his order across and remained where he was, crowding her into a corner with his bulk.

Ken brought the drinks over and cleared away her plate. 'I bet you didn't know our Angus here is a distant relative of Bonnie Prince Charlie. There's blue blood in them veins – a bit thin by now,' Ken joked. 'But royalty no less. Ye'll have to write an article on him next.'

Charlotte smiled politely again. 'I tend to write about antiques. I don't think Angus *quite* comes into that category.'

Her remark brought a lot of laughter and disagreement from the other locals, but Angus just nodded at her, looking down his flared nostrils. 'No, I'm no antique lassy, that I'm not. I've plenty of life in me yet an' no mistake.'

And, to Charlotte's horror, he took himself in hand through his kilt. With his massive truncheon swathed in tartan he waved it about under his sporran, a big lecherous grin parting his red wiry beard.

Burning with embarrassment, Charlotte jumped up, spilling half her drink as she squeezed past the mountainous Scotsman. Just as she was making her escape, he slapped her backside – hard.

It stung and Charlotte only just stopped herself from tipping the remaining contents of her glass over his big, stupid, grinning head. She was fuming. Everyone else seemed to think it was highly amusing. Only the appearance of Jamie stopped her from dashing right back to her room.

'Charlotte, hello. Och, what's the matter? Are ye all right? You're awful flushed.'

'Not really,' she grimaced, glaring daggers at Angus. 'It's him! He's an absolute animal!'

Jamie took her arm and steered her towards the bar. 'Och, he's harmless. But ye can come and stand beside me if ye'd rather.'

'I'd *much* rather,' she breathed, turning her back on Angus who was still grinning and playing with himself under the table. Jamie was like a breath of fresh air in comparison. She took a deep breath, determined that Angus wasn't going to spoil her evening. She smiled at

Jamie and forced herself to relax again. 'So, Jamie, how's the fishing?'

'It's grand,' he answered, pushing his soft sandy hair back from his eyes. 'Mind you, forecasts say some awful weather's heading this way – storms and the like. You'll have to mind, because if it gets too bad they'll stop the ferry and you'll be stuck here.'

'I've room in ma bed,' Angus piped up.

Charlotte cast him a withering glance, glad to see he was no longer touching himself up. God, but he had got a big one! An image of it swathed in tartan suddenly jumped into her head.

'Charlotte, are ye all right?' Jamie murmured, peering intently at her. 'You've a funny look on yer pretty face, hen.'

Charlotte halted her runaway imagination. Stopped herself from picturing Angus's awesome tackle and imagining the damage he could inflict with it. 'Sorry, I was just thinking. It's nothing important.'

Jamie lowered his head to hers. He smelled good, of soap and toothpaste and his own male scent. He spoke in a whisper, his blue eyes twinkling with mischief. 'Do you know what I was thinking?'

Charlotte nibbled on her lower lip and regarded him suspiciously. 'I don't think I want to know.'

He looked hurt. 'I'll no' tell ye then. I'd no' want to offend you.'

She smiled and touched his hand. 'I'm only teasing. Go on, tell me.'

He bent close to her ear, his lips brushing her lobe, sending little tingles up and down her spine. 'What I was thinking, what I've been thinking since ye took them photos of me, is that I'd like to do the same to you.'

'I don't like having my picture taken,' Charlotte replied softly, looking coy.

'Then I'd have to take yer mind off it.'

'And how would you do that?'

His gaze became languid, and his forefinger coiled into the palm of her hand. 'I'd take ye out into the heather, and then I'd undress you, nice and slowly, and kiss every inch of your beautiful body –'

'How do you know I've got a beautiful body?' Charlotte toyed, enjoying his attention.

He lowered his gaze further. 'I could hazard a guess.'

She smiled. He was so easy to smile at. So sweet and gorgeous. He had the most alluring mouth, so close to hers. And lips that just begged to be kissed. 'And then what?' she murmured. 'After you've kissed every inch of my beautiful body? There's not much photography going on as far as I can see.'

'Then I'd make love to ye. And I'd photograph your lovely face while I'm doing it.'

A delicious tingle raced through his body and she bit hard on her lip, not knowing quite how to reply.

'What do ye say to that?'

She felt like saying, 'Yes please.' But what the hell was happening to her? Poor Paul, waiting back home for her. How could she be so unfaithful? Wracked with guilt, she deliberately made light of Jamie's suggestion.

'I'd say your girlfriend is not going to be best pleased with you. Does she know what you're like!'

The hurt look came back into his clear blue eyes. 'I canna help being attracted to a pretty wee lassy, especially when I canna see ma girlfriend that often. She has a job on the next island. It's no' so easy to get together. Here, I've a picture of her, would you like to see?'

'I'd love to,' Charlotte said, deciding a picture of his girlfriend was just what she needed to cool her ardour. She couldn't just go around having sex with anyone she fancied, could she?

Jamie took a crumpled photo from his back pocket. Despite the creases, it showed a very attractive young woman. 'She's lovely, Jamie. You be careful you don't lose her, messing around with other women.'

He gazed down at the photo. 'Aye, you're right. I'd no' like to lose her, she's a bonny lass.'

'There you go, then,' Charlotte sighed, kicking herself. So where was the prize for being a good girl? There wasn't one. Jamie was so gorgeous.

'So how's the work going, Charlotte?' Nancy interrupted, smiling her rosy smile from across the bar. 'What exactly are ye writing about?'

'The Highland Ruby,' Charlotte answered, glad to get off the subject of sex and Jamie. 'It's an ancient pendant which dates back to the tenth century.'

'And our Mr Alexander owns it, I gather,' chipped in Nancy. 'It'll be quite valuable, I daresay.'

'I imagine it is, but it's the legend behind it which interests me,' Charlotte continued, vaguely aware that the hubbub of chatter had died down and everyone was listening to her.

'What legend is that then?' queried Nancy.

Charlotte fidgeted a little uncomfortably, not too sure whether she wanted to talk about it in the company of so many men. They all seemed to be waiting with baited breath, however, and she realised she hadn't much choice now. 'Well, it's pure myth, I have to tell you,' she began, feeling like she was giving a talk to the Men's Institute or some such thing. 'The story goes that if a man places the Highland Ruby around a woman's neck she falls under his power and has to do everything he commands her to do.'

'Who needs a fancy necklace to do that?' Ken joked, giving Nancy's bottom a smack.

Angus stroked his red beard, clearly intrigued. 'Do ye mean Mr Alexander has the Highland Ruby here, at his home? No' in a bank somewhere?'

'Locked away, safe and sound,' Charlotte assured him. 'He has a very sturdy wall safe. Believe me, Mr Alexander is very, very anxious that the Ruby should never fall into the wrong hands.'

'I should hope not,' Angus agreed, his big eyes all wide and innocent. 'Can ye imagine what an unscrupulous character might do with such a thing. No woman would be safe.'

Charlotte shot him an uneasy glance. They didn't come more unscrupulous than him. She hated to think what would happen if he ever got hold of the Highland Ruby. She for one would not like to be enslaveth to *his* every request.

'So is it true?' Jamie asked softly, claiming Charlotte as his own again. 'Is the legend true?'

Charlotte smiled, deciding to keep her own thoughts well out of it. 'There's no such thing as enchanted necklaces, Jamie. It's a good story though.'

He looked wistful. 'I wish I had a necklace like that. I'd put it on you and no mistake.'

Charlotte squeezed his hand. 'Jamie, you wouldn't need a magical necklace. If I wasn't already spoken for, I'd be yours for the asking.'

A big smile spread across his face. 'You would?'

'Definitely.'

This seemed to satisfy him, and Charlotte once more felt like kicking herself for not jumping at the chance for a romp in the heather with Jamie. Still, there was always the woman's prerogative to change her mind. There was a long night ahead of her.

She touched his hand again. 'Jamie . . .'

She got no further. Two more people walked into the bar. Charlotte recognised the man from the ferryboat who'd brought her here that first evening. She didn't know the young woman with him, though, except that she looked vaguely familiar.

It was obvious that Jamie knew her. Turning pink, he uttered, 'It's Diane, ma girlfriend.'

In two strides he'd caught her up in his big arms and

lifted her off the floor. Charlotte hid the sudden dash of disappointment that hit her. So much for her night of passion – which was just as well, she realised with a sigh. They were obviously madly in love and she'd been unfaithful enough to Paul already.

Holding her hand as if he was scared she'd disappear, Jamie introduced the love of his life to Charlotte.

'This is ma girlfriend, Diane. Diane, this is Charlotte, a magazine writer from London.'

'Pleased to meet you,' Charlotte smiled, extending her hand. The girl was just like her photograph. Very pretty, thick long black hair, a nice figure, if a little rounded, and big blue eyes which latched on to Jamie and barely wavered.

'What are ye doing here, Diane?' Jamie said, so clearly delighted at seeing her so unexpectedly that Charlotte felt a touch of the green-eyed monster. 'I wasn't expecting you till the weekend.'

Diane's arms went under Jamie's shirt, and Charlotte felt a sharp pang of regret that some other girl was getting to feel Jamie's hard smooth torso. 'Why do you think?' Diane murmured into Jamie's ear, her teeth practically nibbling on his lobe and ignoring Charlotte's presence completely. 'I couldn't wait till Saturday. I'm just aching for –'

Jamie silenced her with a kiss and an embarrassed little grin in Charlotte's direction. 'Er, can I get ye a drink, Diane?'

Diane's big blue eyes flashed saucily. 'There's only one thing I want down my throat, Jamie, and it's no' a pint of lager!'

And as if anyone could be left in any doubt as to what she meant, Diane's left hand slid around to the front of his jeans and slipped down inside his waistband.

Jamie jumped back, pulling her hand free, his cheeks glowing with embarrassment. 'Och, Diane, will ye no behave y'sel? You're embarrassing ma new friend.'

'Don't mind me,' Charlotte uttered, doing her best to retain her smile.

Jamie held on to his girlfriend's hands, more to keep her under control than anything else. 'She's got an awful wicked sense of humour.'

'So I see,' Charlotte remarked, wondering why Jamie had to bother with other women when he had a nymphomaniac of a girlfriend.

Diane tilted her chin, pouting her lips in a way that was supposed to make Jamie think her awfully cute. It irritated Charlotte immensely. And she could quite happily have told the girl to hop back on the boat and go back to where she came from.

The look on Jamie's face however was one of stunned delight. Charlotte gritted her teeth. How wonderful, Jamie's girlfriend turning up out of the blue, just when they were both wondering if a bit of hanky panky was on the cards.

She sighed under her breath. Hanky panky was on the cards all right. Only now it didn't involve her. Charlotte couldn't help but narrow her eyes as she looked at Diane. She was dressed for the climate rather than for a lover in blue jeans and a chunky sweater. But there was no doubt that beneath the heavy garments there was a red-hot young woman, dying for sex.

Diane began tugging impatiently and childishly at Jamie's hands. 'I want to go, Jamie. Hurry up and finish your drink.'

'But ma mother's at home. She'll still be up. She'll no' give us any time on our own.' Jamie looked helplessly at Charlotte. 'She's a wee bit old-fashioned is ma mother. She doesn't care for me having lassys back.'

Diane interrupted him and looked at Charlotte for the first time. 'Basically, she'd have a screaming fit if she caught us in bed together.'

Charlotte raised her eyebrows. She really didn't want

to hear about their sex life. In fact, she was starting to feel more and more like a wallflower every second.

'Well, I'm sure you'll work something out,' Charlotte remarked with deliberate disinterest. She noticed then, with some relief, that the ferryman who'd brought her here that first night was still hanging around. 'Excuse me, won't you? There's someone I want to speak to.'

'You don't have to go,' Jamie said, seeming genuinely reluctant for her to leave his company. But Diane freed her hands and slid them down his waistband again, demanding his full attention. Over the top of her shiny dark head there was a rueful expression on Jamie's face. 'I'll see you later then, Charlotte.'

Charlotte smiled weakly as she turned her back on them and concentrated on the ferryman. 'Hi. Remember me?'

His weather-beaten face crinkled. 'Aye, that I do lass. How's it going?'

'Good,' she lied, sounding cheerful. 'Actually, I wanted to ask you about Andrew Alexander. You implied that you know him, but I never got the chance to ask you about him. Can I buy you a drink while we talk?'

His crinkled eyes lit up. 'Aye, a drop of whisky would be nice.'

As Charlotte bought him a drink, Diane dragged Jamie to a shadowy little alcove in the far corner of the bar. They sat down practically on top of each other. Charlotte looked away, irritated by the girl's behaviour.

'Ma name's William McTavish by the way,' the ferryman said pleasantly. 'Now what is it you're wanting to know?'

Charlotte took her notebook and pencil from her bag. 'I need a little background on Andrew Alexander. I think you implied when we spoke earlier that he didn't like the press. Why was that?'

William McTavish removed his yellow woollen hat and savoured his drink before speaking. 'Well, it's understandable. No disrespect to your profession, but the press put him through hell when his young bride died of an overdose.'

'Yes, he did tell me something about that,' Charlotte nodded, seeing out of the corner of her eye that Diane and Jamie were kissing passionately.

'The lassy took her own life,' William McTavish continued, sipping his drink. 'Possibly by accident. But for a while Mr Alexander was under suspicion, at least in the eyes of the press. His restaurant chain was going through a sticky patch at the time, and her wealth dropping into his lap so suddenly must have come as a bit of a relief.'

'So the newspapers put two and two together, making five?' Charlotte guessed, noticing that Diane's hand was now quite blatantly on Jamie's crotch, stroking him in a way that made Charlotte's pussy tingle with desire. She bit her lip. Dammit, why did his girlfriend have to come tonight? She heaved a sigh, annoyed with herself for having the chance earlier and blowing it.

William McTavish paid no attention to the young lovers over in the corner. He seemed perfectly happy to concentrate on Charlotte's face and figure. 'Aye, the newspapers weren't kind to the man. It must have been awful. Bad enough his young bride dying, but to get the blame . . .'

'What was she like?' Charlotte asked, seeing that Jamie had curled his randy little girlfriend across the front of him, holding her close, his hand quite clearly on her breast. No one else seemed to be paying them any attention. Except Angus, of course, who sat facing them, legs astride, no doubt giving his monstrous tackle room to expand.

'She was awful wealthy,' William McTavish said after thinking for a moment. 'Not flashy rich. Not his type at all really. He was usually seen with the glamorous, sophisticated, sexy type of lady. There was one he often brought here before he got married. Now, what was her name?' He called across the bar to Nancy. 'Nancy, I'm trying to think of that woman's name who used to knock about with Mr Alexander before he got married. You know, the big buxom one with the long blonde hair and legs up to her armpits.'

Nancy cast him a disapproving glance at his mode of description. 'Ingrid, wasn't it? Swedish as I remember.'

A lecherous glint appeared on practically all the male faces in the bar and conversations sprung up about the size of Ingrid's tits and backside. Charlotte began to wish she'd never asked.

William McTavish sucked in his breath. 'Now, she was the sort Mr Alexander was accustomed to being seen with. She was the sort that loved the limelight while young Fay – the one he married – was a sweet, innocent little thing.'

'Did Mr Alexander and his wife spend a lot of time here?' Charlotte asked, deliberately not looking at what Jamie and his girlfriend were doing now.

'Aye, what little time they had together, they'd come here. But the tragedy happened in London. He had a flat in the West End. He's sold it now, so I heard, and when he's not here living like a recluse, he's living in hotels around Europe where his restaurants are.'

'Do you think he still misses her?' Charlotte asked, wanting to know everything about Andrew Alexander.

'I wouldn't know, lass. I believe he loved her, but who can tell?' he murmured, sipping his drink again. 'They seemed very happy together. But you can never tell what goes on behind closed doors.'

That was true enough, Charlotte thought, glancing at Nancy. Who would guess what she got up to once the doors were locked.

She smiled at her companion. 'Thank you for talking to me.'

'Do ye have to go?' he asked, looking at her hopefully. 'I'd like to hear about your work in London.'

Charlotte hesitated. Perhaps if Diane hadn't turned up, she would have stayed up and enjoyed the evening. But with her practically devouring Jamie in the corner, there didn't seem much point in hanging around. On top of that, her head was full of thoughts of Andrew Alexander. It didn't help to know he also had a Swedish lover at some point in time. No wonder he was able to reject her advances that morning.

A sweet virginal bride or a steamy hot Swedish sexpot. He certainly went to extremes. What chance did she have of interesting him? An ordinary, average twenty-seven year old. Neither virginal nor particularly sexy. Boring, in Andrew's eyes, probably. Suddenly, bed seemed the best place for her.

Thanking William McTavish, Charlotte finished her drink and wandered back to her room. Tomorrow morning she would have to go and see Andrew again. God only knew how she would face him after what had happened. But she really had no choice if she was to get this article finished.

The thought of seeing him again sent odd little shivers up and down her spine. She had no idea what his reaction to her would be. Probably he'd keep her at arm's length, afraid that the Highland Ruby had worked its magic once too often. Or maybe he'd realised by now that it was the effects of the drinks he'd given her. Well, she wasn't going to touch a single drop next time. She would be stone-cold sober and in complete control of her actions and emotions.

She hoped.

But it was hard not to let her mind drift back to that morning. She could picture herself now, kneeling down before a roaring log fire, nestling between Andrew Alexander's outstretched legs, her hands stroking his thighs, her fingertips tracing the outline of his hardening cock.

She gave an ironic little sigh. At least she'd interested him enough for him to get a hard on.

She got ready for bed. Lying in her tartan pyjamas with the sheets tucked under her chin, she wished more than anything that Andrew Alexander was in bed with her.

'If ma mother catches us, there'll be hell to pay,' Jamie continued to fret as he and Diane walked arm in arm along the seafront towards his cottage.

Diane pressed herself close to Jamie as they ambled along by the harbour wall. It was pitch black now, only the moonlight and a few stars casting a silvery glow across the bay. They'd left some of the locals at the Captain's Table for their regular late-night drink. Diane guessed that Jamie stayed over sometimes. She wondered what they found to talk about till all hours of the morning. Still, at least there was no danger of him going off with another woman; there wasn't much competition here on the island. There was Nancy, of course, but she had Ken, and she was too ordinary to interest Jamie.

But that Charlotte Harvey from London was a different matter altogether. She hadn't liked the look of her at all. Far too attractive – and she'd seen the way Jamie had hankered after her. She would have to watch that flame-haired journalist.

For now though, she'd got Jamie all to herself. And she couldn't wait to get his cock in her hand. Sex every other weekend only was beginning to get her down. And even then it was only when his mam went out to do the shopping or visit a neighbour. She treated him like a child, but he wouldn't have a word said against her.

She only hoped the old dear was tucked up in her bed when they got back because if she didn't get Jamie's big hard cock up her within the next half hour she was going to die of longing.

Jamie turned and smiled at her in the moonlight. 'This is a nice surprise, Diane, hen. I've been thinking about ye all day.'

She pulled his head down so she could kiss him again, her hand automatically going down to the front of his trousers to rub against his prick through the thick denim.

'And I've been thinking about you. Jamie, I need you. My whole body is just tingling with longing.'

'Is it?' he murmured, fondling her breast. 'Tell me what ye want me to do then, and I'll see if I can oblige.'

Diane began to giggle. 'Och, you know all right. I want sex.'

'You mean you want fucking,' Jamie said, forcing her back against the harbour wall and pinning her there with his thighs.

Diane gasped as she was crushed against the damp brickwork. Jamie never used words like that. What had got into him? 'That's dirty talk, Jamie,' she scolded.

'It's straightforward talk,' he murmured, slowly gyrating his pelvis against hers so that she could feel the hardening of his erection. 'If you want me to give you a good hard fucking you'd better say so.'

Her heartbeats began to drum against her ribcage. This wasn't like Jamie at all. They usually waited until they got back to his cottage and his mam was snoring. Then they'd make love quietly, so as not to wake her. It wasn't like him at all. Nevertheless, it was what she wanted. With a tremor in her voice she murmured, 'Yes, I do, that's what I want.'

'So say it,' he breathed. 'Say the word.'

'I can't,' she giggled, embarrassed. 'It's rude.'

'No, this is rude,' he uttered, unzipping his fly and pulling out his semi-erect cock. He gripped it in his hand, and Diane's eyes widened in horror in case anybody should come along and see him.

'Jamie, someone might come . . .'

'Aye, you I hope, followed closely by me. Now say it.

Tell me you want fucking. Tell me you want my cock up your cunt. Say the words. Say them.'

She felt on fire. A raging heat began to course through her sex. Her pussy swelled and pressed against her clothing. She writhed against the stiff denim of her jeans, desperately needing to feel him, yet afraid that tonight she may have bitten off more than she could chew.

'Jamie, I can't,' she murmured, feeling the need in her grow. She put her arms around his neck, pulling his head down to hers so that she could kiss his lips.

He allowed her to kiss him just briefly, then pushed his rampant length between her legs, almost lifting her off the ground. She pressed down on it, hating her clothes that stopped the feeling – stopped his penetration.

'Jamie, please,' she began to whimper. 'Oh Jamie, I want you . . .'

'I want fucking,' he spelled out for her, rubbing himself between her legs, his cock now fully erect and hard.

She couldn't bear it any longer. But her voice was soft, just a whisper. 'Jamie, please fuck me.'

'Louder,' he said, looking down into her flushed face. 'Say it louder.'

Her fear of being overheard was overcome with her lust. 'I want fucking, Jamie,' she said huskily. 'Fuck me till I can't sit down.'

He groaned. 'That's better.' He took her hand, glancing back over his shoulder, as he led her down some steps on to the shingle beach, his penis pointing the way.

As she was led down, Diane's wide luminous eyes kept looking from Jamie's face to his big shaft. The tingling between her legs was acute and she ached for it.

He stopped near some upturned boats, quickly unbuckled her jeans and pushed them down past her knees. The cold night air on her bare buttocks and legs made her feel even more sexy. She made no protest as he pressed her backwards until she was sitting on an upturned boat.

Then, as the cold rough wood scratched against her bare bottom, she cried out, 'Jamie, it's all wet and slimy.'

'Just how I like it,' he breathed, pulling off one of her shoes and dragging her jeans and knickers off one leg. He got down on his knees in the shale and parted her legs wide so that her sex glistened with her juices under the starlight. His thumb expertly found the hard bud of her clit while two fingers slipped up her fanny.

She threw her head back as the sensations rocketed through her. He finger-fucked her hard and she cried out, gasping his name, vaguely aware that there could be fishermen not far away, wading in the shallows with their rods.

Jamie's free hand rucked up her sweater, pushing it up around her neck. Then he pushing her bra up, too, exposing her breasts. Diane glanced at her erect nipples in the moonlight and groaned as Jamie's finger and thumb closed around one peak and squeezed it hard.

He eased back from her, then, and took hold of his big hard cock. 'This is what ye want isn't it? Ma cock up your fanny. Tell me you want fucking. Tell me again.'

She needed no encouragement, and thrilled to the sound of the words as they left her lips. 'Fuck me, Jamie, up my cunt. I want your cock up me. Fuck me hard, Jamie, now please.' Her legs widened and her hand slipped down to her open sex lips.

Jamie took hold of her ankles and spread her legs even wider. For agonising moments he stroked his length between her legs. The bulbous head feeling hot and needy against her clit and then teasingly playing at the entrance to her hot sex passage before stroking down to her anus.

'Jamie . . . I can't wait . . . please.'

With a look of total desire on his face he thrust his big cock up her and gasped as she cried out in satisfaction; for at last getting what she wanted: his big lovely penis right up her.

'There, baby. This is what you wanted. A good hard fucking,' he said and he drew back so that only the tip of his penis was inside her. She groaned and tried to pull him closer. Then he thrust his pelvis forward, spearing her once again. She gasped at the power of his thrusts and gripped as best she could to the rocking upturned boat as Jamie began to fuck her hard and fast, his cock ramming in and out of her pussy like a steam train, his groin banging against her clit.

The sensations were so intense that her climax came swiftly and in no way that she was used to. Not a slow build up which she could control and manipulate, but a sudden all-consuming wave of pleasure that had her splayed beneath him. She moaned in delight and satisfaction until he too finally came in her, shooting hot spunk into her with such force that it trickled down her legs and all over the bottom of the boat.

Exhausted, Jamie pulled out of her. There was a smile on his lips and his eyes were closed. 'Was that all right, Char . . . Diane?'

Diane's eyes sprang open. What did he almost call her? Charlotte! 'What did you say?' she demanded accusingly.

He looked embarrassed suddenly. 'I said was that all right for ye?'

'You called me Charlotte!'

'I did not.' He tried to laugh it off, but he was writhing in embarrassment.

Diane's heart was plummeting. Hurriedly, she pulled on her knickers and jeans, and tucked her tits back inside her bra. 'You were thinking of her, weren't you?' she snapped, pushing his hand off her shoulder as he tried to hold her.

'Don't be daft, hen. I wasn't thinking of anyone but you.'

'Liar! You fancy her don't you? You wished it was her you were fucking. That's why you were acting so . . . so differently. You were fantasising about her all the while you were having me!'

'I was not. Now will you stop being so daft. That was just great. You loved it as much as me, so stop tormenting y'self.' And he took her into his arms and kissed her passionately.

Her anger subsided a little. Maybe she had misheard him. Perhaps he hadn't almost said, 'Charlotte' at all. Maybe she imagined it.

'Do you love me, Jamie?' she asked softly, looking at him from beneath her long dark lashes.

'Ye know I do, hen. I'm mad about ye.'

'And you don't fancy any other woman?'

He held her tight, the top of her head tucked under his chin so that she couldn't see the look of torment on his face. 'There's no one but you. Believe me. I wouldn't look at another woman. I promise.'

Breathing in his familiar warm scent, Diane snuggled closer to her lover, forgiving him, but not quite forgetting. 'That's all right then, Jamie,' she breathed into his sweater. 'That's all right.'

He could still feel her. Could still smell her. Andrew Alexander sat in his chair by the fire, picturing Charlotte there at his feet. Kneeling between his legs, her lips around his cock, sucking and lapping like she could have eaten it. It was just as he'd predicted, although he hadn't bargained for just how strongly her actions would affect him.

Despite his anger and turmoil of emotions, Andrew Alexander's excitement rose again as his fevered thoughts went over and over the events of that morning. His hand brushed against the semi-hard penis under his dressing gown.

He couldn't sleep; he'd given up on sleep. His thoughts and longings were too powerful to allow sleep to sweep him into oblivion. Even alcohol had failed in that this time. Now, at three in the morning, he was still awake, still unable to erase thoughts of Charlotte Harvey from his head.

God, what was it about that woman? She was beautiful yes, but no more so than other women he'd slept with. It was more than beauty. Perhaps it was the mixture of her childlike curiosity and her open desire for sex that had touched him. He didn't decry any woman for making it clear when she wanted sex; better that than pretending otherwise.

If only he could be sure her arousal wasn't due to the Highland Ruby. That's why he'd not taken things further. Although he doubted that the naïve Charlotte Harvey could ever imagine the heights he could have taken her.

But it had to be her who wanted his sex. Not the effects of some ancient pendant.

God, the willpower he'd needed to stop himself from just thrusting his cock into her and fucking her like she'd begged him. If ever a man deserved a medal . . .

He glanced across to the wall safe. His hand raked through his hair. It *had* to be the effects of the Ruby which had caused her to behave like that. Up until then she'd shown no interest in him as a man. If anything she'd seemed to dislike him, certainly she'd taken offence earlier when he'd warned her what might happen if she were to wear the Highland Ruby. She'd stormed out and not returned till now.

So what did that tell him? That the Ruby was enchanted. Only he'd never really believed that. There was no such thing as magic, it was just what people wanted to believe – or not believe.

His mouth curled into an ironic little smile. Did that mean Charlotte must subconsciously have fancied him a little? Maybe so.

He allowed his weary eyes to close and he moved his dressing gown aside to stroke the length of his penis.

He'd liked the way she had touched him; the softness of her fingers, the light pressure as her hand had closed around its girth and squeezed. He loved the way she had fondled his balls.

As the memory of it came vividly back, he felt himself harden. He masturbated slowly, stroking his hardening cock as he recalled her pert little bottom, her cheeks parted revealing the delicate pink folds of her eager pussy. He half smiled to himself. She'd got such a cute little arse. Had she ever had a cock up it? Probably not. She'd probably no idea what she was missing.

It would be nice teaching her.

He moaned softly, imagining, while his hand moved quicker, sliding up and down, pulling his foreskin back to rub his thumb over the shiny purple head. They had barely spoken afterwards, once he'd snatched the Ruby from her neck and thrown it across the room. He recalled that look she had given him – as if she were suddenly bereft.

He must have imagined that. More likely, she was suddenly overcome with shame and embarrassment. That whisky had been too strong; he should never have given her that second glass. It must have been the alcohol that made her lose her inhibitions, alcohol and the sexy legends he'd been telling her. Nothing at all to do with an enchanted necklace, and certainly nothing to do with his own personality or looks.

Drink, talk of sex and wearing a pendant which released her from all moral standards was what turned her on to him. Exactly the same circumstances that Fay must have experienced when she cheated on him.

At least Charlotte Harvey wasn't a newly wed, although she had a boyfriend, so she said. Was she feeling guilt-ridden for cheating on him?

He wasn't proud of his own behaviour, even though he'd stopped before taking further advantage of her. He'd still allowed it to go too far. But he was only human. The sight of her standing naked in front of the fire had been the start of it.

Yet how many naked females had he seen? He wouldn't like to even try to calculate. But she had looked so utterly fantastic. Those breasts, that dark red hair, her figure, her pale skin with its sheen of dampness from the rain. She was lovely, but more than looks, she interested him, excited him. He couldn't remember the last time a woman had really excited him.

And knowing how she reacted when aroused, the way she had opened up to him.

His hand tightened around his cock, gripping himself until a tiny droplet of moisture oozed out and stood like a jewel on the crown of his erection. If she was *that* willing with so little stimulation, the prospect of what they could do if their relationship was to develop was fascinating to say the least.

Allowing himself the luxury of fantasising about her, he closed his eyes and pictured himself with her, his thoughts running wild. His hand moving feverishly up and down, bringing himself to climax.

He came. And his cry of release echoed around the stone walls of the isolated house.

Across the moors, Charlotte, with her hands tucked between her legs, dreamed peacefully on.

# Chapter Seven

'It's a better morning than yesterday, you'll be pleased to know,' announced Nancy, rousing Charlotte from her sleep.

Charlotte blinked as Nancy drew back the curtains. A pale watery sunlight flooded in. 'Good,' she murmured, squinting against its glare. There was a breakfast tray by her bed with the usual tea, porridge and cooked breakfast. Lord, but she would have to go on a diet when she got back!

'And what's on our journalist's agenda for today, hen?' Nancy asked, bustling about the room.

'Finishing the article, hopefully,' Charlotte replied, the thought of seeing Andrew again bringing her fully awake. She had dreamed of him last night; dreamed of him making love to her; dreamed that he had stripped her naked and laid her down on the rug before his roaring fire; dreamed of his long beautiful penis entering her. In her dreams she had come, a wonderful warm feeling of utter sexual satisfaction.

It was wishful thinking. He wasn't interested in her. He was used to Swedish bombshells and innocent virginal types. Being neither one nor the other obviously held no attraction for him whatsoever.

She sat up in bed and stretched. Half of her ached to see him again, while the other half dreaded another rejection. At a pinch she probably had enough material to write an acceptable article, except for not knowing for sure whether there was any truth in the legend or not. But she still hadn't photographed the pendant. And that was vital.

Nancy moved the breakfast tray closer. 'Here, this will set ye up a treat.'

Charlotte groaned inwardly at the sight of so much food so early in the morning. A cup of tea was really all she could stomach at the moment.

When Nancy had gone downstairs, Charlotte headed for the bathroom, her thoughts spinning around in her head. What if she still felt that overwhelming urge to touch him? What if like yesterday she just couldn't resist him? What if it hadn't been the effects of the alcohol or the pendant, and she was just completely and utterly under his spell? She wasn't usually in the habit of losing all control. In fact, she couldn't remember ever being so overcome with lust that she'd dragged Paul's clothes off him.

She took off her pyjamas. They were a dark-green tartan pair with a cartoon bear on the breast pocket. She'd bought them especially for this Scottish trip, not sure what the weather would be like, but guessing she would need something warm in bed seeing as Paul wouldn't be beside her.

She groaned and slapped her forehead with her hand. Poor Paul, how would she ever face him after all this?

She took a quick shower, amazed to finish it without any interruptions from Kenneth or Nancy. Back in her room she debated what to wear. Ignoring the cotton pants with the little hearts on, she went for her cream silky G-string and matching bra.

Staring at her reflection in the mirror, she pulled a face. 'And who exactly will be seeing your knickers today, girl?' she asked herself.

Having only brought trousers with her, she pulled on stretch-blue jeans and a pale-blue sweater. She examined her reflection in the mirror and saw how the sweater hugged her breasts so that her nipples were clearly prominent. Usually she only wore this particular sweater for Paul.

She didn't question her motives for wearing it today. But she did have a sudden desperate need to speak to Paul. Surely hearing his voice would bring her back to earth and remind her where her loyalties lay.

She reached for her mobile and tapped in his number, deliberately shutting off all thoughts of her recent sexual exploits in case Paul, somehow, picked up the vibes over the phone.

He was a long time answering and Charlotte was on the point of hanging up when he came on the line. He sounded breathless.

'Hi, did I get you off the loo?' Charlotte joked, imagining him racing in to answer the phone, trousers round his ankles.

'Er, something like that. How are you? Is it going well?'

'Not too bad. I've still got a lot to do. I'm hoping to photograph the Highland Ruby today.'

'Ah, talking of which, oh –' he broke off for a second, then continued. 'I've done a bit of research on the Andrew Alexander I was talking about. Got some old newspaper cuttings. They've all got his photo on them – good-looking guy. I posted them to you yesterday. Hopefully you should get them tomorrow.'

'I think it probably is the same person,' Charlotte answered. 'But actually, Paul, there's nothing suspicious about his wife's death. The papers just hyped it all out of proportion.'

'Oh well, the cuttings are on their way, uh, anyhow.'

'Are you okay?' Charlotte frowned.

'Yep, just stubbed my toe against the table,' he answered, sounding strained.

'Twice?'

'Pardon?'

'You stubbed your toe twice. I heard you groan twice.'

'Just reliving the agony. Anyway, I'm just getting ready for work . . .' His voice faded.

Alarm bells sounded at the back of Charlotte's head. 'Paul, is there someone with you?'

'You're joking aren't you? Anyway, I'm going to be late. Got my first lecture in thirty minutes and you know what the traffic can be like.'

Charlotte pressed the phone closer to her ear. What was that in the background? Rustling, movement of some kind; he didn't sound alone. Her throat felt dry all of a sudden. Surely he hadn't got someone with him.

'So, when are you coming back?' Paul broke the silence. 'You're going to call me and I'll pick you up from the station, right?'

'I can get a taxi,' she murmured dully.

'Wouldn't hear of it. You call me, right! Uh –'

There it was again. Another little groan, almost inaudible. But not quite. 'Paul –'

'Sorry, I've got to get off now. I'll see you soon though.'

'Must you? Oh –' the line went dead. Charlotte stared at her mobile feeling utterly sick to the stomach. He *did* have someone with him. She was positive. Her heart plummeted. How could he? Not her Paul, it was unthinkable.

She slumped down on to the edge of the bed, feeling wretched. Even the pricking of her conscience over her own sexual activities of late didn't make her feel less awful. How could he?

Feeling utterly betrayed, Charlotte somehow managed to finish getting ready and finally dragged herself out of the pub and into the cool morning sunlight. Loaded down with her camera and all her equipment, she wasn't looking forward to a half-hour trek across the moors, particularly when Andrew Alexander wasn't expecting her. And particularly now, feeling so utterly alone and betrayed.

She trusted Paul. He was the one person she could rely on – or so she thought. Only at the first opportunity he'd got another girl with him.

Unless of course, she was mistaken. That groan *could* have been because he'd stubbed his toe. Possibly she was judging him by her own standards. She could be doing him a complete injustice.

She wandered around to the side of the pub. On one side stretched the moors which led eventually to Stonemoor House, while ahead lay the harbour, just starting to come alive as the boats returned from their fishing trips. Overhead seagulls screamed and screeched, circling in the hope of scavenging easy pickings of fish scraps thrown from the boats.

Charlotte leaned against an old wall. Its stones were damp and covered with clumps of green moss and lichen. She clutched her mobile phone. Was she really being fair on Paul? Perhaps she ought to give him the benefit of the doubt. Maybe she should call him again and try to put her mind at ease.

She hesitated. He would probably already have left for college now – surely that ought to reassure her. He would hardly have someone with him if he was going to work.

Unless she'd spent the night with him.

The niggling doubts continued, sapping her faith in him. She heaved an unhappy sigh, unsure what to do. She could ring his flat, and if there was no answer, try and catch him on his mobile. But did she really want to? She tapped in half of his number then stopped. What if a woman answered the phone? What if she ended up feeling even more wretched than she did now?

Her eyes fluttered shut. She clutched her mobile and stared pathetically at the little keypad. To ring or not to ring, that was the question. She only wished she felt noble enough to give Paul the benefit of the doubt.

Miserably, her finger hovered over the numbers as she tried to make up her mind what to do.

'Paul! You are completely insatiable!'

'Not complaining, are you?' Paul asked, grinning, as he lifted the girl's ankle-length skirt, exposing her plump thighs and a triangle of black nylon panties which barely concealed the bush of curly brown pubes.

He'd teased her last night after discovering she wasn't a natural blonde. They'd met in the college library yesterday afternoon when she'd helped him find newspaper cuttings on Andrew Alexander. It was only fair he took her out for a drink afterwards to thank her. Coming back here was her idea, as he recalled. Where, back at his flat, he'd been able to thank her properly. In fact he'd given her a right good *thanking* all night long.

Paul hadn't bothered getting into his trousers yet and stood there in just his shirt with his rampant cock moist and shining from the sucking she'd just given it. Now, with her skirt gathered up in one hand, he reached between her legs and felt the warmth of her sex through the silky fabric of her pants.

She pretended to scowl at him. 'Paul, I'm going to be late for my first lecture. You've had me all night, don't you ever let up?'

He grinned as he pulled the crotch of her pants to one side and slid his finger inside them. Her tangle of brown pubes were moist, her fanny lips still swollen from the shagging he'd given her before they'd got out of bed. 'Never mind let up, I want to *get up* – up you.'

'Was that your girlfriend on the phone?'

124

'Mmm,' he breathed, turning her around. 'Kneel on the sofa, Jenny.'

Jenny, a student of English literature, in her final year at Paul's college, did as she was told. Kneeling, she turned her back on Paul and folded her arms on the back cushion of the sofa. 'The one I did that research for?' she asked, resting her chin on her arms.

'That's right, babe, and this is my way of thanking you,' Paul said, pulling her pants to one side to slip his cock into her. She was hot and wet, and he slid into her easily. 'She's interviewing the bloke up in Scotland. Don't you think I'm a considerate guy in helping her with background information?'

'Oh very considerate,' Jenny uttered as Paul's hips moved feverishly back and forth, sliding in and out of her well-lubricated fanny. 'I'm sure she'll appreciate everything you've done while she's been away.'

'Cheeky,' Paul growled, giving Jenny a particularly hard pelvic thrust. He grunted in satisfaction as it silenced her for a moment and he noticed her purple-painted fingernails digging into his sofa.

His phone rang again but he ignored it. He shouldn't be here anyway. If it was work, they'd assume he'd left and he wasn't expecting any other calls. Bit of bad luck, Charlotte ringing like that. Jenny had just been in the throws of giving him a blow job. Still, Charlotte couldn't have suspected anything. He was pretty certain of that.

After a few minutes the ringing stopped and he was able to concentrate fully on screwing Jenny. But moments later his mobile rang. The little screen lit up to show it was Charlotte again.

'It's her again,' Paul said, reaching for it. 'Don't make a sound, right?'

'Go a bit easier, then,' Jenny gasped.

'No chance,' Paul murmured, getting quite a kick out of shagging someone while talking to the girlfriend on the phone. It wasn't quite the same thrill as when Dominique was controlling him, but it was great nevertheless. He pressed the receive button. 'Hi, babe, did you forget to tell me something?'

She sounded hesitant, which wasn't like her, and he slowed down the rhythm of his hips to a gentle rocking motion, just so the tip of his penis penetrated Jenny's luscious pussy. He could tell by her gently mewing that it was driving her crazy. She was a girl that liked it hard and fast. Jenny was quite a girl to have around. He'd have to remember her.

'Where are you?' Charlotte asked him.

'Driving to work, babe, in the rush hour too. You don't know how lucky you are being on a nice peaceful island. Don't suppose much happens there, does it?'

'Oh, you'd be surprised, Paul. Anyway, I ... I just wanted to hear your voice again. Silly, aren't I?'

'Ah, that's sweet. Are you missing me, babe?' As Charlotte answered, Paul squeezed the cheeks of Jenny's arse and gave her one long, lingering hard thrust as he erupted inside of her.

He covered her cry with a loud cough.

'Paul, are you all right?' Charlotte fretted over the phone.

'Yes, I'm OK, bit of a tickle in the throat. Look, it's a bit difficult to talk right now, can I call you later? Yes, I will, I promise. OK. Bye for now.'

He pressed the red button on his mobile and slipped, satisfied and dripping spunk, out of Jenny's lovely hole.

Jenny straightened, a slow smile spreading across her face as she looked at him. 'You know what you are, Paul?'

'Tell me?'

'You're a pervert. Shagging me and talking to her. Will you be calling me later, too?'

He kissed the end of her freckled nose 'You never know. You'll just have to wait and see.'

An image of himself being thrashed by Dominique

whilst chatting to Jenny appeared in his mind, and his lips parted in a great, wide grin.

Charlotte slipped her phone back into her holdall and stared blindly at a distant fisherman throwing scraps of dead fish on to the shale. A flock of seagulls swooped down to devour the waste. She felt numb. Utterly numb and sick to the stomach. Paul had someone with him, she was positive.

Too hurt to cry, she remained slumped miserably on the wall, her life and future in tatters.

Blinded to everything except tormented thoughts of Paul having sex with some faceless female, she failed to spot the tall striking figure making his way across the moor towards her.

Andrew Alexander, dressed in jeans, good solid shoes and a waterproof jacket, was almost upon her when she snapped out of her daydream. She looked up at him with big doleful eyes.

He seemed about to say something else, then changed his mind after seeing her expression. 'Charlotte? Are you all right? What's happened?'

Despite everything, the close proximity of the man had the effect of sending tingles of desire rampaging through her loins. She hated herself for feeling this way.

'Bad news?' he asked again, glancing down at the mobile she was still clutching.

She wasn't going to tell him. Wild horses wouldn't drag the information from her that her boyfriend was right this minute shagging some tart.

'Nothing I can't handle,' she told him curtly, tossing back her long auburn hair. 'I was just coming to see you actually.'

'I guessed you would, that's why I've come here. Saved you the journey.'

Charlotte felt as if another knife had been plunged through her heart. Wonderful! Her boyfriend was two-timing her, and Andrew Alexander was afraid to be alone with her. Her self-esteem took a steep nosedive.

He continued to look concerned. 'Charlotte, are you sure you're okay? If that bottom lip drops any lower you'll be scraping it off the ground.'

'I'm absolutely fine,' she assured him, dusting the green moss from the seat of her trousers. 'Never better, in fact,' she added, hoping she sounded brighter than she felt. 'And I'm glad you've saved me the journey, because that's what I was actually debating: whether to bother coming over to your place to finish the article or not.' The lie slipped easily off her tongue.

He raised his eyebrows in surprise. 'You don't think the Highland Ruby is worth writing about? After you've come all this way?'

She shrugged, feigning disinterest. There was no way she would allow him to know she'd secretly hoped to be alone with him again in Stonemoor House. Deep down she harboured a faint hope that last night's dream just might come true. Well, there was no chance of that now he was here. And if he didn't want her, then she didn't want him.

'I've enough information to put a feature together,' she shrugged coolly. 'I admit I do need some photographs, though.'

He took a package from the inside pocket of his jacket. 'Lucky for you I brought the Highland Ruby with me, then. What sort of background do you want for your photographs?'

An agonising pang of disappointment hit her like a bullet through the heart. He really had come prepared. Obviously he wanted to get this over and done with as quickly as possible, and not find himself in any compromising situations again. Well that was fine with her. Absolutely fine, the man could go to hell! In fact all men could.

He tilted his head and looked quizzically at her. 'Charlotte, I think we'd better clear the air, don't you, before we go any further?'

She jutted her chin. 'There's nothing to clear as far as I'm concerned.'

His lips twitched into an embarrassed little smile. 'How about yesterday?' he suggested, raising one eyebrow.

She wasn't ready to discuss yesterday. Feeling the way she did, she doubted she would ever want a man to touch her again. Even him.

She made a point of looking at her watch. 'I'd rather forget all about yesterday,' she said irritably. Adding, 'Look, if we're going to do this story, then let's get on with it. I need to take photographs.'

He breathed deeply. 'OK, you're the boss. So, like I say, what sort of background do you want?'

Hoping she had her emotions fully under control, but avoiding his quizzical gaze just in case, she said, 'By a stream, I thought. With pebbles and cascading water, perhaps a little waterfall.' She glanced at him. 'Know anywhere like that?'

He rubbed his chin. He was immaculately cleanshaven. He smelled good too, and his hair looked freshly washed. For a moment she wondered if he'd gone to some trouble especially for her. Then she stopped her silly daydreams. Most likely he was hoping for a quick shag with Nancy before he went home.

'I think we can find you somewhere suitable,' he remarked, setting off, leaving her to follow – a particularly annoying little trait of his. He glanced back over one broad shoulder at her. 'Well, are you coming?'

Charlotte followed, glowering at his back. But her glare soon dissolved into those old feelings of lust. He had such a fine physique. She'd always had a thing for men with a body like his. Broad-shouldered, lean hips, a nice firm, well-shaped bum. She feasted her eyes on his rear as he walked on ahead.

Making her way around rocks and thistles, it seemed that yesterday was no more a reality than her dreams from last night. God, how she'd loved the feel and the taste of the man. How she'd wanted him inside of her.

As she walked in his footsteps through the rain-softened earth, she felt that familiar tingling sensation between her thighs. A dull ache began to throb in her lower abdomen and her pussy became hot and swollen with longing. Her anger with Paul was fading into insignificance. She didn't question her feelings – or rather her lack of feelings towards his infidelity. There seemed to be only one thing on her mind suddenly. One powerful, all-encompassing thing – sex.

Trying her best to concentrate on not slipping in the mud, Charlotte was more aware of how her clit rubbed against the inner fabric of her clothing as she walked. And of how hard her nipples were becoming, protruding proudly through the tight-fitting wool of her sweater. Even her lips felt fuller.

This need for Andrew Alexander was like nothing she had experienced before. Certainly not with Paul, and not even with Jamie. Although as she thought of Jamie her lips twitched into a smile. Impishly, she wondered whether Andrew might strip like Jamie had and pose nude for her. While the highly unlikely prospect made her smile, it also sent shivers of excitement running through her body.

Andrew glanced back suddenly and caught her staring at his backside, no doubt with a silly grin on her face. 'I'm glad to see you're looking a bit happier,' he said, waiting for her to catch up. 'Are you struggling with all that equipment? Here, let me.'

Never one to believe in equality when it came to a man offering to carry heavy bags, she handed her holdall over willingly. She hung on to her camera, just in case.

'Not far now,' he added, striding on, heading down a steep grassy slope. Charlotte picked her way downhill more slowly, afraid her shoes would skid on the wet grass and her feet would shoot from under her, leaving her sprawling on her back. And unless Andrew was to land on top of her, that certainly wasn't her idea of fun.

At the bottom of the slope ran a stream which meandered amongst a dense cluster of fir and birch trees. Beyond them, the land veered sharply upwards, forming a mountainous grey-green incline. She guessed that the stream was Andrew's chosen location.

Boulders and large granite rocks cluttered the little valley. No doubt they had rolled down the mountainside at some point in history, some having bounced across the stream to embed themselves in the ground.

Charlotte followed Andrew as he picked his way between the rocks to the stream. As she got closer, the sound of tinkling, rushing water greeted her and she gasped at the sight of the picturesque setting. The stream was quite shallow and the water sparklingly clear, churning and frothing as it cascaded over rocks and pebbles, singing its way down to the sea.

Excitement bubbled inside of her. It was just the right setting for the Highland Ruby. 'This looks perfect!' she exclaimed, delighted, forgetting for a moment everything else.

'I thought it would be,' Andrew said, watching her as she quickly took out her camera and adjusted its settings.

Charlotte walked along the banks of the stream, selecting what she hoped would be the right place to capture the Ruby in all its natural glory. Kicking off her shoes and rolling up her jeans, she paddled in the clear mountain water, its icy chill making her shriek.

Andrew smiled indulgently, as if she were a small child paddling and having fun. For once he looking relaxed and at ease – but still oh so very sexy.

'Here will be just perfect,' Charlotte exclaimed, balancing herself, legs astride a narrow part of the water. 'Could you pass me the pendant?'

He took the Highland Ruby from his inside pocket. Charlotte hesitated before taking it, wondering if its magic was going to rub off on her again. Not that she believed for one minute that the Ruby had anything to do with her attraction to Andrew. That was physical, not magical. But even so, she couldn't deny that her behaviour yesterday had been out of character.

Andrew appeared to read her mind. 'Afraid, Charlotte?'

She pretended she hadn't a clue what he was talking about. But deep inside a luscious tingle swept through her; she knew he was remembering yesterday, too.

'Afraid of what?' she asked innocently.

His mouth curved into a wry little smile. 'Of falling under its spell again.'

She met his enquiring gaze blatantly. 'So you believe I was enchanted yesterday? That's why I did what I did?'

'Were you?' he asked.

'I thought you didn't believe in the legend.'

He moved one broad shoulder restlessly. 'Enritha fell under its spell. Other women through the ages supposedly did, too.'

Charlotte narrowed her smoky grey eyes. 'I thought we women only used it as an excuse to sleep around.'

'That's why I'm asking,' Andrew remarked, holding her spellbound with his dark, penetrating gaze. 'Were you under its spell yesterday? Or were you using it as an excuse to throw away all your inhibitions and enjoy yourself?'

Charlotte hid behind her long eyelashes, concentrating on a shiny blue pebble lying on the stream bed. She hadn't been under any spell, she knew that. There were three very simple reasons why she was so horny yesterday: the potent whisky, those sexy stories and him.

She could have admitted to the first two excuses, but not the third. She didn't want him to know she fancied the pants off him. Him, Andrew, with his hot Swedish lover and his sweet virginal bride! A girl could only take so much humiliation, and having him reject her yesterday was something she didn't want to repeat.

Charlotte suddenly realised that if he believed she was under the spell of the Highland Ruby yesterday, it would be a perfect way of saving face.

Praying he wouldn't see through the façade, she made sure her eyes remained downcast, and her voice as innocent as she could muster. 'I ... I don't know. I certainly felt odd yesterday when I was wearing the Ruby.'

He looked at her with a mixture of disbelief and disappointment. 'So you're telling me it was the Highland Ruby which made you desperate for sex.'

'I wasn't desperate,' she declared, annoyed. 'I just felt in the mood for it.'

He cocked one eyebrow. 'Charlotte, you were as hot as hell, and you know it.' As she started to protest that it wasn't her fault, he held up his hands. 'Look, I'm really interested to know how you felt. I'm not being perverted. I need to know. For the last five years I've tried to imagine what was going on in Fay's head when she went off and slept with another man. If only I could believe that she had no choice, that she was under the influence of the Highland Ruby, then it would help me come to terms with it.'

Charlotte bit her lip. She didn't like telling lies, only in this case a little fib was probably the best solution. 'All right,' she murmured. 'I'll tell you. I really felt as if I had no control over my actions. Although you didn't actually make any sexual requests of me, all those sexy stories worked in just the same way. I couldn't stop myself.'

He didn't look convinced. 'I wish I could believe you. But let's be honest, it's medieval nonsense. Your behaviour yesterday was probably down to the whisky.'

'Perhaps that added to it,' she admitted, which was the truth. 'But I honestly felt I had no choice but to behave

133

as I did.' For good measure she looked up at him aghast. 'You didn't think I wanted to, did you?'

'Well, I wondered. I kind of thought it was me who'd turned you on. Not just some charmed relic.' He looked vaguely hurt, which pleased Charlotte immensely.

She smiled sweetly and lied blatantly. 'Sorry, no. I'm afraid if you'd been the Hunchback of Notre Dame I would have reacted in exactly the same way.'

Another look of disappointment flashed briefly across his face. Charlotte's hopes soared. She only hoped she'd made the right decision in lying about her true feelings. But surely it was best if Andrew didn't realise the Highland Ruby had nothing to do with her wanting his lovely big cock up her. In fact, if he only but knew it, he could send the thing sailing away downstream and have her right here and now.

That wasn't his intention however. Nevertheless, she had obviously convinced him of the Highland Ruby's powers, because he handed her the pendant with a quirky look on his face. 'Here you are, then, and I guess I'd better keep my mouth well and truly shut while it's in your possession.'

'Yes, that's probably best,' she agreed, turning away before he saw through the façade. Deliberately she focused her attention on positioning the Highland Ruby ready to photograph it.

As she worked she sensed him watching her. His eyes seemed to be burning through her clothing. And as she bent over to place the pendant on a large shiny stone and her jeans tightened around her buttocks, she knew he was looking. Was he imagining her bare-arsed, with her pussy all moist and glistening, the delicate pink folds parted in anticipation of his hard cock?

She remained with her back to him, bent over, hoping the sight of her pert bum in tight jeans would make him as horny as her. She ached for him, absolutely ached. But it had to be Andrew who instigated anything. She just couldn't bear it if he allowed her to go so far, then called a halt as he'd done yesterday.

She continued her work, allowing her creative spirit to take over. These pictures would look fantastic. Although there was still another angle she needed. And that might pose a bit more of a problem.

When at last she'd taken all the pictures in this setting, she gave the Ruby a little shake. 'I hope it doesn't go rusty.'

'Gold can take a bit of water,' he remarked, standing on the banks of the stream, his long legs slightly apart. With the breeze ruffling his hair, he looked utterly magnificent and so, so shaggable.

Charlotte hesitated in giving the Highland Ruby back. This fierce yearning to touch him – and have him touch her – was overwhelming. The desperate need sent her brain working overtime with a ploy to achieve her desires.

'You know, Andrew,' she began almost shyly, as if she really didn't want to suggest this at all, 'If you wanted to be absolutely positive that the Highland Ruby really can enchant women, you could try it out again.' She fidgeted awkwardly as she saw his startled expression. 'I mean, sort of experimental. Under laboratory conditions, so to speak.'

His dark eyes narrowed suspiciously. 'How exactly?'

Charlotte took a deep, steadying breath. Aware that her heart was thudding and her pussy throbbing with anticipation. 'Well, the legend says the woman becomes enslaveth to his every request. So request something, and if I can refuse, then I will. And I'll trust you not to take advantage of me,' she added for good measure. Hoping against hope that he *would* take advantage of her. The naughtier the better.

An odd kind of look ravaged his face momentarily. As if she was asking an awful lot. 'Charlotte, that's not a good idea.'

'But you want to know whether the Highland Ruby really is enchanted or not, don't you?'

'It's not. You were drunk yesterday.'

'I'm not today. So go on, ask me. You need to know. It's only fair on Fay. If she had no choice but to sleep with that man, then you should know that.' She walked barefoot up the grassy slope towards him. From this angle he towered over her, like some gorgeous sex-god. 'Andrew, for your own peace of mind . . .'

He looked down into her eyes, his chest expanding as if he needed his lungs full of air to help him through this moment. His voice was husky. 'If I had any sense, Charlotte, my one request would be for you to hand me back the pendant.'

'Ask then.'

He looked in turmoil, as if he was wrestling with his conscience. Charlotte waited with baited breath, hoping he didn't request she give the pendant back. She would have to comply if she was to be believed. And that would spoil all the fun.

Finally he looked at her with a glint in his eye that should have warned her. 'Are you serious?'

'Yes,' she shrugged, positive she could handle anything *he* requested of her.

He wandered over to a large chunk of granite embedded in the earth, and leaned against it. 'Charlotte, you're suggesting we prove this out of fairness to Fay?'

She followed him, the grass cold and wet between her toes. She faced him defiantly. 'Yes, and for your own peace of mind,' she added, continuing the façade, hoping he'd ask for a blow job. Lord, she'd be on her knees like a shot.

'This isn't a game, Charlotte,' Andrew murmured, looking deadly serious. 'Fay's memory means a lot to me. If you're doing this just for kicks, then I warn you, you'd better stop right now.'

'I'm not,' she lied.

He looked doubtful. 'I've no way of knowing whether you're leading me on or not, have I?'

'Why on earth would I do that?' she exclaimed, growing exasperated and frustrated, more in need of his touch with every passing minute.

He shook his head, looking almost defeated. 'I don't know . . . unless . . . here, give me the pendant.'

She hesitated, disappointed that he wasn't going to make any naughty suggestions. Reluctantly she handed it to him. To her surprise, however, he didn't stow it back in its packaging. Instead, he carefully placed it around her neck, reciting the legend as he lifted her hair from beneath its gold chain.

His voice was clear, every word pronounced so perfectly. 'Modest maidens and virgins beware, before accepting this stone so rare, for he who placeth it on thy breast, thy slaveth to him, his every request. Tho' detestable or loathsome he may be, thy will dissolves, thy belongeth to he.'

The weight of the Highland Ruby seemed to drag her down. It was an effort to raise her eyes and look at him. A shiver ran down her spine, as if he really had cast a spell on her – that she really was a slave to his every request. She struggled to muster all her confidence back. She wanted to have sex with Andrew, there was no problem with that. So why did she feel so anxious all of a sudden?

Andrew stood up straight, folding his arms across his chest, seeming suddenly larger than life. 'And now we shall see,' he said crisply, his words void of emotion. 'Strip for me, Charlotte.'

She staggered, not expecting such a straightforward command. She began to tremble and every nerve-ending started to jangle with nervous energy.

He was waiting, his eyes riveted on her, no doubt expecting her to refuse. For long moments she wrestled with her conscience. If she said no, he would know that yesterday's escapade was of her own choosing. Whereas if she obeyed, he would be more convinced of the power of the Highland Ruby. It would help him come to terms over Fay.

By pretending the Highland Ruby really did possess certain powers Charlotte was doing everyone a favour. Besides, he'd seen her naked once already. What difference did it make to see her in the buff a second time?

Trying to keep her face expressionless, as if truly under a spell, she took off her sweater, being careful not to dislodge the Ruby. The pendant slipped down between her cleavage. It felt cold on her skin. A cool breeze fluttered over her exposed flesh, heightening the strange sensations already coursing through her trembling body.

Andrew said nothing. He remained, motionless, watching her. Waiting.

With tremulous fingers, Charlotte unfastened her jeans and pushed them down. Andrew put out a steadying hand while she stood on one leg to slip them off.

She stood, half naked, in just a lace bra, her hardening nipples clearly visible through the delicate patterned fabric, and a thong which left very little to the imagination.

She hesitated before removing her bra and panties. She was expecting him to say, OK, he was convinced. But he remained silent, simply waiting. Charlotte's heartbeats began racing as she unhooked her bra and took it off.

Andrew's perfect white teeth ground down on his lower lip as her breasts fell free and her nipples hardened visibly. Charlotte glanced at them herself, seeing how erect they stood, dark pink against the creamy paleness of her flesh. She had the urge to touch them herself but resisted. Her panties were next. She gulped, wishing he would say something, or touch her . . . anything! But he was as rigid as a statue.

Shaking now, she took hold of the rim of her lace pants and very slowly slid them over her hips. Then she stood as naked as nature intended before him, her cheeks burning, her clit crying out for attention. She just prayed that none of the locals were out for a morning stroll.

'Now turn around,' Andrew ordered, stepping away from the rock and indicating that she should face it with her back to him.

A shudder of fear tinged with excitement rampaged through her trembling body. Slowly, she complied to his demand, and stood facing the waist high chunk of granite, aware of his eyes scanning her nakedness.

What she wanted now was his touch. She wanted his hands caressing her bare buttocks; she wanted his lips and teeth tugging at her nipples. But he made no move towards her, although his next request sent hot little quivers racing around her loins.

'Part your legs and bend over the rock.'

Charlotte bit down on her lip. Why? She wanted to cry. But if she was to keep up this pretence, she had to obey without question. She shuffled her feet a little apart and put her hands on the rock, bending slightly.

It wasn't enough to satisfy Andrew Alexander. 'Legs further apart,' he instructed. 'Wider . . . that's it, now lean right over the rock, arms above your head.'

She had no choice. The stone was cold and damp against her breasts and stomach; the pendant dug into her. But she obeyed. With her legs wide apart, she knew he had a perfect view of her pussy. The knowledge made her ache to have him touch her. Only as yet he hadn't laid a finger on her, and her nerves were becoming as tight as a drum.

He kept her that way for long interminable minutes. She was beginning to get cold. But his next command brought her out in a hot sweat.

'Charlotte, you will let me have you anally.'

Her eyes almost popped. No, not that! Not up her arse! That couldn't happen. It was just too awful to contemplate. This had all gone far enough; normal sex was one thing, but anal sex had always been her worst nightmare.

She opened her mouth to cry 'no!' Then she snapped her lips shut. How could she say no without admitting that she was lying about the power of the Highland Ruby? Oh God, she thought and squeezed her eyes shut. She had no choice. If he discovered she was pretending he would be furious. Apart from not wanting to make him hate her, Charlotte also had her job to consider. She'd spent enough time on this article; she couldn't jeopardise it now.

'Well, Charlotte. Do you slaveth to my every request. Or can you tell me to go to hell?'

She bit down hard on her lip. If she intending stopping this charade it would have to be now. But in a tiny voice she murmured, 'Yes, I am enslaveth.'

He uttered something indecipherable and Charlotte held her breath, hoping he would be a gentleman and decide her agreement was enough, and that he wouldn't fuck her in the arse. Yesterday he'd refused to go all the way because he thought she was under a spell. Well, wasn't today just the same? Surely he wouldn't go through with this.

But a moment later she heard the unmistakable sound of him unzipping his flies. Her stomach lurched and she turned her head a little to see his semi-erect cock bounce free from the confines of his jeans. It quickly became fully erect to stand proud from his loins.

Charlotte's clit began to tingle in anticipation and she tried to relax her muscles, guessing to fight it would only make it all the more excruciating.

He moved towards her so that his warm smooth cock brushed against the cheeks of her bottom. She writhed, wishing it was going to penetrate her cunt not her arse. To her delight then, he began to stroke her buttocks, coiling one hand around to her front to play with the nub of her clit. He massaged it with expertise and she

140

felt her arousal escalating. His other hand remained at her rear, his fingers playing up and down her crack, slipping over her anus to her pussy, entering her as his other hand still played with her clit.

Massaging her this way enabled him to keep a firm pressure over her back passage. She loved the feel of his hand being there. It was so different from the way Paul tried to touch her. There was nothing awful or disgusting about Andrew's touch. Just the opposite: it was exciting and she ground down on his hand, using her muscles to part her bum cheeks even more so that he could feel her more intimately, his fingers still moist with her own juices.

For long delicious minutes he played and massaged and fondled her in that position. Hot tingling sensations darted through her abdomen, bringing her to the verge of climax. All the while she could feel his hard cock pressed up against the cheek of her bum. And then, as she knew was inevitable, she felt his finger slide up her hole.

True to her initial instincts, Charlotte thought for a second that she was goint to make a feeble attempt to writhe free and push him away. But he was holding her fast, one hand on her mound, expertly teasing her clit, so she remained on the verge of coming, while his finger eased gently up inside of her. She expected pain. That didn't come at first. Not until he massaged her back passage internally. Even then it wasn't exactly pain, more a mixture of agony and ecstasy as he moved his finger left and right, then in little circles, stretching her ready for his big hard cock to penetrate her.

Charlotte remained bent over the rock, her legs wide apart, her eyes squeezed shut in anticipation. Never in her life had she experienced sensations like these. Adrenaline swept through her veins, charging her with fear and excitement and dread for when he entered her properly.

A moment later, he did precisely that. Removing his finger from her back passage she felt his cock pushing against her tiny opening – which was already well lubricated from her own pussy-juice.

She cried out as the initial thrust sent a searing pain through her. He stopped, his arms going instantly around her waist and stomach in a way that comforted. He held her, not moving, waiting for her, and maybe himself too, to grow accustomed to the sensations rocketing through them.

And then he began to move his hips, slowly at first, gently, waiting for her to get used to these feelings, waiting for her pain to subside, then gradually he increased the pressure and quickened the momentum. Charlotte began to relax her muscles, began to move in rhythm with him. The penetration became deeper, the rhythm quicker and harder as his excitement mounted.

His hand slid down her flat stomach to her mound again and his finger and thumb teased the hard little bud of her clit. Charlotte moaned softly as he crushed her against the rock, his hand locked between her hot pussy and the cold hard granite.

There was no let up as he massaged her clit, sending her into spasms of pleasure as he continued to fuck her in the arse. Shivers raced through her body. Shivers of utter delight that tingled from the tip of her toes to the top of her head.

This was exquisite pleasure that she never realised existed, and never wanted to end. He could go on pumping his cock up her arse forever and ever.

She began to groan, to call out his name, to push her bottom against his cock, rocking back and forth, fucking him as hard as he was fucking her. His thumb on her clit finally brought the climax she was desperate for, and as she cried out in release she thrust herself back, spearing herself on his shaft as hard as she could. At the same moment he erupted inside of her. Hot spunk shot up her back passage increasing the pleasure of her climax, lengthening the sheer wonderful feelings that sent her into jerking spasms of bliss.

Andrew held her, both arms around her middle, his weight coiled over her back, breathing hard against her throat. Charlotte didn't move, couldn't move. She savoured the moment – exhausted but totally, totally satisfied and loving now this new feeling of emotional intimacy as he held her so close. She could feel his heart pounding and his legs, which were so muscular and strong, were trembling, just as hers were.

Too soon, he withdrew from her, and the cool Scottish air swept around her overheated skin, making her shiver. A second later he touched her again, but this time it was to wipe her bottom with a tissue. She allowed him this further intimacy before turning around to face him. She was still trembling. Trembling from head to toe.

Andrew Alexander had a look of satisfaction on his face. Whether he was satisfied and happy now he knew his bride had no choice in sleeping with another man, or he was satisfied because he'd fucked her anally, she wasn't sure.

What she did know was she had loved it. Loved it and wanted more – much more.

# Chapter Eight

*F*urther upstream amongst the dense greenery, there was a distinct flash of red tartan. Hiding deep in the undergrowth, Angus McDonald mopped the moisture from his massive cock and tucked his grubby handkerchief into his sporran. He let his kilt fall into place and leaned back on the wide tree trunk, scarcely able to believe his luck in coming across that pretty wee journalist getting a good shagging from his neighbour, Andrew Alexander.

He felt pleased with himself. It wasn't every day that his search for a rabbit for dinner led to such a pleasant little interlude. He'd come across them just right. Just when the lass was stripping off for Mr Alexander.

Angus had quickly ducked out of sight and peered through the foliage as the blood rushed to his nether regions and his fat cock hardened.

Keeping well out of sight he had ogled the goings on, enjoying the view of Charlotte bent naked across the stone. This was the second time he'd seen her in the nude, and the sight of such a pretty pair of tits and lovely rounded arse made him as randy as hell. Lifting his kilt he'd grasped his big cock in his hand and began wanking himself off.

With his hand working overtime, he couldn't believe that Andrew Alexander was just watching the wee lass; not even touching her when she was obviously dying for it. What the hell was the matter with the man? There she was, spread-eagled across the rock with her lovely long legs wide apart, and her fanny so damp he could see her juices glistening from some distance.

He was just thinking he'd go down and do the job for Alexander himself when the man finally got the idea and gave her a good seeing to. And about time too, Angus had thought, as his hand tightened around his own tackle.

Scarcely blinking in case he missed anything, Angus had continued wanking, oblivious to anyone else who might be out for a morning stroll. In particular, Jamie and Diane, walking side by side down to the stream.

'You stink of fish, Jamie,' Diane complained, wrinkling her nose.

'Aye well, if ye'd given me time to nip home and have a bath and change ma clothes, I'd probably be a lot more acceptable to ye. Don't forget I've been out on the boats all morning.'

She cast him a long sideways glance. 'I'll put up with you. Anyway, your mother will be at home, and I wanted you all to myself for a while.'

'Oh, and why's that?' Jamie asked, slipping her arm around her waist.

Diane allowed him to pull her close. She'd put last night's niggling worries to the back of her mind. Jamie hadn't actually called out Charlotte's name as he made love to her. It was just 'Char'. It could have meant anything. There was no point in worrying herself over it. Anyhow Charlotte would be going back home soon and the competition gone. Besides, Diane thought as she snuggled closer to him, she hadn't come all this way to argue.

Slipping her arm around his waist, she suddenly saw something that made her mouth drop open in shock. There in the woods was the biggest truncheon of a cock she had ever seen in her life. 'Och, Jamie, just look at that dirty beast! Look at him playing with himself! My God, look at the size of it!'

'It's Angus,' said Jamie, following her gaze. 'Now what's that old pervert found to get excited about? A couple of sheep having it off I shouldn't wonder.'

Diane was one step ahead, looking to where Angus was looking. She staggered at the sight that met her eyes. That young journalist, the one Jamie had a *thing* for, was bent across a rock, stark naked, and Andrew Alexander was at her rear banging away like there was no tomorrow.

For a second Diane didn't know whether to drag Jamie away, or stay and watch. She'd never seen two people having sex before. It was supposed to be a private thing, not a spectator sport. Although she had to admit the sight of them was making a damp patch on her knickers.

'It's Charlotte!' Jamie gasped, stunned. 'Charlotte and Mr Alexander. My God, he's raping her!'

'He's not!' Diane snapped irritably, annoyed that her boyfriend should instantly jump to Charlotte's defence. Glancing at his horrified expression, and seeing that he was definitely upset that his precious Charlotte was enjoying herself with someone else, Diane's eyes narrowed. 'Och, she's loving it,' she goaded spitefully. 'Look at her, Jamie, your gorgeous wee journalist is having a lovely time getting shagged by the man she's writing about. Is that no' ethical?'

'It's disgusting!' Jamie growled, unable to drag his eyes off them. 'How could she –'

'How could she when you thought she fancied you!' Diane practically spat the words out. 'You fancy her, don't you, Jamie? Admit it. You fancy the pants off her.'

146

'Och, don't start that all over again. I don't fancy her at all.'

Diane folded her arms angrily, still watching the pair having sex, oblivious to the rest of the world. 'You mean you *don't* wish it was you, with your dick up her pussy?'

'There's no need to be coarse, Diane,' Jamie admonished her.

'You wanted me to be coarse last night, when you were thinking about her,' Diane snapped, glaring from the copulating couple to Jamie. 'Is that how she speaks? Oh, fuck me, Jamie dear. Fuck me.'

'Diane, will ye stop this. You're talking daft.'

'Am I?' she retorted.

'Aye, you are. I don't fancy Charlotte at all,' he said, grabbing her hand and practically whipping her off her feet. Ignoring her protests, he pulled her behind a tree and pressed her up against the rough bark, his knee pressed between her legs. 'It's you I fancy.'

Diane twisted her head aside as he tried to kiss her. But he kissed her nevertheless. His lips crushed hers, forcing her angry mouth open to allow his tongue admittance.

'Jamie,' she gasped, knowing why he was so inflamed with lust again. It was seeing that journalist naked and having sex. Same as last night. She was right. Jamie had been fantasising about her, that's why he was so horny.

Angrily, she tried to push him off, but his kiss deepened and his hands went everywhere, squeezing her breasts, fondling her through her clothes. Then his fingers found the zip of her trousers and in a second he had unzipped her. Before she could zip it back up, he'd pushed her trousers down to her knees, taking her knickers with them.

'Jamie, behave yourself!' Diane gasped, as the tree bark scratched the cheeks of her bare bottom and a hot tingling sensation spread around her naked sex. But then she groaned in anticipation.

Behaving himself seemed to be the last thing on Jamie's mind. His hand slid between her legs and no matter how hard she clenched her thighs together, his fingers prised between them, seeking entrance to her.

Despite knowing he was so excited because of his precious Charlotte, Diane couldn't halt the rush of excitement at having him so crazed with lust. She'd wanted sex badly. That was her reason for taking the boat trip over here sooner than they'd arranged. Sex she had wanted and sex she was getting. Twice in twelve hours.

Last night's session had been fantastic – until he'd let that woman's name slip. Now this, with him ravaging her out in the open, and with people about. What if Angus spotted them too, and turned his gargantuan cock in this direction? The idea of someone masturbating while watching them having sex excited her beyond belief. Especially someone like Angus.

She'd never seen one as big as his before, and as Jamie continued fingering her she couldn't help but fantasise what it would be like to have *that* thrust up her.

The thought made her juices flow and her hands went up to Jamie's shoulders and curled around his neck, before dragging his head down so she could kiss him harder. Her thigh muscles relaxed and she allowed him to push her legs apart so that he could get four fingers inside her.

She gasped and clung to him as almost his whole hand went up her. Just his thumb remained out, and that caressed her clit, sending ripples of pleasure darting through her. She bore down on his hand, her pelvis moving back and forth, her climax growing. She could hear the soft slurping of his fingers in her love juices and she gyrated her hips against him, on the verge of coming.

But then Jamie gently eased his fingers out of her, and unzipped his flies. 'Suck ma cock, hen,' he uttered hoarsely, taking his long throbbing length in his hand and rubbing his foreskin back and forth.

Diane moaned, half with desire and half from the frustration of not actually coming when she was so very close. But Jamie's other hand pressed down on her shoulders, forcing her down on to her knees until she was kneeling on the wet grass – one knee in the mud, the other on her trousers. God only knew what kind of mess she was going to end up in. Though to be honest, she didn't care.

And Jamie obviously didn't care, either. His erection was bobbing about in front of her eyes, begging for her to take it in her mouth. He jutted his pelvis forward and with his hand at the back of her head, forced his cock down her throat, almost dislodging her tonsils.

She gagged and gripped his thighs, pushing him back a little so that he didn't actually choke her with it. With him more under control, she sucked hard at the long slippery length, her tongue and lips enjoying the silky feel. She slid her hand underneath his crotch, pressing up through his jeans to follow the fine ridge to his anus. Then her middle finger pushed upwards, knowing she had hit the spot by the increased pressure of Jamie's fingers in her shoulder blades.

She sucked greedily, using her teeth to gently bite him. Then her tongue coiled into the eye of his cock and began lapping at the pearl of moisture that oozed out as his arousal grew.

His hips rocked back and forth and Diane knew he was ready to come. Still annoyed that he fancied that journalist, she pulled free, leaving his cock standing bereft, dark-purple and angry. But she softened his anguish with a coy smile as she turned her back on him, and pressed herself up against the tree, posing just as Charlotte was with her arms raised above her head and her legs astride. She glanced back over her shoulder at Jamie and in a husky, seductive breath, murmured, 'Fuck me, Jamie darling. Fuck me.'

He didn't need telling twice. Bending his knees, he

wriggled about until his rampant cock was up between her legs and into her wet cunt. Diane wrapped her arms around the tree as his hot hard length slid up inside of her.

Crushed against the rough tree bark with Jamie's lovely penis hard up her was enough to satisfy Diane's desires, although, even when he came, she still hadn't climaxed.

As he drew out of her, Diane turned and faced him. Slowly, knowing he was watching her, she slid her hand down between her legs. Knowing exactly where to touch herself, she masturbated in front of him, bringing herself off, her entire body jerking spasmodically.

Her smile of self-satisfaction brought just a tiny frown to Jamie's bright blue eyes.

'Get dressed, Charlotte,' Andrew instructed as he zipped himself back up.

Still trembling, Charlotte did as she was told, swiftly pulling on her panties, jeans and shoes. She avoided his eyes, not knowing how to react to him. What she longed to do was kiss him passionately and let him know how wonderful anal sex was. She'd never have believed it in a million years – enjoying being fucked up the arse!

Only she couldn't tell him that. Supposedly, she wasn't acting out of her own free will. Supposedly she was under the influence of the enchanted pendant. In which case, she ought now to react like Enritha and demand his blood!

She gripped the Highland Ruby, ready to keep up the pretence and tear it off and throw it back at him. But he took hold of her hand. His voice was soft. 'Leave it on,' he said.

A tremor rocked through her body. Did this mean he hadn't finished with her yet? 'Why?' she managed to croak.

His little finger brushed against her naked breast as he

rested the Ruby in the palm of his hand. 'Because it looks good on you.' He glanced towards her camera, lying discarded amongst the damp heather. 'May I?'

She followed his gaze. 'You want to photograph me wearing it?'

'Any objections?'

She hesitated. It fact, she wanted such a pose for her article. Only not of herself, particularly not topless. She had envisaged a tasteful shot with some other woman wearing it.

She had to remember to keep up the charade and remain under its spell, however. 'Why ask?' she uttered curtly. 'You can do whatever you like while I'm wearing it.'

'It's the gentlemanly thing to do,' he told her, half smiling to himself.

Charlotte bit down on her lip. And was it the gentlemanly thing to shag her up the arse? Not that she was complaining.

'Go ahead then, but there's only a couple of shots left,' she sighed, turning aside just in time to see what looked like a flash of tartan disappearing through the trees. She frowned. She must have been imagining it.

'I only want one,' Andrew answered.

Clever Dick, she almost said. Although she should hardly be surprised that he was so confident. He'd certainly been pretty sure of himself earlier. Dishing out his orders: strip for me, Charlotte; part your legs, Charlotte; bend over while I fuck you up the bum, Charlotte.

Her eyes fluttered shut. Oh but God, how she'd loved it!

After a quick examination of her camera, Andrew positioned her, half turned towards him, the Highland Ruby nestling between her breasts. Her nipples were still hard and she felt suddenly very sexy as he pointed the camera at her.

She gazed deep into the lens, not seeing the camera,

but seeing the man behind it. OK, so he wanted a photograph. Well she would give him this one memory of her. Something to remind him of today. Posing as sultry and seductively as she could, she gazed into the lens from beneath a sweep of long eyelashes, recalling the wonderful sensation when his big hard cock penetrated her for the first time.

He would know what she was thinking when he saw this shot. The memory was captured for all time. He would remember her and this day long after she had gone from his life.

He took the picture, a strange expression clouding his face as he handed the camera back to her. 'You will send me that photo, Charlotte, when they're developed.'

'Yes,' she murmured. Dismayed then, to have him lift the Highland Ruby from her neck and rewrap it in its velvet cloth.

She felt naked without it.

After securing it back inside his jacket, he looked steadily into Charlotte's eyes. 'So now we both know. It really does have powers. Are you all right?'

She was far from all right. She was still trembling and fiercely frustrated at being unable to say what she truly felt – that it was wonderful, and that she wanted to do it all over again.

She felt bad about fooling him, too. OK, so maybe he would sleep easier at night believing that Fay hadn't been able to control her actions. But where did that leave her? She couldn't help but feel angry at her own stupidity for not being honest with him. She turned her anger on him. 'Do you care if I'm all right? Do you honestly care?'

'Actually, I do,' he told her, still studying her with those deep dark eyes of his. 'And it's no use hating me. It was your idea we test the theory of the Ruby.'

'Oh yes, and you certainly did that all right, didn't you!'

He sighed and shook his head. 'Charlotte, I knew there

wouldn't be any point in just asking for something which you might be in the habit of giving, like oral or straight-forward sex.'

She gasped at his audacity. 'I'm not in the habit of –'

He raised his hands in surrender. 'OK, but even so, I had the feeling that anal sex wasn't a normal act which you would indulge in. So that's why I plumped for that.' He stared hard at her again. 'I am right aren't I, Charlotte? You haven't had anal sex very often have you?'

'That's none of your damn business,' Charlotte exclaimed, glaring off into the distance where black thunder clouds rolled over the hills. Despite her anger, she wished with all her heart that she could admit the truth. That he was the first. The one to take her anal virginity. And that she had loved it. But she felt she couldn't ever tell him.

Unaware of her inner turmoil, an infuriating smile tugged at the corners of his mouth. 'Come on, you'd better finish dressing. You'll catch your death standing half naked like that.'

'Not that my health worried you five minutes ago,' Charlotte retorted, fumbling with her bra then hastily dragging on her sweater.

'Don't tell me you were cold,' he said, mocking her. 'I thought you were pretty damned hot.'

'Oh shut up!' she snapped, turning her back on him. Her nerves were coiled as tight as a spring. What now, she wondered as she smoothed her sweater over her breasts. Was it goodbye? She had her story and she had some photographs. There was nothing to detain her now. Time to go home and back to Paul. Her heart plummeted. Paul. Dear sweet faithless Paul! Not that she was any better. Perhaps they suited each other.

Andrew's voice broke into her thoughts. 'Do you have everything you need for your article now, Charlotte?'

'Now I have my proof, you mean,' she murmured

miserably, still thinking about Paul. Wondering who the girl was. Was she younger, older, prettier?

Andrew's finger and thumb suddenly cupped her chin, tilting her face upwards. 'What is it, Charlotte? There's something troubling you. Is it because of what we just did?'

'Isn't that enough?' she retaliated, still not intending to tell him about her two-timing boyfriend.

'Charlotte . . .' Andrew murmured softly, caressing her cheek.

She jerked her head away, not trusting herself to allow him to get close now. 'I'm fine, just fine,' she snapped, hastily changing the subject. 'Look, I . . . I still need to photograph the pendant on a woman – not me. Just an attractive woman, perhaps with a handsome man looking lustfully at her. It will just set the whole feature off.' Andrew remained gazing into her face, as if trying to read her true thoughts. She avoided his gaze as she continued purposefully. 'All I need to do now is find a nice-looking couple who are willing to pose for me.'

'That may not be as difficult as you think,' Andrew said, giving her one last lingering look before waving his hand. 'Hey, Jamie! Over here!'

Charlotte swung round and spotted Jamie and his girlfriend sneaking off out of the woods. She gasped. 'Oh, my God! You don't think they saw us, do you?'

Andrew gave a little shrug. 'Does that matter?'

'It certainly does,' Charlotte cried. 'I do have my reputation to consider.'

'Shall I ask them?' he suggested quietly as Jamie and Diane came over, clearly reluctant, and whispering to each other as they approached.

'Don't you dare!' Charlotte hissed, quickly smoothing out her clothes. She couldn't help noticing how muddy Diane's trousers were. She felt hopeful that her secret was still intact. Perhaps Jamie and Diane had been enjoying their own romp in the woods, and had not noticed her and Andrew at all. She forced an awkward smile. 'Jamie, Diane, hi!'

'Hello, Charlotte,' Jamie said, his blue eyes flicking over her breasts. She guessed her nipples were still hard and sticking through her sweater like the proverbial chapel hat pegs. Jamie's gaze switched to Andrew. There was ice in his voice and Charlotte's hopes that they hadn't been observed were dashed. 'Mr Alexander,' he uttered curtly.

Andrew Alexander nodded pleasantly at the pair of them, totally unperturbed that they might have witnessed him fucking Charlotte in the arse. 'You two could just be the folk we're looking for.'

Diane shot Jamie a suspicious glance.

'What do ye want us for?' Jamie asked puzzled and looked warily at Charlotte.

He looked strange, Charlotte thought. Not quite so friendly as usual. But then if he'd just witnessed her getting a good hard fucking when she'd turned him down last night he had every right to feel pissed off. As for his girlfriend, she was positively glaring daggers at her.

Andrew, however, had never seemed more relaxed and at ease. Obviously anal sex was just what the doctor had ordered. 'Charlotte's looking for two people to pose for photographs with the piece of jewellery she's writing about. We thought you two would be ideal.'

'Charlotte's already taken ma photo,' Jamie replied, staring hard at her, as if willing her to understand some unspoken message. Charlotte could hazard a guess as to what it was. Why have sex with Andrew, but not with me?

She glanced away, wishing she could say sorry. Wishing he hadn't seen her. The last thing she wanted to do was upset or hurt him.

Diane cast him a sharp, questioning look, no doubt wondering what photos he was talking about. Andrew was watching her oddly too. In fact everybody seemed intrigued. She opened her mouth to explain, then thought better of it. She could hardly tell Diane and the man who'd just introduced her to the best sexual experience of her life that Jamie had stripped naked and posed nude for her.

She decided instead to tell them about the feature she was working on. It seemed to get Jamie more het up than before.

'So let me get this straight,' Jamie began after she'd explained about the legend of the Highland Ruby. 'Let's say if he –' he glared at Andrew '– put this Highland Ruby on you, Charlotte, and told you to . . . to –'

'Bend over and let him fuck you,' Diane finished for him, causing everyone to stare aghast at her. 'What?' she asked innocently. 'Oh, all right, make love then. Make love, Jamie, would you rather talk about Mr Alexander and Charlotte making love or having a fuck?'

'Diane, will ye pack it up!' Jamie said, flashing her a furious look.

She shrugged innocently. 'Sorry.'

Jamie took a deep breath. 'So, what does it mean, Charlotte? Would the woman go through with it even if she didn't want to?'

'So it seems . . . er, according to the legend,' Charlotte replied, glancing at Andrew.

'But there canna really be any truth behind the legend?' Jamie persisted.

Charlotte knew he was trying to find out whether she'd wanted sex with Andrew, or whether she had no choice.

'I would say it's true, Jamie,' she replied, hoping that would make him feel less upset. Only now Andrew was looking curiously at her and Jamie, obviously trying to figure out what was going on between them. Diane was glaring again too. Charlotte groaned inwardly. This was ridiculous. It was impossible to please one person without upsetting another.

She decided to stop trying and simply please herself. She forced a bright, couldn't-care-less smile. 'Anyway, I wonder if Diane would pose wearing the pendant, and you, Jamie, could look lustfully at her, as if you'd like to have her under your spell.'

Diane cast him a coy smile and linked his arm. 'I'm already under your spell, aren't I, Jamie?'

Her smile reminded Charlotte of a Siamese cat which her aunt had once owned. It was a vicious creature that used to purr contentedly while you stroked it, then lashed out with its claws when you stopped.

Miss Feline Features wanted more information. 'And will my photograph be in a glossy magazine?'

'Yes, *Antiques and Legends*. It's a very well-established magazine. Quite up-market,' Charlotte told her, watching out for the claws.

The idea of being featured in a glossy magazine seemed to pacify Diane. 'Ma white frock's still at your place, Jamie, and you could wear your kilt.'

Charlotte still felt wary, wondering whether involving them was a good idea or not. Still, they'd agreed now, so there was nothing she could do – except sound enthusiastic. 'That's great. How long will it take you to get ready? I'd like to get these photographs done today before it rains again.'

'About an hour or so,' said Diane. 'We could catch up with you in the pub.'

'Or why not come over to Stonemoor,' Andrew suggested, glancing at Charlotte, making her feel jittery inside again. 'It would be perfect as a backdrop, either indoors or out. It can look quite atmospheric – can't it, Charlotte?'

'Yes,' she breathed, recalling the flickering candelight and the heat from the roaring fire on her naked skin. Goosebumps suddenly erupted all over her, and she had to force herself to concentrate on Jamie and Diane. 'Would that be okay with you two?'

'Aye, that's fine,' said Diane. 'Will you wait while we get our clothes, or shall we see you over there?'

Andrew seemed to be making all the decisions suddenly. 'Charlotte and I will go over now; you two catch us up when you're ready.'

Charlotte's stomach lurched, but she warned herself not to get excited. He had just satisfied himself shagging her so he was hardly likely to want sex again so soon. No, this was a photo shoot, plain and simple.

'We'll see you later then,' Diane said, tugging at Jamie's arm. He seemed reluctant to go. Another feline look flashed across Diane's face, sharpening her features. 'Come on, Jamie, what are we waiting for?'

Jamie was clearly reluctant to leave Charlotte alone with Andrew and Diane had to practically drag him away. He glanced back constantly until Charlotte finally turned away, biting down on her lip.

Andrew stared at her. 'Something going on here I should know about?'

'No,' she answered stiffly.

'I could put the Highland Ruby around your neck and make you tell me the truth.'

'The answer would still be no,' Charlotte told him irritably. 'Jamie quite likes me, that's all. I think they must have seen us.'

'Having anal sex,' Andrew added.

Her cheeks began to glow. 'Yes that. Anyway, I think he's feeling a bit put out, that's all.'

Andrew looked vaguely amused. 'Put out? I'd say he was smitten.'

'Well there's nothing going on,' Charlotte retorted hotly. 'He's got a girlfriend. He ought to concentrate on her.'

'Just like you've been concentrating on your sweetheart,' Andrew remarked blandly, not taking his eyes off her face.

'I haven't had a lot of choice, have I?' she replied, turning aside as her cheeks began to burn.

He touched her elbow. 'I think maybe I should apologise,' he said in a gentle voice.

Charlotte stared off into the distance. 'Yes, maybe you should.'

'Although you didn't seem to find it too repulsive.'

She chewed her bottom lip, aware of a raging heat springing up between her legs. 'It wasn't that bad.'

'Not the sort of thing you'd regularly indulge in, though?'

She shrugged. 'Perhaps, with the right man.'

'So you'll be going home to what's his name – Paul – with a brand new experience to share with him?'

Charlotte shot him a quick look. It instantly gave away her misery over Paul.

'Hello? What's happened to loverboy then?'

Her eyelids fluttered shut. The last thing she was going to do was cry.

'Charlotte?'

Staring down at the earth, she murmured. 'It's over. I think he's been seeing someone else while I've been here.'

'How do you know?'

'When I rang him, there was someone with him ... you know ...'

There was humour in his voice. 'Whereas you've been such a good girl.'

'I was under the influence of your magic pendant!' she shot at him, aware that it was a blatant lie.

He nodded his dark head. 'Ah yes, so you were.'

Charlotte suddenly had a vague feeling that he still didn't altogether believe in its magic. Her cheeks flamed and she swiftly gathered her bags together, not trusting herself to continue to lie blatantly.

He took the bags from her, like a true gentleman. 'Shall

we go, Charlotte? If we get back now, I can show you around the house and let you choose the right background for the shots.'

'Yes, fine,' she agreed curtly and walked a step behind him as they set off across the moors.

They walked without speaking for a while, then Andrew broke the silence. 'I guess you're pretty cut up about him two timing you.'

'We'd been together for two years,' Charlotte replied, deciding that was sufficient to tell him. Right now she couldn't quite understand her own feelings. She ought to feel bad about Paul, but the truth was, the only thing on her mind at the moment was whether Andrew would want sex again when they reached his house. The prospect made her pussy tingle in anticipation.

'Have you told him it's over?' Andrew asked then, taking her hand to help her over a particularly muddy patch of earth.

Even the touch of his hand sent tingles shooting through her. 'Not yet,' she answered, trying to sound normal. 'I expect he'll deny everything. It's not as if I have proof or anything. Instinct isn't proof, is it?'

'No it's not. You're certain he was with someone then?'

'Positive,' she said quietly.

'First job when you get back then?'

She nodded.

'And when will that be?'

She felt utterly miserable suddenly. The thought of not seeing Andrew again filled her with dismay. 'Tomorrow probably. There's nothing to keep me once I have these pictures.'

'You have all the information you need for your feature?'

'I think so.'

'And you even have your own proof. At least you can write it from experience now.' There was a dangerous twinkle in his eyes. 'Will you be writing it from your own personal viewpoint, Charlotte?'

Heat raced through her veins. 'Not in every detail.'

'You're not going to admit to your readers that the Highland Ruby caused you to have anal sex then?'

'No,' she uttered, biting hard on her lower lip, almost tasting blood.

'And you won't be writing about how, as you listened to the stories behind the legend, you were driven by uncontrollable lust to drag my clothes off me and suck my cock down your throat?'

She could feel a pulse, like a heartbeat, throbbing around the entrance to her pussy. 'I don't think so, somehow.'

'Nor how you crouched on hands and knees, practically naked, and offered your sweet little cunt up to me so that I could ravish you?'

She thumped him hard, not that it made any impact on him. 'Will you stop it!'

He grinned. 'What's wrong, Charlotte? You can't blame the Highland Ruby this time; it's still tucked away in my pocket.'

'You're embarrassing me, that's all I meant.'

'Not that I'm turning you on again.'

'Not a bit,' she lied, her entire lower abdomen now throbbing as her blood pumped through her veins; her desire to feel his cock up her again became a craving.

He threw back his head so that the breeze caught his thick dark hair, giving him a wild, untamed look. 'You know, this could wreck a man's self esteem, thinking the only reason a woman came on to him was because she was under a spell. We do like to think our own charms have something to do with the attraction.'

She couldn't help smiling to herself. 'If you're fishing for compliments you're out of luck. I told you, the Hunchback of Notre Dame would have had the same reaction from me once I was wearing that Ruby.'

His eyes narrowed thoughtfully. 'So perhaps I should do my own test, under laboratory conditions, so to speak.'

Charlotte cast him a wary look. 'How exactly?'

'One way is like this . . .'

Without warning, Andrew pulled her into his arms and kissed her. For a second she was so startled that she hung there limply, allowing herself to be kissed. And then she found herself responding, not only with her lips, but with her body as she melted into him, loving the size and strength of the man. He had a divine mouth and a way of kissing that she could well get used to.

His arms encircled her, his hands slipping down to her buttocks, moulding her pelvis to pelvis, so there was no mistaking the distinct bulge of his cock. Charlotte could hardly believe he was ready for action again so quickly. Yet there was no denying the hot quivers darting up through her own body as her excitement grew.

He finally stopped kissing her, but remained holding her close to him as he looked down into her flushed face. 'That's blown your Hunchback theory, Charlotte.'

'It was just a kiss,' she murmured, but the look in her eyes dared him to go further.

He looked upwards towards the heavens for a moment, as if seeking an answer to some unspoken question. And, then as if gripped by some sudden, desperate urgency, he grasped her hand tightly. Without another word, he marched purposefully towards Stonemoor House. Taking Charlotte with him.

# Chapter Nine

*B*y the time they reached Stonemoor House, Charlotte felt sick with apprehension. Not a single word had been spoken after she had given him that look, and the tension between them was electric.

Andrew turned the key and gave the door a sharp kick to open it. As always his house felt chillier than the air outside and Charlotte shivered both with cold and with nerves.

The remnants of a fire still smouldered in the grate and Andrew raked it with a poker before he added more logs while Charlotte waited nervously by, not sure what to do or say. She felt decidedly odd. Bubbling inside with nervous energy, her breasts and inner thighs prickling.

'It will soon warm up in here,' Andrew said, taking off his outdoor jacket with the Highland Ruby still inside his pocket. He glanced at her and she found herself holding her breath, wondering if he would make a move on her now. What he suggested, however, was not at all what she expected.

'Perhaps you'd like to see the rest of the house while we're waiting for young Jamie and his girlfriend.'

'Yes, why not?' she agreed, hiding the rush of disappointment. The last thing she wanted was a conducted tour of his house. The only place she wanted to explore was inside his jeans.

Clearly not reading her mind, he led the way into the next room. 'This is the kitchen – basic but sufficient.'

Charlotte nodded her approval. He had all the usual mod cons: fridge-freezer, washing machine, cooker, all of which had a vaguely tarnished and well-used look. Definitely a man's kitchen, she thought, no hint of a woman's touch. 'I'm surprised you have gas and electricity, living so far from civilisation.'

He nodded towards the window and Charlotte peered out. There was a generator and a large gas cylinder outside, linked to the house. 'I have my own power supply.'

'I see,' Charlotte mused, wondering then about the other side to his life. He owned a chain of international restaurants. He could probably afford a mansion in any part of the world, yet he was stuck here, in the back of beyond. 'Do you live here all year round?'

'These last few years I've spent a lot of time here. Here and travelling to my restaurants. I've a string of them around this country and Europe, but then you probably already know that, being a journalist. Fortunately I have a very loyal and trustworthy staff who I can rely on, so I don't have to be on top of them every minute.'

'So where do you live when you're not here?'

'Hotels mostly,' he remarked, showing her into another room. It turned out to be a study. The centre of the room was occupied by a large leather-topped desk cluttered by a conglomeration of papers and folders along with a laptop computer. Bookcases lined the walls. 'I had a place in London, but sold that after Fay died. All my furniture and belongings are in storage, in case I ever set up home back in the land of the living.'

'And is that likely?' Charlotte asked as she perused his collection of books.

'I hope so, one day,' he remarked. 'If I settle down with anyone ever again.

Charlotte nodded, realising that settling down with someone like Andrew Alexander would lead to a very different life than settling down with Paul. For one thing sex would be the number one priority if she had anything to do with it. She halted her train of thought. There was hardly any point in considering a long-term relationship with someone she wouldn't see again after the next day or so.

She changed the subject. 'You have a nice selection of cook books.'

'I enjoy cooking. Perhaps before you leave. I'll have the opportunity to cook for you.'

'That would be nice,' she agreed, keeping her voice casual. But in her mind she was already visualising a candlelit meal for two, and afterwards, retiring to the lounge and the rug in front of his fire, where they would both strip naked and feast on each other's bodies.

'I'll show you upstairs, Charlotte,' he said then, a quirky little smile on his face. 'Don't worry, you're quite safe. The Highland Ruby is still in my jacket.'

Charlotte forced a smile, having the feeling it looked more like a grimace. She didn't want to be safe. She wanted him. Only it seemed that unless she made the first move, they would be going nowhere. 'I thought we'd blown the legend out of the window,' she remarked, deliberately giving him a long enquiring stare.

He was at the bottom of the stairs, one hand on the banister knob. He hesitated. 'With that kiss, you mean?'

Her tingling pussy was practically crying out for attention. 'I responded to your kiss when I wasn't wearing the pendant, didn't I?'

He gazed steadily at her for some moments, then took her hand and drew her up the stairs until she was one step higher than him, her face on a level with his. 'Perhaps we should check it out again.'

'Perhaps we should,' Charlotte murmured, aware now that she was so close to him how long his lashes were, and how heady his male scent was. His arms encircled her slender waist, moulding her into him. She felt the hard masculinity of his chest, the strength of his arms and the promising bulge in his trousers.

He kissed her. His lips were soft and moist, and just brushed against hers with the most featherlight of kisses. It had the same effect as being hit by a fire rocket.

He was just impossible to resist and her arms went instinctively around his neck, his fingers tangling in her hair. He looked steadily into her eyes, as if trying to read her mind. Then he kissed her again. This time deeper, a sensuous kiss that sent her pulse racing.

With his lips still brushing hers he murmured, 'I wonder what would happen if I asked you to strip for me now, Charlotte? Now that there's no magic pendant to hide behind.'

She was in turmoil again. Now what was she supposed to do? Admit that it hadn't been magic that made her give in to him earlier. That it was just her own lustful needs. Only what about Fay? She couldn't admit to the truth now; it would be letting Fay down. It was stupid, she knew, particularly when she didn't even know the girl. But she knew Andrew. If she could help him rid the ghost of his dead wife then she would.

Gathering all her willpower she smiled. 'Andrew, I'm not going to strip for you this time.'

He didn't seem convinced and his hands around her hips slipped down to her buttocks, curling beneath them, cupping the cheeks of her bottom in his palms as he drew her closer to him.

'Oh, God,' she moaned under her breath. She was going to need a whole bag-full of willpower to stop herself from giving into him now.

He kissed her again, and she couldn't stop herself from enjoying it. Holding her this way, she could feel his rection hardening against her flat stomach. It was impossible to stop herself from pressing herself into him, loving the feel of his fingers stroking the small of her back and her buttocks.

'So these stay on?' Andrew breathed against her parted lips, giving a little tug at her trousers.

She nodded reluctantly, hoping he wouldn't take no for an answer and simply rip them off her.

He gave her a long lingering look and then moved away from her, going on ahead up the stairs. 'Then we may as well finish the tour.'

'Yes, if you like,' she uttered, irritated with herself for ever admitting to being under the influence of the Ruby.

Upstairs he opened the first door on the landing. 'This is just the bathroom. As you see, nothing spectacular. But this room,' he added, crossing the landing. 'This room is one I'm particularly proud of. Hours of enjoyment can be had in here.'

He opened the door and Charlotte instantly saw how he managed to keep in trim. He had installed a compact gymnasium. The room itself had mirrors everywhere, from floor to ceiling. And it was kitted out with all kinds of keep-fit equipment, from a rowing machine to a bench press, weights, a punchbag, even a multigym. On the walls which weren't mirrored were posters of muscle-men and women in tiny little leotards, their big rippling muscles oiled and gleaming.

Charlotte looked around in amazement. 'So this is how you keep that physique?' she complimented him good-naturedly.

'I try.'

'She glanced at one of the muscle-men posters. 'And is that what your body looks like under those clothes?'

He laughed. 'Not quite. You have to dedicate your life to getting a body like that. I just like to keep myself in shape, just basically keeping fit.'

Charlotte cast her eye over the pictures of female body builders. 'I don't think I'd really like to look like that.'

'You have a gorgeous body,' he said, his dark eyes raking the length of her, making goose pimples erupt all over her skin. He moved closer, his voice husky. 'And the more I look at you, the more I'm thinking I want to put that enchanted relic around your neck and have you stripped naked and legs apart for me again.'

A flaming heat roared suddenly through her veins. The shock of his unexpected suggestion made her head reel. She tried to remain calm and under control. But she couldn't help but imagine what it would be like to have sex here, in this room, with all these mirrors surrounding them, so that she would be able to watch herself getting shagged from every angle possible.

He gazed languidly at her. 'Well, Charlotte, what do you say to that? Should I get the Ruby?'

Her throat was dry, making speech difficult. 'I don' know,' she barely murmured.

'Would you like to be under its spell again, Charlotte? Giving in to all those deep dark desires you keep locked away?'

She was on fire. Every nerve-ending was tingling with longing. Wearing the Highland Ruby again had to be the answer. She could keep up the pretence. Her smoky grey eyes narrowed. Did he realise he was giving her this way out? Had he guessed the power of the Ruby was ground less, that it was really in the mind of the woman?

She looked into his eyes, not sure. Yet he was an intelligent man. Could he really be taken in by a legend? But of course it served his purpose too. Whether play acting or not, Charlotte was allowing him intimacy when wearing it, and that was clearly what he wanted too.

'Well, Charlotte, what's your answer to be? I'll at least give you that choice because when the Highland Ruby is around your neck, I warn you you'll be at my mercy.'

She moistened her lips with the tip of her tongue. He

watched with eyes that were undressing her with every passing second.

She was tingling. Tingling from head to toe as she gathered the courage to give him her answer. Then at last she said the word. Quietly and simply. 'Yes,' she breathed, and her heart began to thud, pounding right down into her sex.

Although it was barely a whisper, her response caused Andrew to exhale a long sigh. And then, without another word, he turned and hurried down the stairs. Charlotte stood, staring at her reflection in a long mirror. Her cheeks were flushed and her long red hair tousled from being outside all morning. And even from here, she could see her breasts heaving and distinctly see the outline of her hard nipples.

Moments later Andrew returned holding that familiar velvet package. He unwrapped it carefully, watching Charlotte's face all the time, his eyes not wavering from hers.

'Still time to back out,' he whispered hoarsely as he tossed the velvet aside and held the pendant in both hands.

Charlotte gulped, remembering what he had just said: 'You'll be at my mercy.' But there was no question of her backing out now. She ached for him. Silently, she walked towards him and raised her chin, allowing him to slip the pendant over her head.

Breathing deeply, his chest rising and falling with every breath, Andrew slowly placed the Highland Ruby around her neck. Speaking softly he recited, 'Thy will dissolves, thy belongeth to me.'

He took her hand and led her out of the gym and into his bedroom. Inside was a massive oak bed with heavy drapes at one end giving it the appearance of a four-poster. The drapes in dark green velvet swathed the wall, the curtains were of a matching fabric, and were closed, as if this room never saw the light of day.

The rest of the furnishings were also in old oak, heavy masculine furniture. Even the smell of the room was of that distinct male scent. There was nothing feminine in here to even hint of a woman's presence and Charlotte had the feeling that it had been a long time since a woman walked through these doors. Or felt that mattress beneath her.

Andrew kicked the door shut, and stood for a moment just gazing at her, as if he could barely believe his good fortune. Charlotte met his gaze with eyes that were languid and ready for love.

'I want you naked, Charlotte,' Andrew said huskily. And as she went to pull her sweater off, he stopped her. 'Only this time, I shall undress you.'

She swallowed hard, then began to tremble as he lifted her sweater up and over her head. He moved behind her and carefully unhooked her bra, letting it fall on to the rug. His hands slipped around to her front and cupped her naked breasts.

Charlotte gasped as he took their weight in the palms of his hands and began to gently mould and squeeze them. He was standing so close behind her that she could feel the bulge at his crotch grow larger, pushing into her buttocks. It seemed to be hardening and becoming bigger with every second, so that she was positive it would burst through his jeans at any moment.

He turned her around to face him then and looked down at her breasts, his finger and thumbs capturing her nipples and squeezing hard until she cried out.

'You have beautiful breasts, Charlotte,' Andrew murmured, easing her backwards on to his bed.

The mattress was firm beneath her back, but the bed dipped as Andrew kneeled astride her, his weight pinning her thighs down so there was no escape. He fondled her tingling breasts again, delighting in squeezing her nipples so hard that she whimpered. Then, lowering his head, he took her right nipple into his mouth, capturing

170

it between his white teeth, with his eyes raised to hers, watching her changing expressions.

With his weight pinning her down, Charlotte's hands slid on to his thighs, stroking him. Her gaze flicked from his face down to the huge bulge at the front of his jeans. She desperately wanted to unzip him and let him bounce free.

'Does he want to come out and play?' Charlotte asked, stroking her hand over his confined erection.

'All in good time,' he murmured, getting up from her and standing at the side of the bed. Gazing down at her with eyes that practically smouldered, he began to unfasten her trousers. Effortlessly he lifted her bottom off the bed to slip the trousers and panties from under her. Her shoes followed.

Charlotte lay there completely naked, her body tingling, her pussy just aching to be touched.

'Turn over, Charlotte,' Andrew told her.
She did as she was told and lay face down on his duvet. She could smell that distinct male scent of his and it drove her crazy.

'Up on your knees and lean on your elbows.'

'Oh, God,' she breathed, kneeling up, with her bottom turned towards him.

'Mmm, that's nice,' he murmured, stroking her bum cheeks and tickling her labia. He then parted the lips so that he could insert two fingers between her delicate pink folds.

Charlotte groaned, loving the feel of him fingering her. Then she gasped as he removed his fingers and she felt his warm moist tongue lap around her, his face pressed between the cheeks of her bottom. He licked her like an affectionate dog.

'Oh, God, yes, Andrew, that's lovely,' she breathed into the duvet.

His tongue explored her more, darting into her pussy,

171

snaking hot and moist towards her anus, licking and sucking at that tight little orifice too.

Her fists were tangled into the duvet cover and her knuckles bled white as he continued to drive her crazy with his tongue.

He turned her over then, on to her back and lifted her legs up around his neck to bury his head into her pussy. Charlotte arched into him, already on the verge of coming. He knew precisely where to apply the pressure of his mouth, knew the very spot that would drive her completely over the edge. Her climax reached feverpitch within seconds.

As ripples of pleasure erupted inside of her, Charlotte clung to his head, wrapping her legs around his neck and forcing herself on to his mouth; she kept gyrating hard against him as he continued to suck her dry.

As her pelvis jerked against him in uncontrollable spasms of pleasure, Charlotte cried out his name, her long legs shooting out rigidly, then coiling back around his neck.

'Andrew, that's heaven. Don't stop, please . . .'

A second climax followed her first, and she satisfied herself on his willing mouth. Never in her life had she felt so fantastically fulfilled.

She eventually relaxed and allowed Andrew to emerge, his face glistening with her juices. His eyes gleamed dangerously.

'My turn,' he growled. 'On your feet, young lady, and strip me naked.'

Charlotte couldn't wait. But even so, she decided that she wouldn't rush things. No doubt he was dying to have his cock freed from his trousers and given a sucking. Well, he would wait a little longer, so that when she did suck him, he would be gagging for it.

Standing before him, she slid her hands under his sweatshirt, delighting as she saw how the brush of her cold fingers on his hot skin made him shiver. She pushed the shirt upwards and eased it over his head. Her eyes raked over his naked torso. He had a perfect physique, in her opinion. Not as muscled as the men on the posters, but muscled enough for her. She ran her hands up over his flesh.

'You do keep yourself in trim, don't you,' she murmured. 'At least up here. I wonder just how powerful that other muscle of yours is now?'

'I thought you'd found that out earlier, young lady, when I pushed it up your arse.'

His words enflamed her, but she remained in control. 'And are you going to make me do that again?'

'Wait and see,' he growled, standing quite still, his erection straining at his zip and dying for release.

Charlotte narrowed her eyes as she looked at him. 'Maybe I shouldn't let him out then, not if he's going to be a naughty boy and force his way up my little bottom again. It hurt, you know.'

His mouth twitched. 'But I've just kissed your bottom better. So I think it's ready to have a little more punishment, don't you?'

She wagged her finger. 'Not yet, that's being greedy.'

'And you weren't greedy,' he asked, looking down at her nakedness, 'when you came in my mouth a couple of minutes ago? How many times was it?'

'Only two.'

'Only two,' he repeated dangerously. 'So twice isn't enough. So we shall have to rectify that before this afternoon is through. Now get my trousers off, Charlotte, before they split at the seams.'

He was wearing a belt, which she unbuckled, and then very slowly she eased down his zip. The bulge inside his underpants expanded out through the flaps of his open jeans, and Charlotte delighted in running her finger all along the thick outline of his cock. It stiffened even more.

Urgently then, she pushed his jeans down to his ankles

and he stepped out of them. With delicate precision, she slid his underpants down.

His stiff cock bounced free and stood erect, its bulbous head already glistening with a gem of moisture; his balls were tight and hard.

Charlotte moaned under her breath, desperately wanting to get her lips around him and taste him again. But before she could stoop down to take him into her mouth, Andrew eased her back on to the bed.

Once more he straddled her, kneeling this time over her midriff, so that his rampant length bobbed right over her face. He reached across for a pillow and lifted her head so that he could put it under her.

'Comfortable?' he asked softly.

'Perfect,' she uttered, her tongue quivering to lick that dark purple knob – so smooth and shiny.

'Suck my cock, Charlotte,' Andrew said, shifting himself forward just enough for him to poke his penis into her mouth. It filled her, and she sucked it in, loving the feel of it. Her tongue snaked around it as she sucked and licked him, while one free hand came up to tickle his balls.

He kneeled up a little, so that he wasn't crushing her, and rocked his pelvis back and forth, thrusting his cock in and out.

'Oh baby, that's good, that's so good,' he breathed. 'Suck me, Charlotte, suck my cock hard, baby.'

She moved her hands around to his buttocks and stroked them as she continued to eat his dick. With his cheeks parted, she tickled his anus, thrilling to the way his body jerked in response. She kept it up, knowing he was loving it.

But her own desires were creeping up on her again, her libido taking only a few moments to start craving for her sex to be touched once more. With him kneeling over her chest, his hard cock half down her throat, it was impossible for her to even touch her clit herself. She bent her knees, her legs apart, tingling with the need to be fondled.

A moment later, she began to wonder whether the Highland Ruby also had the power to grant wishes.

Without retracting himself from her mouth, he reached across to a dressing table drawer by the side of his bed and took something out. Charlotte glanced up and her eyes almost popped.

It was an extremely life-like penis-shaped vibrator, which began to shake and tremble at the click of a switch.

She gagged, trying to ask what he was going to do. But it was impossible to speak with a mouth full of cock, and a second later she didn't need to ask. She discovered for herself what his plans were.

Arching back a little he put the buzzing rubber cock between her parted legs. At first he just rubbed it against her clit. Then he stroked it down between her lips, opening them, and gently slid it up her.

Charlotte gasped against the real thing in her mouth and the hard length of rubber vibrating deliciously up her fanny. Andrew held it in place, his thumb touching her clit as she moved her hips in time with his gentle thrusts.

She felt herself coming almost instantly, and her thoughts centred on her sex, for a second simply squeezing Andrew's hot cock between her lips as she ground herself on to the vibrator and his hand. Seconds later she came, her whole abdomen quivering, thrilling to the darts of pleasure that rocketed through her.

She arched stiffly, and as the first intense sensations ebbed, she began to suck him fiercely again, wanting him to experience the same wonderful sensations.

Clearly his willpower was stronger than hers. When she had relaxed again, Andrew extracted his cock from her lips and got off the bed.

'So you like two cocks at once?' he asked.

'Oh yes,' she murmured. 'I loved it.'

'Good,' he said, taking her hand and helping her to her feet.

She was surprised to find how unsteady she was, and she held on to him as she steadied herself. Her legs were like jelly. Her whole body was trembling.

'Come with me,' he said softly, keeping hold of her hand.

Charlotte followed him obediently, knowing she couldn't and wouldn't stop him from doing whatever he wanted. She was surprised to find that he was leading her into his gym.

'I don't think I've the strength for a workout,' she managed to joke.

He said nothing, but went over to a piece of equipment which had a long curved handle coming up off the end of its bench seat. Unscrewing the end of the vibrator, and removing the batteries, he then slid the rubber cock over the end of the handle.

Charlotte instantly sensed what was in store, and her eyes popped. 'You're joking!'

'You'll love it, I promise,' he said, smoothing some lubrication gel over the imitation cock and his hands. 'Now kneel down on the bench, Charlotte, and back up against the vibrator.'

She could scarcely breathe with a mixture of fear and excitement. But she did as she was told, kneeling and then shuffling along the bench until she felt the rubber cock between her legs. Andrew made an adjustment to the handle, so that the sex gadget was a little lower and aimed directly towards her pussy.

Standing directly behind her, Andrew eased her backwards so that the rubber cock very slowly slipped into her slit. Almost instantly Charlotte began to gyrate against it.

Knowing that he was watching her enjoying herself on the vibrator made her feel as horny as hell. But then, in the next second, she felt Andrew's own hot prick pushing against her anus.

'Oh, my God, no!' Charlotte squealed as the realisation dawned on her what was about to happen. His words came tumbling back. *'So you like two cocks at once?'*

This couldn't be happening. Surely she wasn't going to be fucked both ways at the same time.

Quite clearly she was.

His finger entered her tiny little opening first and she felt the cold lubrication gel. He slid his finger back and forth, and round and round, to lubricate and prepare her. Then his cock, pressed hard against her, demanded entrance.

Charlotte held her breath and cried out as he penetrated her. Andrew gasped too, and held on to her hips for a moment. Slowly then, he began to rock her, building up the rhythm so that both his penis and the imitation one were thrusting up her arse and fanny.

Charlotte clung on to the bench. Her eyes squeezed tightly shut, as she felt the two big hard rods giving her the fucking of her life. At first it was almost too much to bear, but when she saw that it wasn't going to kill her, or rip her in two, she started to relax and enjoy it, loving the sensations flooding through her. Goosebumps sprang up all over her naked flesh and tingles ran through her from her toes up to the top of her head.

Holding on to her hips, Andrew asked huskily. 'Do you like my cock up your arse?'

She could barely speak but somehow she murmured, 'I love it. Andrew, it's unbelievable.'

His movements quickened, thrusting into her with long powerful strokes. Charlotte gasped, wondering if anyone had ever died from pleasure such as this. But then suddenly they were interrupted by someone banging on the front door, and shouting up at the window.

'Hello! Are you there? Let us in, it's starting to rain out here.'

Andrew stopped, but remained hard inside of her. 'It's Jamie and his girlfriend. Don't move.'

'What?' she whimpered, as he withdrew from her arse, and cleaned himself up with a tissue.

'I'll get them settled and I'll be back,' he promised, pulling on a tracksuit and trainers. He came around to the front of the contraption she was kneeling on, and stooped down so that his face was close to hers. 'Don't stop enjoying yourself,' he said with a wink, then kissed the tip of her nose.

From this angle, Charlotte couldn't see him leave the room. And there wasn't a mirror facing her here. But she heard his footsteps go down the stairs and then heard him letting Jamie and Diane into the front room.

The rubber cock was still inside her, and her clit was prickling with the desire to come. There didn't seem any point in wasting the moment, so she continued to rock back and forth on her knees, thrusting the fake penis in and out. Then, altering her position, she pulled back a little so that the tip of the vibrator rubbed against her clit, wanking her wantonly. She was on the verge of coming, but she held back, waiting for Andrew to return.

She didn't hear him come back into the room, but he was suddenly at her rear again, and the handle with the rubber penis was folded downwards out of the way so that without a word, his long length rammed hard up her hot moist pussy.

Charlotte gasped as he penetrated her with such determined thrusts they practically forced the breath out of her lungs. She gasped and clung on to the end of the apparatus. She hadn't expected him to have her quite like this; there was something different about him somehow. Like he was in a hurried frenzy. Not that she was complaining really. She loved him shagging her doggy fashion. It was just that she expected him to be a little more loving. This just seemed like hard, raw sex, without the care and emotion he had shown earlier.

178

He seemed almost like a different person.

A shiver ran through her and she struggled to see behind her. All she could glimpse was his foot and leg. But it wasn't Andrew's trainer and tracksuit bottoms. It was a muddy leather boot and dark-blue denim jeans that were damp around the hems.

She twisted and turned, and finally glimpsed, not Andrew shafting her – but Jamie.

She shrieked and darted forward, almost doing him a mishap. On her feet, she shot across the room and stared wide-eyed at Jamie. He stood there, flushed with shame, his cock all hard and glistening with her juices.

'How dare you!' Charlotte hissed, terrified of what Andrew or Diane would do if they came in now. 'What on earth are you thinking of?'

Jamie looked suddenly helpless. 'I'm sorry, Charlotte, I couldn't help myself. I came up looking for the toilet and came in here by mistake. When I saw ye bent over with your lovely wee arse in the air, and playing with that thing, I just couldn't stop myself. I'm awful sorry.'

'Sorry! Jamie you can't just go having sex, uninvited.'

He hung his head in shame, and Charlotte felt a twinge of forgiveness. He looked so vulnerable standing there, shamefaced, head hung low and his big erect penis still standing to attention.

'Oh, Jamie,' she sighed, wandering back to him. She spoke gently. 'Jamie, you'll have to stop fantasising about me. I like you, I really do. But to be honest, it's Andrew that I'm interested in. He's the one I want.'

Jamie nodded miserably. 'Aye, I guessed that. Are ye going to tell him what I did?'

'I ought to,' she scolded. 'Only what purpose would that serve? It would only upset everyone. Especially your girlfriend.'

'Aye, that it would, and I've upset her enough already.'

Charlotte smiled. 'Well you'd better go and make up with her. You don't want to lose her, Jamie.'

179

He raised his baby-blue eyes hopefully. 'Do ye forgive me?'

'Yes, I forgive you. And I'm flattered. It's not every day that I get two men wanting to make love to me.'

He smiled and Charlotte's eyes glanced down to his big long shaft, looking so bereft with no one to comfort it. Impulsively, she reached out and stroked its long smooth length. Allowing her hand to lightly slide up to the very tip, and then slowly back down to its base. Her hand circled beneath it then and gently cradled his balls, giving them the tiniest of squeezes. For good measure, she stooped and planted a little kiss on the end of his shaft.

For a second, she was sorely tempted to open her mouth and suck him fully in. Her clit began to prickle again and she had to use every ounce of willpower to straighten up and move away from him.

'Go downstairs, Jamie. You have Diane and I, well, I haven't got Andrew, but at least I've got him for today.'

Jamie heaved a sigh as he squeezed his cock between thumb and finger. 'Och, Charlotte, you've got no idea what you're doing to me.'

'Go downstairs,' Charlotte ordered, afraid her own willpower was going to crumble and collapse at any second. 'Go on. Please.'

With another sigh, he squeezed his erection back inside his jeans and zipped himself up. As he left the room, Charlotte sank down on to the cold plastic seat of the multigym.

She felt as tense as the cables linking all these weights and levers. Her body literally prickled with the need for some long, uninterrupted fucking.

To calm herself down and work off some of the nervous energy she started to exercise on the multigym. Adjusting the weights down to something manageable, Charlotte reached up for the bars above her head and slowly brought them down. Watching herself in the

180

mirror she saw her breasts rise and harden as her muscles got to work. She pumped them twenty times, then released the bars to do something different.

She settled on the hip and thigh abductor and opened her legs to place them around the two pads. She sat facing herself in the mirror, offering a perfect view of her pussy as she slowly opened and closed her legs, working her thigh muscles.

Concentrating hard, she closed her eyes. When she opened them, there was another reflection in the mirror, watching her. Andrew.

'Don't stop,' he breathed, gazing at the reflected image of her uninhibited sex lips.

A heat erupted inside her again. She was burning, knowing he was watching her. Somehow she managed to continue to open and close her legs, pushing hard against the abductors, watching him in the mirror – watching her. Her thigh muscles began to quiver. She was tingling and was positive there would be a very damp patch left on the seat when she got up.

Andrew eventually moved to stand in front of her. And as she continued the workout, she found herself staring, not at her own naked sex, but at Andrew's, as he slipped his jogging bottoms down and stepped out of them.

His cock stood fiercely to attention, curving upwards with his knob already wet and glistening. Taking Charlotte's hands, he helped her disentangle her legs from the multigym and led her across the room.

Charlotte glanced at their reflection in the mirrored walls, quivering with anticipation at the sight of herself naked, hand in hand with Andrew, his rampant cock projected forward like a baton.

He sat down on the bench press and drew Charlotte towards him until she was standing over him, one leg either side of him. His cock stood to attention and Charlotte knew what was expected of her.

'Sit on me, Charlotte,' he breathed, holding on to the base of his shaft. Charlotte lowered herself down on to him.

She gasped as his long hot length slid easily into her pussy. His hands reached out and cupped her tits, squeezing her nipples until she whimpered. She began to ride him, slowly at first and then, unable to contain herself, she fucked him hard and fast, arching herself backwards so her clit ground against the base of his shaft, bringing her to a shuddering climax.

Gripping her hips, Andrew groaned and squeezed his eyes tightly shut as he too came, spurting hot spunk up her. Charlotte collapsed against his heaving chest, totally sated, exhausted and utterly, utterly satisfied.

The Highland Ruby dug into her breastbone and she shifted it aside. She had quite forgotten she was wearing it.

# Chapter Ten

Diane wandered around Andrew Alexander's living room, a small glass of malt whisky in her hand. 'It's no' very posh here, considering he's a wealthy man.' She glanced at Jamie, who was sitting moodily in the chair by the fire. He'd hardly said a word since they arrived, and since coming down from the toilet he had been worse. No doubt he was still thinking about his precious journalist. 'Jamie, I'm talking to you. I said it's no' very posh. It's sort of barren, don't you think?'

Jamie said nothing, but remained hunched over his half-empty glass, staring broodily into it.

'Jamie!' Diane snapped, glaring at him. 'I'm talking to you.'

'Aye, all right, it's no' posh. So what?'

'What's the matter with you? You're a real misery.'

He drained his glass and went to the cabinet to pour himself another.

'Jamie, you can't do that!' Diane gasped, horrified. 'You can't just help yourself to his drinks!'

'Can I no'?' he growled moodily. 'I thought he said make y'selves at home, so I will. Do ye want a top up?'

'No I don't. It's awful strong anyway, and you shouldn't be having all that.'

Ignoring her, Jamie filled his glass to the brim, spilling some whisky on the floorboards. 'What's keeping them anyway. They've been upstairs ages. Diane, go and tell them we haven't all day.'

'I will not,' Diane argued. 'Anyway, we've nothing else to do today. Your mam will be at home, so we can't even have your place to ourselves.' She caught the sound of footsteps coming downstairs. 'Here, they're coming. Drink some of that whisky quick; we don't want him knowing you've had a refill.'

Placing herself between Jamie and the couple coming into the room, Diane smiled awkwardly, although she soon realised they couldn't care a hoot if she and Jamie had been at the booze. By their flushed faces, it seemed they'd had other things on their minds.

She glanced at Jamie. The look on his face said he'd come to the same conclusion. Only while she couldn't care less what they got up to, Jamie looked totally forlorn.

Diane's eyes narrowed jealously. God, she was getting really fed up with Jamie mooning after that Charlotte woman. She wasn't *that* special; she probably dyed her hair that colour anyway.

Jamie was supposed to be *her* boyfriend. He had no right being jealous over some other woman. Look at her, standing there all coy, like butter wouldn't melt in her mouth, glancing at Mr Alexander like they were in love. She probably guessed that her Jamie fancied her as well. Well, if she didn't watch out, she would have that smug expression wiped clean off her face. Two could play at this game. How would Charlotte and Jamie like it if she made a play for Andrew Alexander and flirted with him a while? What would they have to say about that?

A cunning little smile tugged at the corners of her mouth. There was only one way to find out.

She positioned herself directly in Andrew's path and

peeled off her waterproof jacket. 'I'll need somewhere to change into my white frock,' she informed him. Standing two inches in front of him, she had his full attention, and she smoothed her sweater down over her breasts, letting her hands linger suggestively over her curves while smiling seductively.

'There's a spare room upstairs with a mirror. I'll show you,' Andrew said, leading the way back to the stairs.

'Are you changing too, Jamie?' Charlotte asked as Diane followed Andrew Alexander along the hall.

Diane glanced back at Jamie. She'd hoped he wouldn't need telling. But obviously he'd rather stay downstairs with Charlotte than come upstairs with her. She couldn't keep the snap from her voice. 'Aye, he does. Jamie, come on will you.'

She waited until Jamie had reluctantly caught her up, then deliberately she placed her hand on Andrew's arm. 'What a quaint house this is, Mr Alexander, or can I call you Andrew? We can hardly be formal if I'm going to share your bedroom.'

'Diane!' Jamie hissed.

Diane ignored him. At least he'd noticed she was flirting. That was a start. 'So tell me more about this mysterious Highland Ruby,' she asked Andrew. 'Is it really true that a woman falls under its spell so she can't refuse a man anything?'

'So the legend goes,' Andrew replied, opening the door to the spare bedroom. 'Here you are. I'll leave you to it. Come down when you're ready.'

But Diane caught hold of his arm again. 'So it robs her of her willpower? Can't she just take the Highland Ruby off?'

'Apparently not,' said Andrew, glancing at Jamie, who was starting to look vaguely annoyed.

'And you own it?' Diane asked, feigning astonishment and fluttering her eyelashes ridiculously.

'I do.'

185

She giggled. 'I can't imagine you've ever had to use it. Someone as attractive as you would have no problem in getting a girl into bed.'

Jamie had turned bright pink. 'Diane, will you let the man go. We've got to get changed. Charlotte's waiting.'

Diane's teeth grated at the sound of Charlotte's name but she held on to her smile – and Andrew. 'I can't wait to wear it. I wonder if I'll fall under your spell. Och, Jamie, can you imagine it? Andrew might command me to do something really naughty, and I won't be able to refuse him.'

Jamie and Andrew exchanged glances. Jamie looked like he was going to explode, while Andrew seemed amused.

'In which case,' Andrew began, backing towards the door. 'I think maybe Jamie should be the one to put it around your neck.'

'Aye,' Jamie said irritably. 'And the first thing I'll command her to do is to stop acting so stupidly!'

'I'm not acting in any way,' Diane retorted, as Andrew Alexander made a quick exit before she could stop him. She spun round at Jamie. And don't call me stupid. Just because he's a gorgeous-looking man and he likes me.'

'He likes Charlotte,' Jamie argued.

'He's shagging Charlotte. It's obvious he likes me too. Did you not see the way he was looking at me.'

'Och you're imagining things,' Jamie snapped, turning away and taking off his clothes.

'You're jealous,' Diane goaded, taking her white frock from her bag and shaking the creases out.

'I am not! Now hurry up and get ready.'

Diane's eyes narrowed. 'Of course, mustn't keep your precious journalist waiting. And by the way, what photographs did she take of you?'

'Just snapshots,' Jamie answered, concentrating on putting on a ruffled white shirt. 'She was taking a picture of a Highland cow, and decided to take ma photo while she was at it.'

'I wonder how she'll tell the difference!' Diane said impishly as she started to undress.

'You! Young lady,' Jamie growled, moving swiftly and forcing her back on the bed. 'You are getting awful cheeky, and if you don't behave, you're going to be very sorry.'

Diane found herself pressed back on her elbows, looking up at him. A fierce tingling sensation had sprung up between her thighs. 'Och, I'm so frightened. What do you intend doing to me?'

'Well, for a start,' he warned, standing over her, legs astride. 'I've a good mind to take your pants down and put ye across ma knee and give you a good spanking.'

Diane felt a rising heat in her cheeks. She had never been spanked, not in all her twenty-one years. She edged up the bed a little away from him. 'Don't you dare Jamie.'

'Then behave yourself, young lady, or that's the least you'll be getting from me, and I warn you, you'll no' sit down for a week.'

A spanked bottom wasn't quite what she had in mind, although she doubted Jamie would have the nerve to go through with it.

Someone tapped the door then. It was Charlotte. 'Hello in there. Are you two ready yet?'

Jamie looked down at Diane. 'Saved by the bell. But I'm telling you, any more of your flirting and you'll be over ma knee.'

Diane swung off the bed and dashed across to the door. She called through. 'Almost ready; two minutes.' She glanced at Jamie, looking gorgeous in a shirt and nothing else so that the tip of his penis dangled just below the hem of the shirt. It was him that ought to get a spanking, Diane thought. He started all this by fancying Charlotte. Well, if he thought he was going to make her behave by threats, he was in for a shock.

She undressed down to her undies then slipped the white frock over her head. As she brushed her thick, dark hair in the mirror, she caught Jamie looking at her. She hid her smile. He was still interested. For one thing, his dick had perked up a bit and was lifting the hem of the shirt. If she could just take it one step more and actually make him jealous enough to stop thinking about Charlotte, she would be happy.

'I'm ready,' she said, pulling the neckline of her frock down over her shoulders so that more of her breasts were exposed. 'Shall we go down?'

Jamie glared at her cleavage. 'I can almost see your titties. Pull your frock up a bit.'

But Diane tossed back her hair and deliberately did the opposite, revealing even more flesh. 'We'll see what Andrew has to say shall we?'

She was out of the door in a flash, leaving Jamie to put on his kilt and sporran and tidy himself up. Downstairs, she made what she hoped was a grand entrance. Charlotte and Andrew turned and stared at her. Then Charlotte rushed forward.

'Oh, that is beautiful. Just perfect.'

'Thank you,' Diane said, smiling past Charlotte to Andrew. She felt a rush of achievement as she spotted Charlotte glancing back to see if Andrew had returned her smile. 'So, where is it then? The Highland Ruby. I can't wait to see it.'

Andrew took it from his jacket pocket. It was swathed in velvet, and when he unwrapped it Diane's eyes almost popped out.

She gasped. 'Oh, that is the most beautiful thing I've ever seen.'

Charlotte went across the room to fetch her camera. 'I'd like you and Jamie standing beneath the candlelight. That should create the effect I'm trying to capture.'

'Aye, fine,' Diane murmured, still gazing in awe at the most beautiful necklace she had ever seen. She lifted her hair, ready for Andrew to place the Ruby around her neck. But he simply held it out to her.

'Best if you put it on,' he said quietly.

She smiled wickedly. 'Don't you want me under your power?'

He said nothing, but simply raised his eyebrows, glancing briefly at Charlotte.

Diane wasn't quite sure what was going on between them. Left with little choice, she took the pendant and put it over her head. 'There!'

Andrew looked at her and sighed. 'You have the Ruby the wrong way round.'

'Have I?' she fretted, trying to get it off, and managing to tangle her hair up in the chain.

As she'd hoped, Andrew had no choice but to help her. As he put it right, and the pendant rested cold against her breasts, she smiled seductively at him and whispered, 'And now I am under your power.'

Charlotte swung round, having heard, and Diane cast her a brazen little stare.

Seconds later Jamie dashed down, still tucking himself in. 'Will I do, Charlotte?'

'You look wonderful. You both do,' Charlotte replied, not sounding so full of herself now.

Diane flaunted herself in front of Jamie. 'Look Jamie, isn't it beautiful? Andrew himself put it on me, so now I'm under his spell. Whatever he commands of me I must obey.' She spun around to Andrew. 'Let's try it out shall we. Ask me to do something. Go on, ask me.'

Charlotte stepped forward. 'Diane, that's not a good idea.'

'Why? What are you scared of?'

'I'm not scared of anything. I'm just thinking of you.'

Diane laughed. 'Och, I'll be fine. Go on, ask me something.'

Andrew stared hard at her, and Diane was positive he was going to suggest something wicked. The others must have sensed it too. They looked like they were holding their breath.

At last Andrew spoke. 'All right, Diane. I command you to go and stand beneath that candle with Jamie so Charlotte can get her photographs done.'

Jamie burst out laughing.

Diane was seething, and in two minds whether to storm out and let them find someone else to wear the stupid necklace. But Jamie put his arm around her waist and, still chuckling to himself, led her to where Charlotte wanted them beneath the candle.

Charlotte began taking photographs. Then she stopped and sighed. 'Diane, You're right not to smile in these shots, but could you try and look sultry rather than grumpy?'

Jamie laughed again and Diane jabbed him in the ribs with her elbow.

To her surprise, Andrew came to the rescue. He stepped forward and readjusted the Highland Ruby around her throat. His fingers brushed against her skin making goosebumps erupt all over her flesh. She found herself gazing into his eyes, feeling his warm breath on her cheek.

Jamie and Charlotte fell silent.

'There, that's better,' Andrew murmured, focusing directly on Diane. 'You look so beautiful, Diane. Now I want you to think beautiful thoughts. Concentrate on what you desire most in all the world. See it Diane, touch it. Taste it.'

Diane felt her anger melt away. He had such a soothing voice, so calming, so sexy. What did she desire most? That was easy: Jamie's undying love and devotion – without him lusting after another woman. As Andrew's voice crooned on, and she felt Jamie bristling at her side as she reacted to Andrew, she started to think of her heart's desire. Of being adored by Jamie. Of him on bended knee swearing to love and honour her forever.

The camera shutter clicked time after time. Before she knew it, Charlotte had finished. She put her camera aside, an odd expression on her face.

'Thank you,' Charlotte said stiffly, deliberately not looking at Andrew. 'I'm sure I've got some wonderful shots there. I'll send you some copies to keep.'

Andrew walked to the drinks cabinet. 'Another drink, anyone, to celebrate another successful photo shoot? Charlotte?'

'A small one,' she said, still not looking at him as she continued, busying herself with her camera.

Diane felt a delicious warm glow inside. Charlotte was jealous! She was jealous of the way Andrew had spoken to her. Yes! She almost yelled out in triumph. Now it was just Jamie to contend with, to make sure it was her he was lusting after, not the journalist. Jealousy was a powerful weapon, and she intended using it to the full.

She wandered over to Andrew, glancing first in the mirror to make sure her neckline was pulled as low as possible. She stood close to Andrew, so that her breast was brushing his arm. He didn't move away.

'Thank you for saying what you said,' she murmured, speaking softly so the others would wonder what she was whispering about. 'You helped me to relax.'

'No problem.'

'I'm wondering if this necklace was making me do as you said? I suppose it must, seeing as it has those powers.'

'Who knows?' Andrew shrugged, turning to hand a glass of malt whisky to Jamie and Charlotte. Charlotte put hers straight down on the table, and continued packing her camera away. Jamie watched them over the rim of his glass.

Ignoring them, Diane continued, keeping her voice as low and seductive as she could. 'It's hard to say whether it was you or this necklace. I suppose if you would ask me something really, really naughty, then I'd know.'

'Such as?' Andrew asked, his voice carrying across the room.

Diane glanced at Jamie and Charlotte. They were both staring now. Enjoying the attention, Diane let her head roll back, her thick dark hair cascading over her naked shoulders. 'You could command me to seduce you –'

Before she had even finished speaking, Jamie had angrily slammed his glass down on the table, making everyone jump. He strode furiously towards Diane. Seeing his expression, she dived behind Andrew for protection, but Jamie grabbed her around the waist and pulled her away from him. Charlotte and Andrew tried to intervene.

'Stand aside,' Jamie commanded, his eyes glittering, and in the next breath, he had half carried, half dragged a protesting Diane over to a chair and sat himself down on it, pulling her down across his knee and holding her there with one arm.

Lying there, Diane looked up to see the others watching, startled looks on their faces but no one lifting a finger to save her. The next moment, she felt Jamie lifting up her frock.

She squealed. 'Jamie, no! Don't you dare! Jamie!'

'Didn't I warn you what I'd do,' he growled.

Diane was mortified. No matter how hard she struggled, Jamie was holding her down so hard over his knee she couldn't get away. And now she felt her frock lifted up over her back so that the heat from the fire warmed her thighs. His hand gripped the rim of her knickers and with a flick of knee and hand she felt them dragged down to her ankles. Her bare bottom was on show to all and sundry.

If the humiliation wasn't bad enough, Jamie's hand came down with a loud smack on her bottom and she squealed. One smack wasn't enough for him, however.

'Naughty girls who flirt deserve a good spanking,' he

said, accompanying each word with a smack on her bare arse.

Her bottom was stinging, and her cheeks were as red as a beetroot. Writhing, she glimpsed Charlotte and Andrew's faces – they obviously found the whole thing very amusing. Another half dozen smacks came down on her bare bottom before Jamie decided she'd had enough.

He lifted her on to her feet, and immediately covered his head to avoid her arm as she swung at him. Despite everything, Diane saw by the bulge at the front of his jeans that he was pretty aroused.

'Now get your clothes; I'm taking you home,' Jamie ordered. 'I'm sorry it's ended like this, Mr Alexander, Charlotte. Only I did warn her. Upstairs, Diane, and when I get you home, there's something else I'm going to give you.'

Red-faced, and her backside tingling, Diane raced upstairs. The spanking may have been embarrassing, but it had also made her as horny as hell. She threw all their clothes into a bag and grabbed their coats. Only as she fastened her coat up did she remember she was still wearing the Highland Ruby.

With a mischievous little smile, she buttoned her coat to the neck. She would only borrow it. Andrew Alexander could have it back later.

Stunned and slightly turned on by seeing Diane spanked, Charlotte stood dumbly by as Jamie ushered his girlfriend out of Stonemoor House, slamming the door after them. Then she and Andrew watched them from the window. Diane went storming on ahead with Jamie hot on her heels. Then, catching her up, his arm went around her waist. For a minute Diane didn't want to know, then her arm snaked around him and mischievously lifted the back of his kilt to give *his* bottom a smack. They disappeared into the distance, wrapped up in each other's arms.

Shaking her head, Charlotte looked into Andrew's face. 'I think she got what she was after, don't you?'

Andrew laughed. 'Actually I think she got a bit more than she bargained for. She had a nice bum though – chubby and cute.'

Charlotte gave him a thump. She'd been quite jealous, particularly watching Andrew speaking so seductively to Diane. Deep down, she knew why. He was in fact helping her get the photos she wanted. Even so, she'd felt a little envious.

Andrew raised his hands. 'Ah ha! No violence, or I may have to put you across my knee.' He moved a little closer to her. 'Would you like that, Charlotte? Would you like me to spank your bare bottom?'

Tingles ran down her spine. The thought made her clit prickle. 'No I would not,' she lied.

'Good, all the more reason for me to do it,' he growled, giving her a little smack and then keeping his hand on her buttock, pulling her into him.

Her arm slid around his waist and down to his buttocks. 'I could spank you just as easily. It's not a man-only thing you know.'

He smiled. 'Mmm, that might be quite nice.'

Her mobile phone began to ring and reluctantly she broke free from him. 'It's Paul,' she said before pressing the little green 'receive' button. 'Paul. Hi,' she said, knowing she sounded flat. She raised her eyes to Andrew and saw that he was heading her way.

'Charlotte, babe, are you OK?' Paul asked. 'God I'm missing you so much.'

'Are you?' Charlotte murmured.

'Oh, more than you could possibly know. So, how's it going? Bet you can't wait to get back to civilisation.'

Andrew was right behind her. The next second his

hands slid up her jumper, fondling her breasts through her bra.

Charlotte arched back against him, the mobile phone still pressed to her ear. 'Actually, Paul, it's not so bad here. The people are very friendly.' She craned her head back so that Andrew could kiss her lips lightly. 'It can be a bit hard going at times though –' and she pressed her bottom back against his groin, feeling the bulge of his cock through their clothing. 'In fact, it can sometimes be a bit of a pain in the arse.'

Andrew spluttered.

'Charlotte, is there someone with you?'

'There is actually, Paul. This probably isn't a good time to talk. I'll call you later.'

'But you're OK? No problems with anything?'

Something hot and hard was pushing into her back. Charlotte glanced back to see Andrew standing there with his cock in his hand.

Stroking it with her left hand, while holding the phone with her right, she said: 'No problems as such, Paul, but something big has just come up which I've just got to get to grips with. I'll call you. Bye.' She pressed the red disconnect button and threw the mobile on the chair.

'Feel better?' Andrew smiled.

'Much,' Charlotte said, going down on her knees and taking his big semi-hard cock in her mouth. She sucked him in, deeply loving the way his penis seemed to erupt inside her mouth. It filled her and she loved it.

Andrew stood there, legs apart, allowing Charlotte to feast on his hardening erection. And she sucked and licked and tickled his balls until she was dripping wet in her panties.

Sliding his dick out of her mouth she stood up. 'God, Andrew, what have you done to me? I've gone into overdrive. I'm becoming a sex maniac!'

He growled into her neck and nibbled her ear lobe. 'Lovely! Sex maniacs are my favourite people.'

For a fleeting second, perhaps because he had said *people*, in plural, meaning more than just her, she had a fleeting image of his past lovers. Fay and the Swedish bombshell. Were they sex maniacs too?

She suddenly felt irrationally jealous. Then realised she was being silly. Poor Fay was out of his life for good, and the Swedish girl was history. For the time being, Andrew was hers and she was going to enjoy every moment with him.

He stripped her trousers off her. 'It's a waste of time you wearing these.'

'Maybe I should get Velcro ones that just rip off,' she joked. 'It would save time.'

His expression darkened as his hand slid down her flat stomach and his fingers tangled in her dark pubic hairs. 'And we haven't a lot of time have we now?'

She swallowed hard. The thought of leaving the island and never setting eyes or hands on Andrew again caused an incredible pain in her heart. 'I, I have to get back soon. I've a job to go to, and a flat.'

'No boyfriend though?' Andrew asked, studying her closely.

She shook her head. 'No, no boyfriend.'

He began stroking her mound, his fingers sliding either side of her clit, and then squeezing it, so that she groaned in pleasure. She parted her legs, standing on tiptoe, clinging to his neck as he continued to stroke and squeeze her clit, driving her crazy.

He walked her backwards to his chair by the fire and sat her down on its edge. He kneeled before her, the firelight in his eyes making them glow as he looked at her.

'I want to suck your cunt, Charlotte Harvey. Open your legs and let me eat you.'

Breathing heavily, Charlotte raised her legs and wrapped them around his neck. With a smouldering glance, he buried his head into her fanny and his tongue began licking and sucking at her. She felt ecstatic.

He brought her to a climax easily, and ground his mouth hard on to her pussy as she clung on to his head; sensations erupted through her as she cried out his name.

Exhausted, she collapsed back in the chair, but Andrew got up from his knees and pulled her to her feet. He laid her down on the floor, and stretched himself out over her, his long shaft pointing down and hovering just over her mouth. Then he buried his face once more into her hot wet sex.

He lowered his body on to her as if he was doing press-ups and Charlotte sucked his cock into her mouth, so lost to everything now except her passion. She wanted to eat him. To explore every inch of him. Eagerly her hands stroked his bottom, squeezing his bum cheeks as he continued to lap at her. Daringly, her fingers traced down the crack of his bum until they found his anus. She tickled it softly, aware that his whole body had suddenly tensed. Finding more courage Charlotte pushed her finger just inside him. He gasped and his hot breath tickled her inner thighs.

Remembering what he had done to her, she made little circles with her finger inside him. Exploring him. Thrilled by her own daring. She wanted suddenly to lick him there, and she raised him up a little with her hands. He moved to how she wanted him, and as tingles shot through her, she licked lightly around his anus, just daring to allow her tongue to probe a tiny way into him.

Levered up a little from her, he groaned as she continued to give him some of the anal pleasure he had lavished on her. But it was clearly too much and he adjusted his position a little so that his cock was back in her mouth.

'I need to come, Charlotte. Suck me, honey, suck me off, please.'

She gagged as she took him into her hot, willing mouth

and as her lips closed around his hard length she felt the pumping release of his ejaculation. She gagged and clung on to him as his foaming come ran down her throat.

She lay, with his still-hard cock in her mouth. And she gently sucked him. This time in a way she hoped would soothe rather than excite. He lay there, keeping his full weight off her, but relaxed against her soft body. In no hurry to move.

Eventually he did move, and got to his knees, drawing Charlotte up beside him. His arms went around her and she clung to him.

There was no need for words, but as she felt his thudding heart pounding against her breasts, she had to ask herself: was this love?

# Chapter Eleven

'Let me cook for you, Charlotte,' Andrew said, after she was dressed and he had readjusted himself so he was decent again. 'What sort of food do you like?'

'I like most things. You could surprise me,' she said, smiling happily at him as he kneeled to bank up the fire again.

'I may just do that,' he said, glancing around the room. 'Did you notice where Diane left the Highland Ruby?'

Charlotte frowned. 'No, I didn't. She had it on when Jamie spanked her, then she ran upstairs.'

Andrew headed for the door. 'She'll have left it upstairs in the spare room. I'll go and get it. I'll be happier when it's back in that safe and out of harm's way.'

Charlotte sat down by the fire, watching the flames licking up the chimney. She knew what he meant. Although the Highland Ruby wasn't truly enchanted, somehow, by its very reputation, it affected people. It caused them to do and say things which they normally would not.

Andrew was some time in coming down. When he did finally return, his expression was grave. 'It's not there.'

'You mean she's taken it?'

'Must have,' he said, snatching up his jacket.

Charlotte jumped to her feet. 'Don't panic, I bet she's just forgot she was wearing it. Tell you what, why don't I catch up with her in the harbour? She's staying with Jamie, so she won't go far with it. I need to change anyway if you're cooking a meal for me later.'

He visibly relaxed and took her hands. In a velvet-soft voice he murmured, 'Bring your toothbrush for the morning.'

She raised her eyes to his. 'And my pyjamas?'

He pulled her close to him, wrapping his arms around her waist. 'You won't be needing them. I'll keep you warm.'

A delicious glow of happiness flooded through her. She had never felt so good. Reluctantly, she pulled away. 'I'll get back now then. What time is dinner?'

'Seven. Shall I come and fetch you?'

She smiled. 'No, it will still be light; I'll be fine.' She stood on tiptoe and kissed him. 'And I'll bring the Highland Ruby back.'

Taking her hand, he walked her to the door. 'Well at least it's not raining at the moment. Are you sure you'll be OK?'

'Positive,' she said, stepping outside. 'See you at seven.'

He blew her a kiss. 'I'll be waiting.'

With a final wave, Charlotte set off back across the moors. There was a spring in her step and she felt like singing. Love or just pure lust, she couldn't be sure. The only thing she did know was that it was wonderful.

Picking a few sprigs of heather as she meandered her way across the moors, she couldn't stop thinking about Andrew and what they had done together. Paul seemed so unimportant now. How odd that she had been satisfied to be his girlfriend for the past two years, actually believing she was in love with him – and him with her.

What a joke. How many times, she wondered, had he been unfaithful to her during that time?

Charlotte was back at the harbour just as the first spots of rain fell again. She ducked into the doorway of the Captain's Table pub. 'Just made it,' she sighed, finding Nancy putting on her waterproofs. 'Ah, you'll need them, it's just starting to rain again.'

'Charlotte! Good, you're back!' Nancy exclaimed, tucking her hair under a rain-hat. 'Would ye mind watching the pub for a wee while. Ken and I are off to get some provisions from the next island. There's a boat waiting to take us.'

'Yes, of course,' Charlotte replied.

'There'll not be many customers this time of day, and them that do come will know how to pull a pint. They'll leave their money by the till.'

'No problem. Only I need to find Diane quite urgently.'

'Diane? Och, she'll be stopping with Jamie and his mother. They've a cottage at the far end of the quay. They've got a mobile phone if that will help.'

'Well, yes, it would help to start with.'

'I'll find the number,' Nancy said nipping into the back room. She returned with a scrap of paper and a large brown envelope. 'Here, I've written it down. And this package came for ye on the afternoon ferry. Miss High and Mighty brought it in with her.'

'Who?' Charlotte puzzled, recognising Paul's handwriting on the envelope. It would be the press cuttings. Well, she wasn't interested in reading a pack of lies about Andrew. She ripped it open to make sure it wasn't anything important, and seeing the stack of newspaper clippings, shoved it all into her holdall.

Ken came bounding downstairs then. Like Nancy, he was clad in oilskins and hat. 'Hello, Charlotte. We're just off to get some provisions. Is there anything ye'd like bringing back?'

'No, I don't think so. By the way, who's Miss High and Mighty?'

Nancy cast Ken a warning glance and he grinned. 'I'll tell ye later. She's upstairs anyway, so if ye hear anyone moving about it's only her.'

Ken's grin spread wider and Nancy thumped him. Charlotte shook her head, not a clue as to what they were on about. She dialled Diane's phone number instead, more concerned with contacting Diane and getting the Highland Ruby back than bothering herself about some opinionated guest.

'We'll see ye later, Charlotte,' Nancy waved. 'Just make y'self at home.'

Ken winked. 'Bye, hen.'

Charlotte waved vaguely, listening to the phone dialling out. Seconds later Diane answered it.

'Diane, hi. It's Charlotte.'

'Ah,' Diane murmured, sounding cagey. 'The Highland Ruby – yes?'

'Got it in one,' Charlotte replied.

'Is Mr Alexander awful angry?'

'More worried than angry. Have you still got it?'

'Aye. I'm awful sorry, Charlotte. I sort of forgot I was still wearing it. Then Jamie and I had a little bit of fun with it when we got back. Can you believe it, he even told his mam that we were going upstairs to bed, and when she tried to stop us, he got all masterful and said, mam, I'm over eighteen. I'd like you to respect my privacy.'

'Well, good for him,' Charlotte remarked, meaning it. 'He really is asserting his manhood today.'

Diane started giggling. 'Aye, well Jamie and his manhood are having a bit of a rest at the moment. He's sleeping. I think I've worn him out.'

Charlotte wasn't in the least surprised. Shagged out, was the expression that sprung to mind. Making a concerted effort, she concentrated on the matter in hand.

'Diane, could I come and fetch the Highland Ruby? Andrew is pretty anxious to get it back.'

'Where are you?'

'At the Captain's Table pub.'

'I'll bring it over,' Diane stated. 'I could do with a drink anyway. See you in ten minutes.'

'Fine,' Charlotte agreed, glad she didn't have to get soaked again.

With a few minutes to spare, she poured herself a glass of lager, leaving the money by the till, and got out her notebook. If she could make a start on writing the article it would be a help.

She spread her work over the little circular table and began reading through her notes and jotting ideas down. She'd got the opening paragraph written when Diane burst in.

She peeled off her waterproof hooded jacket and shook her damp hair free. 'It's tipping it down again. Lucky we went to Mr Alexander's house when we did.'

'Well, I hope it clears up,' said Charlotte. 'Because I'm going back for dinner at seven.'

'Lucky you,' Diane remarked, hanging her coat on a peg. 'You two are a bit of an item then?'

Charlotte shrugged, not sure whether it was a good idea to admit anything to Diane. Yet oddly, the girl didn't seem to have that conniving look about her any more.

'Don't deny it,' Diane grinned. 'Anyone can see you fancy the pants off each other.'

Charlotte couldn't help smiling. 'I suppose I'd be lying if I denied it. You know, it's funny, I've never felt so attracted to a man so quickly, nor so, so passionately before. I just hope it's not the effects of the Highland Ruby.'

'Talking of which,' Diane said and grimaced, placing a plastic bag on the table. 'Sorry.'

Charlotte peeped inside, relieved to see it was the

Highland Ruby. 'Thank goodness! Andrew will be so glad to get this back.'

'Tell him I'm awful sorry. I just forgot I had it on,' Diane said, wandering over to the bar. 'Is there nobody serving?'

'No. Nancy and Ken went out,' Charlotte explained, following her. 'They asked me to keep an eye on things. What would you like to drink?'

Diane smiled and folded her arms over the bar top. 'That lager you're drinking looks good. I'll have a half pint too, please.'

'Coming up,' Charlotte said, pulling on the bar pump. 'So you and Jamie are OK again?'

Diane chewed her lip. 'Aye, we're all right now. I think I ought to apologise for my behaviour earlier – flirting like that with Mr Alexander. Only I thought Jamie fancied you so I decided to make him jealous. And get one over on you too. I'm really sorry, Charlotte.'

'Don't worry about it,' Charlotte murmured, returning to their table. God, if Diane knew that Jamie has slipped his cock up her that afternoon she'd have a fit!

Diane sipped her drink, then fiddled with the bag containing the Highland Ruby. 'It's a strange old necklace isn't it? I wonder if it really is magical.'

Charlotte shook her head. 'I don't know. I've only worn it when Andrew's put it around my neck, and to be honest, there's nothing I wouldn't do for him.'

'I know what you mean. When Jamie and I got back to his bedroom earlier, I asked him to put the necklace on me, and make me do whatever he commanded.'

Charlotte raised her eyebrows. 'And did he?'

Diane blushed. 'Aye, he did that all right. He had me in every position you can imagine!'

Charlotte stared into her lager, well imagining Jamie's lovely cock thrusting in and out. She couldn't help thinking she was quite an expert on Jamie's private parts. He'd posed naked for her. She'd watched him in action with

Nancy, and experienced his sexual prowess first hand. If she had never met Andrew, she would certainly have had a fling with Jamie. As it was, compared to Andrew, everyone else paled to insignificance.

Diane took the Highland Ruby out of the bag and held it up to the light, admiring the fantastic sparkle of crystal and ruby. 'The thing is, Charlotte,' Diane murmured. 'Like you and Mr Alexander, I'd have given in to Jamie, Highland Ruby or no Highland Ruby.'

Charlotte nodded. 'So it's no real test of the Highland Ruby's true power, is it?'

Diane pulled a face. 'No it's not. What we need is someone obnoxious and disgusting and vile to try it out on us.'

No sooner had she spoken than Angus McDonald lumbered in. Charlotte and Diane looked at each other and burst out laughing.

The big red-haired Scotsman stood looking at them falling about in hysterics. He beamed a yellow-toothed smile. 'Well, girlies, are ye having a nice time? I like to see pretty lassies havin' a bit o' a laugh.'

Diane wiped the tears from her cheeks. 'Good,' she cackled, before bursting into uncontrolled laughter again.

Charlotte regained her self control first. Rubbing her damp eyes, she got up. 'Nancy and Ken are out. I'll get your drink, Angus. Scotch is it?'

'Aye, a double,' he said, settling himself on a stool at a table next to theirs, his big hairy legs spread wide.

Diane staggered up to the bar with her. She lowered her voice to a whisper. 'I don't know if you know, but he has got the most enormous dick I have ever seen in my life!'

Casting him a quick glance and seeing that he was already fiddling under his sporran, Charlotte replied, 'I know, I saw him in here on my first night. He was watching–' she drew herself up quick. 'Er, watching Nancy and Ken making love.'

Diane's eyes popped. 'Where? Not in here?'

'Er, yes. They must have thought everyone had gone. I came down for a nightcap and Angus was peeping from behind the door, playing with himself.'

'What a pervert!' Diane hissed, glancing back at him. 'And I bet you didn't know he was spying on you this morning.'

Charlotte felt her cheeks turning pink. 'You mean down by the stream?'

Diane grinned. 'I don't mean to embarrass you. I could see you were oblivious to everything except Mr Alexander. But honestly, Charlotte, you could have sold tickets.'

Charlotte groaned. 'Oh God. You and Jamie saw us?'

Diane nodded, still grinning.

'And Angus was watching too?'

She nodded again. 'And having a good old wank in the process.'

'The dirty old man!'

'He's a right creep,' Diane said, pulling a face. 'A perfect candidate for us to test out the Highland Ruby, don't you think?'

Charlotte wrinkled her nose in disgust, although it was no more than she'd thought herself. If Angus McDonald could persuade her to even touch him with a barge pole, she would believe the Ruby had mystical powers. At the moment, she still didn't really know if the Ruby was enchanted or not. If she could find that out, it would be brilliant for her article.

Keeping her voice low, she whispered, 'How can we do it though?'

'Leave it to me,' Diane breathed, taking the drink to Angus. 'There you go, Angus.' She sat back down with Charlotte. 'So, how's the research on that magical necklace going Charlotte?'

Charlotte cast her a shifty glance. 'Oh, yes, it's okay – I think.'

Diane took the Highland Ruby out of the bag. 'You just wouldn't believe it, would you? That if a man put this around a woman's neck, she would fall under his spell and not be able to refuse him anything.'

'I know,' Charlotte murmured, seeing Angus's bulbous eyes lighting up. 'It's amazing isn't it.'

Angus cleared his throat. 'So that's this famous necklace. Can I see it for a moment?'

The girls exchanged glances. Diane shook her head. 'Oh no. It's got magical powers, and you're a man and we're women. It's too risky.'

He shifted on his stool, his fingers practically itching to get at it. 'Och, for pity's sake, I just want to look at it. I'll no' run away with it.'

Charlotte and Diane exchanged long, thoughtful glances. Finally Diane said, 'What do you think? Shall we let him see it?' She winked one eye mischievously.

'Well, so long as he doesn't slip it over our heads,' agreed Charlotte.

Diane began to writhe a little on her stool. 'And providing he doesn't start asking us to do lurid things.'

Angus's sporran began to move of its own accord in his lap, as if some powerful force beneath it was pushing it up. Charlotte couldn't help noticing that Diane was staring at it goggle-eyed. She nudged her but she simply continued to gaze down into the red-haired Scotsman's lap. A moment later she was holding the Highland Ruby out for Angus to take a closer look at.

His eyes lit up. 'My! It's awful bonny. It looks heavy too. Can I hold it?'

'Just for a moment,' Diane agreed, a strange look on her face.

Licking his lips, Angus took the Highland Ruby in his grubby fat hands. Instantly Charlotte knew she should never have allowed it. But it was too late now. In a flash, Angus had it over Diane's head. She gasped in mock surprise.

Angus jumped to his feet, towering over her with his mighty bulk. 'Now let's see if the magic works for me, shall we, lass?'

'No!' Charlotte cried, going to remove the Ruby from around Diane's neck.

But Diane clung on to it. Glancing at Charlotte, she said under her breath, 'Hang on, let's see what happens.'

Charlotte stepped back, shaking her head. This was not a good idea. No wonder Andrew kept it under lock and key. The way people behaved when they had it!

Angus was grinning like the letch he was. It was all he could do to stop himself from rubbing his cock right there and then. He rubbed his hands together instead. 'Now then, my pretty wee lassie, what shall I make you do?' He didn't have to think too long. 'I know. Right then, I command you to lift up your jumper so I can see your tits.'

With a little glance at Charlotte, Diane did as she was bid, lifting her sweater up to her chin so that Angus could ogle her breasts.

'Get your brassier out of the way,' he said, slavering at the mouth.

'Don't do it, Diane,' Charlotte cried fiercely.

But Diane simply pushed her bra up and let her breasts fall free. Charlotte groaned and turned away.

'Now I'm going to fondle them,' Angus growled, 'and you're not going to stop me.'

Diane certainly did nothing to stop him. She faced him, holding her clothes out of the way while his chunky hands squeezed her tits and tweaked her nipples until they stood to attention.

'A bit of arse now,' Angus practically dribbled. 'Get them trousers and knickers off, lass.'

To Charlotte's horror, Diane unfastened her trousers and slipped them down past her knees, followed by her knickers. 'Diane, give me the Highland Ruby. This has gone too far. It's really influencing you.'

'I'm all right,' Diane murmured, attempting to convince Charlotte with a long confident stare.

Once more Charlotte stood back, shaking her head.

Angus leered at the half-naked woman before him. But it wasn't long before leering wasn't all he was content to do. His hand went between her legs, almost lifting her off the floor. She uttered a gasp but still didn't ask for Charlotte's help. 'Sit on that table, lass,' said Angus, wiping his hand across his mouth. And get them legs open for me; I'm going to give your fanny a gobble.'

Charlotte felt sick.

Diane however, did as she was told. Sitting down on the edge of the table, she slipped her trousers and knickers right off, and parted her legs as wide as they would go. Angus got down on his knees and buried his big red head into her pussy.

Charlotte groaned as his mass of red curls bobbed up and down in time with his slurping and Diane's moans, which, admittedly, sounded very much like moans of pleasure.

Angus finally got up from his knees. He pulled Diane to her feet. 'Now lass, see what I've got under ma kilt for ye!'

'Oh, Diane, don't!' Charlotte wailed.

But Diane just cast her a brief, if slightly glazed stare, and lifted the front of Angus's kilt up. A huge truncheon of a cock bounded free, rising up like the raising of the Titanic's mast.

'Suck it, hen,' was Angus's simple request, which turned out to be almost impossible as Diane just couldn't get her mouth around it no matter how hard she tried.

Angus had turned a darker shade of red all over. 'It's a big one, isn't it, lassies? Well if it won't go in your mouth, let's see if it'll fit up your cunt.'

Charlotte couldn't let Diane go through with it. Grabbing the Highland Ruby she tried to drag it off Diane's

neck. But Diane gripped on to it for all she was worth
and refused to let it go.

Afraid they would break it, Charlotte was forced to
release it. Diane smiled at her. 'It's OK, honestly,' she
whispered, and turned back to Angus. 'Are you com-
manding me to have sex with you?'

'Aye, I'm going to shag the arse off you. Bend y'self
over that table.'

Charlotte covered her eyes. This couldn't be happening. It was supposed to be just a bit of fun. But now it
had gone the whole way. Oh, God, Andrew would kill
her if he knew she'd allowed the Highland Ruby to be
misused this way.

Peeping through her fingers at the sound of someone
panting and groaning, she saw Angus ram his massive
cock into Diane's pussy. Like a big old steam train,
Angus's weapon thrust in and out of her like a piston,
his balls making loud thwacking sounds as they slapped
against her thighs.

Despite her abhorrence of the situation, Charlotte felt
her own clit starting to prickle. The sight of Diane getting
such a good, hard shagging made her ache for Andrew's
cock up her again.

Only Andrew wasn't here, and her clit was crying out
for attention. Staggering back against another table, Charlotte's hand went involuntarily between her thighs. She
rubbed hard on her mound as she watched Angus continue to fuck Diane doggy fashion.

As Diane's gasps became louder, the table started to
rock and groan under the pressure. The thwacking
slapped harder and faster. And Charlotte's hand rubbed
feverishly at her clit, bringing herself off at precisely the
same moment as Angus came, sending spunk all across
the bar floor, and dribbling down Diane's inner thighs.

Diane straightened up from lying plastered across the
table. There was a stupid grin across her face. Taking the
Highland Ruby from around her neck, she passed it to

Charlotte. Looking glazed but infinitely satisfied, she said, 'Test over. And I have to report – it doesn't work.'

Charlotte gasped. 'You mean you wanted him to fuck you?'

Diane grinned wider and nodded. 'Aye. It's something I can always remember whenever Jamie makes me jealous over other women.'

Charlotte sank down into a chair, totally at a loss. At the same moment, there was a sound of clapping. It came from the open doorway that led upstairs.

Everyone spun around.

A woman stood there. A startlingly good-looking woman in her mid thirties, with long straight blonde, hair and blue eyes that twinkled with devilment.

'Bravo,' she clapped in an accent that was neither English nor Scottish. 'How very entertaining.'

She had disappeared back upstairs before anybody could blink. Horrified that her antics had been witnessed, Diane struggled back into her clothing and was off like a shot.

'You too, Angus,' Charlotte ordered, pointing towards the door.

'I've no' finished ma drink.'

'I don't care. The pub's shut. Out!' She gave him a shove which, although it probably felt like a fly bumping him, convinced him she meant business.

Downing his Scotch in one gulp, he ambled out of the pub and into the rain. Closing her eyes, Charlotte groaned miserably. Andrew would go crazy if he ever heard about this.

Stowing the Highland Ruby back into the plastic bag, she just hoped and prayed that he never, ever, got to hear about it.

Still shaking her head, she dragged herself up to her room.

After showering and washing her hair, she tried to do

a little more work on her article, but it was useless. She just couldn't concentrate.

As the afternoon wore on, Charlotte began to dress for her dinner date with Andrew. She quickly realised however that she hadn't brought anything remotely suitable for a date. Her wardrobe consisted solely of trousers and sweaters. She had one sleeveless top – a black, skinny-ribbed polo-neck. She heaved a sigh. Combined with her black trousers, it would have to do.

At least her hair looked good. The soft highland water suited her, and her complexion looked healthier, too; probably all this fresh clean mountain air.

She pinned her hair loosely up, allowing wisps to dangle around her cheeks. Gold hoop earrings and a simple gold chain completed the ensemble.

At six thirty, she went downstairs, finding Nancy and Ken enjoying a meal at the very table Diane had been shagged over.

Guilt shot through her. Not that either Nancy or Ken would have disapproved. Probably if they'd been around they would have joined in. But even so, Charlotte still felt bad about it all. As if she'd let them all down – especially Andrew.

'Was everything OK this afternoon, hen?' Nancy asked, pausing with a forkful of food halfway to her mouth.

'Yes, no problem,' Charlotte lied, glancing out at the rain. 'Did you get all your shopping done?'

'Aye, that's it for another month,' Ken said, smiling at her. 'Are ye off somewhere nice?'

'Yes, dinner with Andrew Alexander,' Charlotte replied, wondering why they exchanged glances suddenly. 'Why? Is that a problem?'

'Well –' Ken began, but Nancy interrupted him.

'Have a lovely time. Och, but you're not going to walk across the moors in those little boots are you?'

Charlotte peered down at her ankle boots. 'I haven't brought anything else with me.'

212

Nancy got up and went through to the back room. She returned with a pair of black Wellington boots. 'Take these, hen. It'll be a quagmire out there.'

Charlotte stared at them and groaned. She was going to look a sight.

'And I hate to say it,' Nancy fretted. 'Only the rain will go straight through that coat you're wearing. You can borrow my oilskin. It'll keep out a force-nine gale.'

Reluctantly, Charlotte dragged on the waterproof clothes. They weighed a ton, and she looked like something from a shipwreck.

'You'd rather be dry when you get there, wouldn't you?' Nancy asked, seeing her forlorn expression.

Charlotte tried to look grateful. 'It's very kind of you. You won't be needing them till tomorrow will you, only Andrew said I could stop the night.' She couldn't stop the blush from spreading up her throat into her cheeks. 'It will be too dark to walk back over the moors later, you see.'

Ken and Nancy exchanged glances again.

Ken winked. 'Aye, that it will. Enjoy yourself then, and we'll see you tomorrow sometime.'

Charlotte was quite glad to get out of the pub. They really were looking at her strangely tonight. Perhaps they'd already heard of the goings on with Angus. Maybe their blonde guest had told tales already.

With a sigh, Charlotte headed around the side of the pub and set off in the direction of Stonemoor House. The rain was coming down in torrents now, sweeping across the moors on a chilling wind. It lashed into her face, washing the mascara from her lashes so it dripped into her eyes, blurring her vision. She trudged on, knowing she was going to look an absolute mess again by the time she reached Andrew's house.

Still, at least she didn't have to make the return journey tonight. The prospect of what she might be doing instead brought a warm glow to her insides and put a smile back on her face again.

Trying to peer through the downpour, Charlotte half expected to meet Andrew along the way. It would have been nice if he'd made the effort to come and meet her, even though she told him not to bother. A journey shared in these kinds of conditions was a journey halved.

Picturing him snug and warm indoors, with the fire blazing, and her out here, soaked and chilled to the bone, made her feel just the slightest bit indignant. It wouldn't have killed him to come and meet her.

There was no sign of him and eventually Stonemoor House emerged through a bleak grey mist. Charlotte dragged her rubber-clad feet the last few steps and banged weakly on his door. She had hoped he would be waiting, welcoming her with open arms and a dry towel. But she stood at the closed door, with the rain lashing down her face, waiting for him to answer her knock.

She was forced to bang again louder, thumping her fist so hard it hurt. Eventually he slid back the bolt and opened the door. For a second, he looked almost surprised at seeing her, and Charlotte's heart sank. Surely he hadn't forgotten.

'I didn't think you'd come when the weather got this bad,' he said, moving aside for her to enter.

'I, I was in two minds whether to bother,' she uttered, feeling sick inside. 'Particularly as I'm going home tomorrow. I really ought to have stayed at the pub and got packed.'

She had no idea where that little lot came from. The pain and humiliation of not getting the welcome she expected drove her to fight back, to try and hurt him, like he was hurting her.

'You're going home tomorrow?' he murmured, sounding vaguely like he cared.

She shrugged inside her huge oilskin coat. 'Nothing to keep me now. My work's done.' She noticed then he already had a drink in his hand. It rankled to think he'd been relaxing with a drink whilst not knowing if she was going to stand him up or not.

The whole euphoria of the day evaporated like Scotch mist.

'Let me help you out of these clothes,' he said, putting his glass aside and fiddling with her buttons and toggles. 'Then I've something to tell you.'

'Oh, what's that?' she murmured, knowing it was going to be something awful. She wasn't wrong.

After hanging up her hefty coat and hat and stepping out of her Wellingtons into ankle boots, she followed him through to the living room. She had to concede that he looked utterly gorgeous in black slacks and black shirt.

The fire was lit. It roared up the chimney brighter than ever. Candles flickered, casting shadows and yellow dancing light around the walls. And despite him not knowing if she would come, the table looked beautiful with candles, gleaming silver and crystal glasses. Set perfectly – for three.

So this was what he had to tell her. A moment later the third person for dinner sauntered in from the kitchen, like Andrew, with a drink in her hand. Charlotte instantly recognised her as the blonde woman at the pub who had witnessed the episode with Angus. As soon as she spoke, Charlotte also recognised the accent. It was Swedish.

'Why, it is you. Hello again!' the Swede exclaimed, tossing back her mane as if it was so annoying having such beautiful long blonde hair. 'My, my, but you were having fun this afternoon with your friends.'

Charlotte's eyes widened in horror. Surely she wasn't going to blab out what she'd seen. Oh, God, no! If Charlotte had to come clean about it, she would do it in her own way, in her own words. But she soon discovered that the Swedish girl was either totally insensitive or downright malicious.

She sidled up to Andrew and slipped her arm through his. 'Andrew, you should have seen the naughty things your young friend was doing this afternoon.'

'I wasn't.' Charlotte protested, but a dark frown formed across Andrew's forehead.

'Naughty things?' he repeated, staring at Charlotte.

'It was Diane,' Charlotte gabbled. 'She wanted to test the Highland Ruby on someone obnoxious. She picked on Angus and, well, she ended up having sex with him.'

'God in heaven!' Andrew spat, turning aside to stare into the fire.

Charlotte stood there trembling, wanting desperately to go to him. To say how sorry she was. But he stood there, shoulders squared, looking totally unapproachable.

'I tried to stop her,' Charlotte began, making an effort to explain, but the Swedish girl burst out laughing.

'But you were turned on too. I saw you masturbating while you watched them.'

Mortified, Charlotte hung her head. Andrew turned to spear her with a look of utter hatred.

'I'm sorry,' was all she could utter. 'I, I think I'd better go.' She hurried back into the hall, and desperately tried to clamber into her big wet oilskins. But Andrew was right behind her. He dragged them off her and threw them on the floor.

'Running away, Charlotte? I don't think so. I've cooked you dinner. Let's eat.' His arm was around her middle and he forced her back into the living room. The Swede was waiting, sipping her drink and smirking.

She looked like she had fallen out of a glossy fashion magazine. Her dress was royal-blue sparkling Lurex which fitted like a second skin. It was cut low at the neck, enhancing her large breasts, with a deep 'v' at the back cut right down to the dimples of her bottom. Then a large cheeky bow before the whole thing split open again to give anyone behind her a revealing look at her long sun-tanned legs.

216

In comparison, Charlotte felt like Cinderella – only this was no ugly sister.

'Andrew, darling, you haven't introduced us yet. I'm sure your little friend must be wondering who on earth I am.'

Andrew's chest rose and fell. Like his Swedish companion, he looked stunning. If Charlotte had brought her camera, she could have photographed the pair of them to illustrate the Highland Ruby article. They looked so perfect together. Her so blond and him so dark. Charlotte wondered whether he had dressed so sexily for her or the blond bombshell.

'I'm forgetting my manners,' Andrew said icily. 'Charlotte, this is Ingrid Hansson, an old friend of mine.'

Charlotte nodded, recognising her as Andrew's old girlfriend. The one that everyone in the pub was talking and letching about.

'Ingrid, this is Charlotte Harvey,' Andrew continued the introductions. 'Charlotte is a journalist. She's here to write about the Highland Ruby.'

His words cut like a knife. Was that all she was to him? What about earlier, didn't that count for anything? Or was he just filling time until his girlfriend arrived.

'So pleased to meet you, Charlotte. I hope I haven't embarrassed you by telling Andrew of your exploits this afternoon.'

Too hurt to care any more, Charlotte gritted her teeth. 'It really has nothing to do with Andrew what I do in my own time.'

Her words hit home. 'When it concerns the Highland Ruby it bloody well does concern me. Haven't I drummed it into you how dangerous it is in the wrong hands? After all I've said, couldn't you see that?'

'I had no choice,' Charlotte retaliated. 'If you'd let me explain exactly what happened –'

'I can imagine what happened. At least I think I can.'

He glared at her. 'And did you put the Ruby on and let him fuck you too? Who was it anyway?'

'It was Angus and no, I damn well didn't!'

'Angus!' he spat. 'Angus – and you were so high and mighty when he peeped in the window at you.'

'If you'd let me explain.'

'Please.' Ingrid stepped in between them. 'Why are you getting so upset? I thought we were having a nice meal together. I think you are being a little unkind, Andrew, speaking to your guest like this.'

Andrew clamped his mouth shut, and Charlotte folded her arms and stared blindly into the fire.

'Why don't you pour Charlotte a drink, Andrew? I am sure she could do with one.'

He glared as if he'd rather murder Charlotte, then stormed over to the cabinet and poured her an aperitif. She took it unappreciatively, and swigged half back in one go, almost choking as it caught her throat.

He didn't seem to care.

'Sit down, the meal's ready.'

'I'm not hungry,' Charlotte uttered, desperately wanting to get out of there. 'I've brought your precious Highland Ruby back. That's all you care about, isn't it?' And she turned and marched back into the hall again.

Once again Andrew followed her. 'I've cooked you a meal, the least you can do is stay and eat it.'

Tears began to prick the back of her eyes and she fumbled in her bag for a tissue. 'If I'd known I was playing gooseberry, I'd have told you to stick your rotten meal!'

'I didn't know she was coming,' Andrew hissed, surprising her.

Charlotte stared at him. 'And I'm supposed to believe that? With you all done up like a dog's dinner.'

'I dressed for you, Charlotte, which is more than you've done for me.'

She felt mortified. 'This is all I'd got with me. I'm sorry

if I'm not good enough for you and your posh friend. We haven't all got dresses with slits up to the backside.'

Ingrid stood in the doorway. 'I have the answer. Come with me, Charlotte.'

'Why?' Charlotte demanded angrily, not caring that she'd been overheard.

'Because I have brought some other dresses with me. They will fit you.'

Charlotte's eyebrows shot up as she glared hatefully at Andrew. So he wasn't expecting her, yet she'd come with umpteen changes of clothing.

'Are you staying over?' Charlotte asked bluntly.

'But of course.' Ingrid chuckled. Then glanced from Andrew to Charlotte. 'Oh, I see. You also expect to stay here tonight?'

Charlotte folded her arms. 'Seeing as Andrew asked me to bring my toothbrush I assumed as much.'

Ingrid smiled wickedly. 'Oh my, then I can see we are in for some fun tonight. As far as I remember, Andrew only has one spare bedroom. I wonder which of us will be sleeping there alone tonight?' She laughed again. 'Or perhaps we shall all get on so wonderfully, we shall all sleep together in Andrew's big bed like good friends.'

Charlotte glared daggers at Andrew, hating him for his double standards. It was all right for him to have another woman over and sleep with her, but not all right for Charlotte to indulge in sexual activity with anyone else. Not that she had anyway. Not really.

He seemed to be calming down slightly. 'Charlotte, I suggest you go upstairs with Ingrid and find something suitable to wear. You're making me feel uncomfortable dressed like this when you're casual.'

If looks could kill she would have sent arrows through his heart. How could he be so stuck-up and pompous? She hated him. Absolutely hated him. Ingrid was welcome to him.

Charlotte stomped up the stairs, her blood boiling. The

door to his gym was open and as she went to go past, she faltered, remembering the fun they'd had in there earlier. Was it really only a few hours ago? It seemed like another lifetime.

To her surprise, Ingrid's clothes were actually in the spare bedroom. Charlotte had honestly expected them to be in Andrew's room. Charlotte couldn't resist saying something. 'I see Andrew has already allocated the rooms. He's put you here in the spare room.'

'For the present,' Ingrid replied smiling. Her smile failed to touch her eyes. They remained icy blue. 'Now let me show you my dresses. I am sure they will fit you. You are tall and slim like me. Ah! The green would look perfect with your hair, or the silver maybe?'

Charlotte somehow stopped herself from gasping at the sight of the dresses – or rather gowns would have been a more appropriate description. They must have cost hundreds.

'Try them on. I have sandals which match. Even if they are not a perfect fit, they will do. You are not walking far tonight, I think.'

To be honest, the green dress was an absolute dream. But seeing that Ingrid wasn't going to give her any privacy to try it on, Charlotte had to undress with her watching. Quickly, she stepped out of her clothes and slid the green Lurex gown over her head.

'Without the bra,' Ingrid suggested, coming forward to untwist a shoulder strap.

It was obvious the bra would have to come off: the dress was low-cut with delicate straps. Charlotte wriggled out of it, managing to keep her modesty. She examined her reflection in the mirror.

The clinging, sparkling fabric enhanced her curves more than Charlotte would have liked. Glancing at Ingrid she thought they both looked like beautiful sparkling dolls that had fallen off the Christmas tree. She shook her head in amazement.

'You do not like?' Ingrid exclaimed, astonished.

Charlotte uttered a harsh laugh. 'Oh, I like, all right. I've never seen anything so beautiful.'

'*You* look beautiful, Charlotte,' Ingrid said sweetly, lifting Charlotte's long flame hair from her neck, a painted fingernail scratching very lightly at her skin as she did so. 'And now that we are both looking our best, I believe we can compete for Andrew on equal terms.' Her blue eyes flashed their challenge. 'I do so like a fair contest.'

So this was war, Charlotte gathered, as she turned her attention to redoing her hair and make-up. There was a battle to be fought and won. And the prize was Andrew.

Staring at her reflection in the bedroom mirror, Charlotte asked herself, was he worth fighting for? Did she really want him after his treatment of her tonight?

The answer hit her like a ton of bricks. Yes! Yes! Yes!

If he was telling the truth about Ingrid turning up unexpectedly, then she could understand and forgive his anger after hearing about her exploits that afternoon. She knew he was going to be angry. She'd expected that all along. And if he hadn't cared if she'd had sex with Angus, that would have been downright insulting.

The decision was made. If Ingrid wanted a fight, then a fight she was going to get.

Applying a final coat of lip gloss, Charlotte finally turned and faced Ingrid, her smoky grey eyes smouldering. With a look of determination, she announced: 'Let battle commence!'

# Chapter Twelve

$A$s Charlotte and Ingrid entered the room together they were met by an expression of stunned approval on Andrew's face. For a second he looked like a child on Christmas morning, spoiled for choice as to which present to open first.

At least his anger and animosity towards Charlotte seemed to have gone, which she was relieved about. And whether he felt it or not, he began acting like the perfect host. Pulling back two chairs at the dining table, he murmured politely, 'Ladies.'

Charlotte found herself facing Ingrid with Andrew between them at the head of the table. It wasn't a particularly large table, and the atmosphere, when Andrew had served soup and poured wine, was intimate.

'Andrew, this soup is delicious,' Ingrid complimented him as they ate.

'It's from a tin,' Andrew replied. 'The company have been making soup for decades; they ought to have the recipe right by now.'

Ingrid laughed, as if it was the joke of the century, then turned her ice-blue eyes in Charlotte's direction. 'So you are a journalist, Charlotte. What is this Highland Ruby you are writing about?'

Charlotte shot Andrew a surprised glance, amazed he hadn't used it on her at some time. Obviously he was serious when he'd told her it needed to be under lock and key.

'It's just a very old pendant,' Charlotte explained, keeping an eye on Andrew for approval or disapproval. 'I write for an antiques magazine and my editor thought it would make a good feature.'

Andrew seemed relieved she hadn't mentioned the legend. Deep down, Charlotte was glad he'd never told Ingrid of its reputation. She could well imagine her reaction if he had.

'Do you really go home tomorrow, Charlotte?' Andrew asked, and for the first time that evening she heard that softness in his tone. Her hopes lifted slightly.

She shrugged. 'My work's finished here. It's time I went back. I do have other features to write.'

His black eyebrows joined over the bridge of his nose. 'We've hardly spoken about your work. It must be very interesting.'

'Sometimes,' she admitted, staring down into her soup. But never before had it been heartbreaking.

It quickly became obvious that Ingrid preferred to be the centre of attraction and at the heart of the conversation. She began talking about her own career. It didn't surprise Charlotte to discover she was a model. Modelling anything from clothes to cars to make-up.

While Andrew went into the kitchen to prepare the next course, Charlotte delved further into Ingrid's relationship with Andrew. 'Have you known Andrew long?'

'For three years. We met through an advertising campaign when he opened a restaurant in my country.'

Three years! Not three days. Charlotte's heart sank. She had no chance of winning Andrew's heart – or any other bit of him.

However, the next bit of information had Charlotte becoming more hopeful again.

'But I have not seen him for six months,' Ingrid complained. 'So I decided I would visit him. Many people have trouble in tracking Andrew down, but I am known to his personal secretary who works in a main office in London. She told me he was staying here in Scotland at the moment.'

'Yes, that's how I eventually tracked him down,' Charlotte acknowledged. 'So, you just took a ferry over on the off-chance he would still be here?'

Ingrid looked delighted with herself. 'I am an impulsive woman. When I want something, I go for it. I do not let anything stand in my way.'

Meaning me, Charlotte observed, seeing the flash of determination in her cold blue eyes.

Andrew returned then with a platter of lamb cutlets, roast potatoes and steaming vegetables. As he served the meal, his hand brushed against Charlotte's bare shoulder. Goosebumps broke out all over her and she needed every scrap of willpower not to reach out and touch him.

Conversation flowed as they ate. Mainly it was Ingrid recounting stories of their past activities together, excluding Charlotte, whose only experiences of being with Andrew were certainly not for general airing.

After they had eaten, Andrew poured brandies and assembled three armchairs around the roaring fire.

'What now?' Ingrid asked brightly, crossing her legs so that her dress fell open and, to Charlotte's amazement, revealed she wasn't wearing knickers.

Andrew couldn't fail to notice, and he shifted a little in his seat, his legs parting a little more. Charlotte knew it was because his erection would be hardening at the sight of Ingrid's blond pubes.

Not bothered that her sex was on public view, Ingrid opened her purse and took out a large wooden dice. She smiled at Andrew. 'I know. We could play a little game?'

Andrew's eyebrows arched. 'I know your little games Ingrid. I don't really think that would be fair on Charlotte.'

'Then she can go up to bed. The spare room is waiting.'

Charlotte gritted her teeth. 'But I wouldn't dream of missing out on the fun. Why don't you explain the rules, Ingrid.'

Andrew took another sip of brandy and Charlotte did likewise. Aware suddenly that she was going to need all the Dutch courage she could muster.

'We should sit on the floor,' Ingrid announced, slipping down on to the rug. She waited while Charlotte and Andrew did likewise. 'Lovely! This is so cosy. Now here I have a dice, which we all take turns in throwing. Whatever it lands on you must obey.'

'And what happens if you don't obey?' Charlotte asked, studying the dice. It was engraved with the words: *truth, dare, fantasise, kiss, promise* and *strip*.

'Simple. You leave. You go to the spare room and spend the night alone, leaving the others down here to play.'

Charlotte swallowed hard. It hardly left her with much choice. Ingrid certainly would have no intention of spoiling her own game and she doubted Andrew would back out either. She took another gulp of brandy. 'Let's play then.'

'I shall go first, Ingrid exclaimed excitedly. 'To show you I am willing to be made a fool of, if you wish.' She took the dice in both hands, shook it and released it into the centre of the rug. It rolled a couple of times and then stopped on *truth*. 'There, one of you must ask me a question, and I must tell the truth.'

Charlotte jumped straight in. 'Is it true that you came here uninvited?'

'Yes, it is true.' She looked at Andrew. 'You can verify that, can't you Andrew?'

'I already did,' he retorted quite sharply, looking at Charlotte.

Ingrid handed the dice to Andrew. 'Your turn, darling.'

He rolled the dice. It landed on *kiss*.

Ingrid barely had time to draw breath. 'Kiss me, Andrew.'

He didn't need asking twice. He leaned across and kissed her lightly on the lips. Charlotte glanced away, relieved he hadn't snogged her. Although seeing him kiss her like that was enough. He certainly hadn't needed any persuasion. She started to get a bad feeling about this game.

'And now it is Charlotte's turn,' said Ingrid.

Charlotte felt her nerves tighten. Her heartbeat was thudding as she rolled the dice. It landed on *strip*. She blushed crimson.

'Don't worry, just one item of clothing at this stage,' Ingrid explained. 'Your sandals will do.'

Andrew caught Charlotte's eye as she took off the shoes. 'Spoilsport,' he remarked good-naturedly.

Ingrid rolled the dice again. Once more it landed on *truth*. 'Ah! Ask me something a little more exciting this time. Perhaps you wish to know the truth about the best sex I ever had. Andrew, shall I tell you the very best sex I ever had?'

'What about the worst?' Charlotte suggested. Preferring not to hear about her sexual activities with Andrew.

'No, I have a different question,' Andrew interrupted. 'The truth now, Ingrid. What's your favourite sexual position?'

Charlotte gasped, but he merely smiled and sipped more brandy.

'Darling, have you forgotten?' Ingrid remarked coyly, glancing at Charlotte to see if she was hitting home. 'You know I like being on top. Straddling the man so I can ride him crazily, and feel his hard length right up me, driving me insane with desire.'

Andrew readjusted himself again, and Charlotte tried not to let the green eyed monster of jealousy get the better of her.

'Hmm,' was all Andrew gave in response. He picked up the dice and rolled it. It settled on *strip*.

'Take your trousers off!' Ingrid squealed, really getting into the spirit of the game.

Charlotte chewed on her lip as he got to his feet and unzipped his trousers. As they dropped to the floor, she couldn't help but notice that the bulge in his underpants was huge. A tingling sensation sprang up between her legs. God, how she would love to caress his cock right this minute. She couldn't help wonder what Ingrid's reaction would be if she released it from his pants and sucked and fondled it right here in front of her.

'Stop staring, Charlotte,' Ingrid jolted her from her daydream. 'It is your turn.'

Dragging her gaze away, Charlotte rolled the dice. It landed on *strip* again. 'It's loaded, she exclaimed.

'It's not, I promise,' Ingrid said, glancing down at Charlotte's breasts. 'The dress must come off now. What a shame you did not get to wear it for longer. It suits you.'

In fact, Charlotte didn't mind stripping in the least. At least semi-naked she would be on a par with Ingrid again, with her blonde pubes on show for Andrew to see.

Getting to her feet. Charlotte slipped the shoulder straps off and wriggled out of the dress. Standing there in just tiny thong panties, she revelled in the sensation of Andrew gazing up at her.

Ingrid rolled *dare* before Charlotte had even sat down. 'It's dare everybody.'

Andrew came up with something. 'I dare you, Ingrid, to finish stripping Charlotte.'

Charlotte gasped. 'Is that fair?'

'Absolutely,' Ingrid exclaimed, getting on to her knees and dragging Charlotte's pants off before she could stop her.

Stark naked, Charlotte felt as if her flesh was on fire as both Andrew and Ingrid examined her nudity.

'Your turn, Charlotte.'

Swallowing hard, she rolled the dice. It landed on *dare* once more.

Andrew was first to speak out. 'Now I dare you to strip Ingrid naked,' he said and raised one eyebrow suggestively. 'Time to get your own back.'

Ingrid seemed delighted by the dare but Charlotte was far from happy. She didn't want Ingrid naked. Her figure was probably a hundred times better than hers. Andrew would compare them both and she would come out the loser.

But Ingrid was already on her feet, lifting her hair out of the way. 'Come along, Charlotte. Andrew wants you to undress me.'

She had no choice. There was a tiny zip at the base of Ingrid's spine. After sliding it down the dress simply fell off her. 'That was easy!' she couldn't help but exclaim as Ingrid stood there, just as Charlotte had predicted, looking stunning. Although her breasts were large they were firm with not a hint of a sag, and she had a bottom that was completely cellulite free.

Charlotte glanced at Andrew. Once more he looked like a child at Christmas spoiled for choice – especially now that the sparkling gifts had been unwrapped. All he had to do now was decide which one to play with first.

Seating herself cross-legged again, Ingrid rubbed her hands together gleefully. 'My turn.' She rolled the dice in her hands and blew on it for luck. It landed on *promise*.

'Promise me,' Andrew began with barely a moment's thought. 'Promise me you won't leave it another six months before you come and see me again.'

Ingrid looked pleased with the request, but for Charlotte it was another arrow through the heart.

'I promise, darling,' Ingrid said, lowering her knees so Andrew had an even better view of her pussy.

Dragging his gaze from the sight of her pink pussy lips, Andrew rolled the dice. *Kiss* came up again. For a second no one said anything and Charlotte knew she had ample time to ask Andrew to kiss her. But something held her back. She didn't want his kisses when he was more interested in his blonde bombshell.

Finally Ingrid said, 'Kiss me on the lips, Andrew.'

As he stretched across to do just that, she waggled her finger then pointed down between her thighs. 'These lips, darling.'

Andrew hesitated, looking at Charlotte. She turned away, her heart thudding. Surely he wouldn't, not after today and everything they had shared together. But to her horror, he got on to his knees and looking as if he was about to do a press up, put his head between Ingrid's thighs. Squealing with delight, she opened her legs wider for him to kiss her and then crossed her legs again and clasped her hands over her blond pubes.

Charlotte sensed Andrew looking at her. She turned away, hating him.

'Your turn, Charlotte,' he said softly, putting the dice into her hand.

She rolled it blindly, not even looking to see what it had landed on.

'Kiss,' he murmured. 'May I kiss your lips too?'

She swallowed hard. 'I can't object, can I? Or I'll be out of the game.'

He gazed at her, then taking her hands, he raised her to her feet and sat her on a chair. He went down on to his knees in front of her. Then, to her astonishment, he opened her legs and with his eyes transfixed on hers, slowly lowered his face into her fanny.

Charlotte gasped as his warm mouth engulfed the whole of her sex, before he nibbled gently on her clit. She clutched the arms of the chair, her startled eyes switching to Ingrid who watched with a fierce look on her face.

Andrew continued to kiss and lick and suck at her, driving her insane with the desire to come. Just as she was on the verge of coming he released her. He sat down on the rug again, leaving her to follow; she was trembling from head to toe.

'That was hardly a kiss, Andrew,' Ingrid chastised him. 'I do not think you are playing fair.'

'Do you want me to leave the game?' he asked roguishly.

Ingrid's eyes flashed icily. 'It would not be quite so much fun without you. My turn again, I think.' She rolled on to *fantasise*. And immediately she perked up. 'Ah yes, my favourite! Now, you two must indulge my fantasy or it will not be fair.'

Charlotte glance at Andrew, noticing his erection had become quite enormous inside his pants. Lord, how she wanted to free it and give it the sucking it deserved. However, Ingrid had taken the floor and Andrew for one was riveted.

'I shall need some stage props for my fantasy,' Ingrid announced, looking around the room. 'Andrew, bring me some of your ties and a scarf.'

His eyebrows arched. 'If I'm going to be dressed up should I put my trousers back on?'

'Don't you dare!' Ingrid warned him. 'Go quickly. Shall Charlotte and I get acquainted while we are waiting?'

'Feel free,' he said, leaving the room.

Charlotte watched him, deciding he looked utterly adorable in his pants and shirt. She only wished she could strip them off him, and take his big cock in her hands. She badly needed to stroke and play with it, and feel it up her bottom once more.

Her eyes fluttered shut at the thought of anal sex, and she felt herself getting wet between the thighs.

'You look flustered,' said Ingrid, 'but I'll bet you're a little tingly down here. She stooped down and stroked her hand in between Charlotte's legs, her middle finger lightly rubbing against her clit.

Charlotte jumped, startled at being touched by another woman. Nancy had been one thing, but lesbian love

230

wasn't something she wanted to make a habit of. Particularly when all she really wanted was Andrew and his beautiful big hard cock up her bum.

He returned then with the required items. 'Now what?'

'Now Charlotte and I will get to know each other a little better. We've already started, haven't we, darling?'

Charlotte was beginning to feel light-headed. She only hoped she didn't pass out, because all the sexual tension in the air was making her feel faint.

She staggered to her feet. Andrew steadied her.

'Are you all right, Charlotte?'

'A bit tired, I think,' she said.

Andrew continued to hold her steady. 'I think the game's over, Ingrid. Charlotte's not in any fit state to carry on.'

Ingrid pouted. 'Oh, but it's my fantasy. Please, just this one last thing and then she can go to bed.'

'Charlotte?' Andrew asked, peering into Charlotte's eyes.

She had no intention of being sent to the spare room. Mustering all her self-control she extracted herself from Andrew's arms. 'I'm fine, she lied, realising then she'd been in his arms, naked, and hadn't appreciated it. 'Go on Ingrid, I want to hear about your fantasy.'

'You won't just hear about it, darlings, you are both in it. Now you must do exactly as I say. Promise?'

Charlotte agreed unreservedly. Andrew simply arched one eyebrow.

Ingrid clapped her hands together. 'First we must set the scene. You two are a married couple . . .'

Charlotte instantly glanced at Andrew. He rubbed the side of his nose, half smiling to himself.

'You are alone in the house,' Ingrid continued, 'when a knock comes to the door. Andrew answers it. You hear a scuffle then suddenly I appear. Only I am a thief with a gun. I'm after the Highland Ruby. But you refuse to open the safe, so I tie you both up while I work on discovering the combination.'

'Is that what the ties are for?' Charlotte asked, wobbling slightly.

'That is correct.'

Andrew looked puzzled. 'Shouldn't you be the one tied up? It's your fantasy after all.'

'No,' she said simply. 'Now, are we ready? Yes? So you and Charlotte are here in your house. You are a normal married couple.'

'What do we do?' Charlotte asked helplessly.

'Do what all married couples do,' Ingrid shrugged, heading for the door. 'Argue or something.'

The moment she was gone Andrew stepped towards Charlotte. 'Arguing isn't all that married couples do,' he said, his voice husky as he undid his shirt.'

'No?' Charlotte murmured, as he threw his shirt over a chair and took his underpants off. Immediately, his semi-erect cock bounced upwards, hardening and lengthening before her eyes.

'Come here, wife,' he said softly, pulling her close.

She liked the sound of the word and moulded herself into him, loving the feel of his warm smooth skin against hers. Her arms went around his waist and slipped down to his buttocks, adoring the sensation of his cock pressing hard against her flat stomach.

'As your husband, I demand my conjugal rights,' Andrew said, taking her breasts in both hands and squeezing her nipples between his finger and thumb.

It was easy for her to indulge in a little play-acting too. 'Well, I did promise to obey you, husband dear. Shall I lie on my back, or would you like me to bend over the table?'

Her words inflamed him and he crushed her back against the table, lifting her up so her bare bottom was on the cold shiny wood. Dishes clattered against each other as her posterior cleared them aside. He held her thighs open so that he was standing in between her, his rampant length pressing against her pussy lips, demanding entrance.

'I think I shall have you like this tonight, wife. But tomorrow I fancy I shall fuck you anally. I think a good arse-fucking at least every other day is sufficient to keep you under control.'

She was on fire; her whole pussy was throbbing with the need to have him inside of her.

A loud knocking at the living-room door stopped them in their tracks. Charlotte groaned. Ingrid! Damn, she'd really had enough of her and her games. This was what she wanted, to make love with Andrew.

Only it appeared that he was merely play-acting all the time. Totally unperturbed at being interrupted, he glanced towards the door. 'Hello? I wonder who that is.'

Charlotte clung on to his neck. 'Andrew, don't, I want you.'

'All in good time. I'd better see who it is.'

'Please, Andrew, I don't want to play games any more.'

But he simply lowered her to the floor and walked over to the living-room door. Ingrid leaped in holding something covered by a silk scarf. It looked like a gun and for a second, Charlotte's stomach lurched.

'All right, where's the Highland Ruby,' Ingrid demanded in her most menacing voice. Which considering she was naked, wasn't menacing at all. But seeing as Andrew was going along with all this, Charlotte thought he'd better too. She held up her hands.

Ingrid waved the gun at Andrew. 'OK, buster, you're going to tie the little lady up. On the chair, lady, hands behind your back.'

Andrew led Charlotte to a dining chair. Making her sit, he tied her hands behind her back. A little tremor of fear crept through her. 'Andrew, I really can't move them.'

He winked. 'Indulge her.'

'It's not really a gun, is it?' she hissed.

'It's a banana,' he murmured.

'Stop whispering,' Ingrid said sharply. 'Now her feet. No, not together. Legs apart, tie each ankle to a chair leg.'

Andrew did as he was told, and Charlotte found herself bound naked, with her legs held apart by the ties.

Ingrid strolled forward, breasts and hips swaying provocatively, her bush of blond pubes neatly trimmed. She removed the silk scarf from the gun, and Charlotte was relieved to find it was only a banana. Her relief was short lived. Ingrid moved to stand directly behind Charlotte.

'What are you doing?' Charlotte asked, growing more and more uneasy about this. She really needed all her faculties about her in this situation.

A moment later, Ingrid tied the scarf around her eyes. Charlotte screamed and struggled as her world turned black. Her heart thudded. 'No, Ingrid, don't. I don't like this!'

Ingrid ignored her cries and Andrew didn't make a move to help her either. Of course, thought Charlotte – they think I'm acting. Her heartbeat pounded with fear.

*Some say he murdered his wife.*

She felt cold and shivery. 'Please, let me go.'

'Tell me where you keep the Highland Ruby,' Ingrid continued in her tough voice.

'Andrew, tell her it's in the wall safe.'

'Sshh!' Andrew murmured. 'Don't tell her the combination.'

'So, you won't talk, huh,' Ingrid growled. 'OK, so I'll have to make you talk.'

'What are you going to do,' Charlotte cried, becoming really frightened now.

'You're going to give me that combination, honey,' Ingrid continued in her tough drawl. 'I'll force it out of you. You'll be begging to tell me by the time I've finished with you.'

234

'Don't hurt me,' Charlotte whimpered. Her voice sounded vulnerable, even to her own ears.

There was silence suddenly. And in her dark world, Charlotte strained her ears to hear what was going on. She caught whisperings and the sound of someone leaving the room. Silence filled her head. Had they both gone? Was she alone? Then a moment later, something touched her nipple and Charlotte almost shot through the roof.

The touch was soft and light. It tickled.

A tongue.

'Andrew?'

The tongue made circles around her hard little bud, then teeth clamped it firmly and gently pulled. She whimpered. The sensation triggered a hot deep need around her pussy. She writhed, opening and closing her knees. She could sense someone's naked body, but she wasn't sure if it was Andrew.

Then a hand touched her between her legs. A small soft hand with long fingernails. A finger stroked the very nub of her clit.

'Ingrid!' Though to be honest, Charlotte was far too aroused to care. And the thought that the blonde Swede had already tasted her made her even hotter.

Ingrid trailed her finger down the side of her clit, knowing just the spot to apply pressure. Then lower, sliding between Charlotte's pussy lips, slipping up into her hot damp slit. Charlotte couldn't stop writhing on the chair, pushing herself forward making her sex more available to the invading hand.

The masturbation went on, with Ingrid fingering her pussy relentlessly while at the same time sucking at her nipples. Charlotte was shivering and tingling from head to toe. Had Andrew gone? Was he watching? Maybe even masturbating as he watched Ingrid doing this to her?

Ingrid stopped what she was doing. Charlotte held her

235

breath afraid of what might come next. She sensed her moving across the room. Then came the sound of liquid being poured into a glass. Ingrid returned. Then two slender hands were on Charlotte's thighs, parting her legs further, and the softness of Ingrid's head moved between her legs.

Ingrid began to suck her clit, and as her hot mouth wrapped itself around the open pink folds of Charlotte's labia, she was engulfed in a burning swirling sensation as Ingrid released what must have been whisky into Charlotte's fanny. Charlotte gasped, clenching her hands into knuckles as Ingrid then licked it all out again.

It was impossible to stop the reaction and Charlotte's body arched against Ingrid, her climax erupting suddenly and uncontrollably. Her whole body jerking and shuddering as sensations engulfed her.

Ingrid moved away from her. 'So, you refuse to give me the combination to the safe. Well, now I shall see how much your husband can take before he cracks.'

Trembling from head to toe, Charlotte listened to the sound of her footsteps leaving the room and going upstairs and finally heard the sound of a bedroom door closing.

'Andrew!' she cried. 'Andrew!'

There was no reply.

Charlotte sat waiting, seeing only blackness. The intensity of her climax had left her drained and shaking with pleasure and humiliation. Now the Swede was upstairs with Andrew and God only knew what they would do. Tears pricked the backs of Charlotte's eyes. 'Untie me someone, please,' she called out.

No one came.

She sat, as the minutes ticked by. She started to feel cold. The fire no longer crackled in the grate. The heat had died from the room. She began to wonder if she would be left tied up all night. But eventually someone came downstairs.

She knew it was Andrew the second he touched her

He removed the blindfold and she was so relieved that she burst into tears, despite the fact that her whole body still resonated with pleasure.

'Are you all right?' he asked as he kneeled to untie her.

'Did you see what happened?'

'No, I didn't see, she made me go upstairs.'

'She made you go upstairs!' Charlotte mocked, jumping up from the chair and rubbing at her wrists and ankles. 'You mean you weren't in here when she, when she –'

'She ordered me upstairs as soon as I'd tied you up,' Andrew explained, rubbing her wrists with his thumbs. 'I'm sorry if she hurt you.'

'She didn't hurt me,' Charlotte admitted. 'She, she touched me and licked me. I loved it.' She stared at him then. 'And what did she do to you?'

He shook his head. 'Nothing very exciting, believe me.'

'Why should I believe you?' Charlotte cried, eaten up with jealousy, knowing that Ingrid had probably had oral sex with him at the very least. She searched around for a dress to throw on, hating her nudity.

Andrew's penis was flaccid now and Charlotte's heart plummeted. He'd had sex, that was obvious. She hated him. Angrily she pushed past him as she ran to the door.

'I'm going to bed. The spare room is vacant I assume?'

'Charlotte!'

She raced upstairs. In the vaguest of hopes, she glimpsed into Andrew's bedroom. But just as she'd guessed, Ingrid was lying naked in his bed, the sheets just draping one leg, her face a picture of sleeping serenity.

Sobbing, Charlotte slammed the spare bedroom door and turned the key in the lock.

She cried herself to sleep.

# Chapter Thirteen

*A*t the first light of dawn, Charlotte dragged herself from her bed. Her head throbbed and her eyes were puffed from her miserable night's sleep.

She dressed and crept along the landing. Andrew's bedroom door was shut. Desperately Charlotte tried to close her tortured mind to images of him lying there with Ingrid.

Downstairs in the hall she dragged on her Wellingtons and waterproofs. If she left now, she wouldn't have to face either one of them again. The thought sent a spear through her heart. But there was no alternative. No other way.

As she picked up her holdall, the kitchen door opened suddenly. Charlotte jumped. Andrew emerged, wearing a T-shirt and nothing else. His eyes raked over her, from top to toe.

'You were leaving without saying goodbye?'

She swallowed hard, her heart thudding furiously. 'Why shouldn't I?'

'Because I thought we might have something special. Something worth hanging around for.'

Charlotte tilted her chin defiantly. 'Don't be greedy, Andrew. You've got Ingrid, you don't need me.'

He took a step towards her but Charlotte backed away. 'I don't want her. Charlotte, for God's sake, it's you I want.'

'So why sleep with her?' Charlotte shouted.

'I didn't.'

'Liar! I saw her in your bed last night.'

'But I slept downstairs in the chair.'

Charlotte bit her lip, wanting so badly to believe him. 'Well, what about last night. Don't deny you had sex with her.'

'*You* had sex with her,' he reminded her, sounding almost amused.

'So what did you two do, when she was acting out her little fantasy?'

He rubbed his chin. 'I admit, she tried to give me a blow job.' Charlotte turned away and finished doing up her coat. 'Listen to me,' Andrew continued, turning her around to face him. 'But it didn't work for me, she just had no affect and gave me up as a hopeless case.'

'Oh sure!' Charlotte murmured in disbelief.

His hands came down on her shoulders. 'It's the truth.'

She tried to shrug him off her, only managing to dislodged her holdall from her shoulder. It fell to the floor, scattering its contents everywhere. 'You expect me to believe that?' she retorted, bending down to gather all her belongings, including the large brown envelope full of press cuttings. She picked it up from the wrong end and a dozen or more newspaper cuttings scattered out.

'Hello, what are those?'

She felt hot suddenly, and scrabbled around guiltily, trying to gather them up. 'Oh, nothing, just work.'

He picked some up.

She felt the colour rushing to her cheeks. 'Paul sent them. I didn't ask him to. Only when he knew I was meeting you he said he'd get some background infor-

mation . . .' Her voice trailed away. There was a strang
look on Andrew's face. The colour had drained from hi
lips. A harsh look of betrayal was in his eyes.

'These are all cuttings from when Fay died.'

'Are they? I, I don't know, I haven't bothered looking

'These are the stories which put me through hell.'

She felt sick inside, sensing the fury that was buildin
in him.

He stared at her with eyes that glittered with disbelie
and shock. 'You're just like all the other journalists. Yo
weren't interested in the Highland Ruby at all. You jus
want to dish the dirt on me again. It's coming up to th
anniversary of Fay's death and you want a story on wha
the merry widower is doing now.'

'Andrew no! That's not true.'

'Isn't it?' he growled, glaring furiously at her. 'I be
you don't work for *Antiques and Legends* at all, yo
probably work for some Sunday sleaze-paper.' And h
took her arm suddenly and marched her into his study
kicking the door shut behind them. 'Well, young lady
you're not running away before I've finished with you
And to her horror, he stripped the big oilskinned coa
from her back and tossed it across the room.

'Andrew!'

'What hurts me is that I actually believed you,' h
uttered coldly, towering over her. 'Not only that, but
even started to feel something for you. Do you know
how long it is since I felt anything other than lust for
woman?'

'No,' she breathed, biting hard on her lip.

'Five years,' he uttered, squeezing her upper arm
backing her towards his desk. 'I never thought I'd car
for another woman after Fay died. Then you walked int
my life.'

'Andrew, those cuttings are nothing. Paul sent ther
thinking he was being useful, but I didn't want them. M
article has nothing to do with your background.'

He wasn't listening. His fingers dug into her flesh, and not only his fingers. Another part of his anatomy was sticking into her groin too.

'You wanted sex with me,' he blazed, crushing her against his desk. 'You pretended to want me.'

'I do!' she cried.

'You even let me fuck you up the arse,' he uttered, holding her captive with his thighs and snatching her arms behind her back, holding both wrists together with one hand. 'Why did you let me? Is that part of your technique? Part of the job? Are those the lengths you journalists will go for a story?'

'No, it's not,' she shouted back indignantly, writhing against him to be free, but only managing to make his shaft harden against her stomach.

'Because if it is, I think I should get a repeat performance, don't you? Shall I fuck you again, Charlotte? Another hard fuck up your backside? Shall I shag your arse so hard you'll remember me all the way back home every time you try to sit down?'

'Andrew, stop it,' Charlotte whimpered. She was in no state to fight him. Wanting him so badly all last night had taken its toll. Like a drug, she wanted anal sex with him whatever way she could get it. Even with him like this, furious with her.

'Well shall I?' He didn't wait for an answer but dragged her trousers and pants down and spun her around so she was spreadeagled across his desk. Papers, folders, pens and books scattered everywhere. His hand went straight down between her legs, his fingers sliding up her cunt and back passage simultaneously.

'You're wet Charlotte,' he breathed dangerously in her ear. 'You're wet and dying for it, aren't you? Does it excite you, getting fucked up the arse, does it?'

'Yes,' she breathed, pushing her bottom towards his rampant cock. 'Yes it excites me. Fuck me, Andrew. I

241

want you to fuck me, but please don't hate me. I've done nothing wrong.'

He uttered something under his breath and for a second, Charlotte had the feeling he was going to stop all this. To release her, even to apologise. The thought of that was even worse, and she arched backwards, twisting her head to kiss him. There was no kiss but she did feel the hot tip of his cock pushing at her anus, then the burning sensation of his erection forcing its way inside her. She cried out as he penetrated her.

For a second, he stood motionless, growing accustomed to the electrifying sensations. And then, slowly at first, but gradually increasing the momentum, he began to rock his pelvis back and forth, his cock driving in and out of her. The rhythm built, becoming hard angry thrusts that knocked the breath from her lungs and made her gasp.

Charlotte clung on to the edges of the desk, spread-eagled; from her waist up she lay flattened on the leather-topped desk. Never in her life had she known sensations like the ones thundering through her. Everything was on fire. Her whole body was tingling, right through to her skull.

There was no let up, his engorged cock continued to ravage her, shocking everything else from her head other than this. And for that moment there was nothing else she wanted more.

When he came, his fingers dug painfully into the flesh on her hips. His entire body jerked as his penis throbbed inside of her, discharging its load. Charlotte bit down on her lip, her eyes huge, her body trembling.

When he finally withdrew from her, she couldn't move. She lay across the desk, breathless and shaking, not even trusting herself to try and stand. Eventually she eased herself up, discovering an impression of her torso imprinted in sweat on the leather desktop.

She turned around. Andrew was gone.

\* \* \*

The moors were swathed in a blanket of wet mist, like a cloud that had fallen from the sky obliterating everything. It swiftly cloaked Charlotte as she ran from Stonemoor House.

Miraculously she found her way back. The foggy outlines of the harbour houses and boats slowly emerged from the grey mist and she gave thanks that she hadn't wandered the wrong way and become lost. Finding the door to the pub unlocked, Charlotte went quietly in and up to her room.

There were no tears to fall, but deep inside, she felt like someone had planted a lead weight in her chest. She packed swiftly, scribbled a cheque to cover her stay at the pub along with a brief 'thank you' letter and left.

Down at the quayside the fishing boats had returned and been winched up the shale beach to unload their catch. She spotted Jamie as he worked alongside the other crew members sorting through the fish. Charlotte picked her way across the stones as seagulls swooped and screeched all around her, fighting for scraps.

'Jamie!' she shouted, trying to make herself heard over their harrowing cries. 'Jamie!'

He finally spotted her and, wiping his hands, clambered down off the boat. 'Charlotte! What are ye doing here this time o' day?'

'I need a lift, Jamie,' she said, finding the tears were close now. 'I'm catching the ferry back to Oban today, but I want to get off this island as soon as I can. Can you get me a boat across to one of the other islands.'

His face softened. 'What's happened? Something to do with Mr Alexander?'

Charlotte could only nod as her chin crumpled. Jamie went to hold her then stopped.

'I'm covered in fish and muck, hen. I'd better not touch 'e.'

'I'm OK, honestly,' she uttered, swallowing hard. 'Can

243

you help me, Jamie? Is there anyone who'd ferry me across to another island? I'd pay them.'

'Are ye sure that's what ye want to do?'

'Positive.'

Looking doubtful, Jamie told her to wait while he asked around. He came back a few minutes later with the news that he'd found her a lift.

Ten minutes later, she was in a rowing boat, being rowed towards a small boat anchored further out in the bay. She recognised the white-whiskered fisherman and one or two others.

'You'll be alright with these,' Jamie assured her, helping her clamber up a ladder slung over the side of the craft, following close behind her 'Will ye write to me, Charlotte?'

'Of course. And I'll send those photographs – only take my advice and don't let Diane ever see them.'

'I won't,' he said, helping her on to the deck. He took her hands, holding her at arm's length, but Charlotte pulled him into her arms.

'I'll never forget you, Jamie.'

'You just take care of yourself.'

'I will.'

She kissed him, and watched as he clambered back into the rowing boat and set off for shore. The white-whiskered fisherman dusted a bench with his woolly hat and sat her down. The motors started and they chugged slowly away from the quayside. Away from Andrew.

As the island became nothing more than a dark, distant outline in the mist, Charlotte was glad of the sea spray in her face. It hid the tears.

# Chapter Fourteen

*P*aul counted himself lucky that Dominique had agreed to see him again so soon after their last session together. Only by the way Charlotte had acted on the phone, he had the feeling he was going to have to be especially attentive towards her over the next few weeks. And that would mean no extras on the side.

Another fling with Dominique would set him up nicely for a while, particularly as he had managed to persuade her to come over to his flat. It had cost him extra, but it was worth it. The thought of having her here under his own roof made him feel as randy as hell. If he'd had the nerve, he'd have asked her to meet him at Charlotte's. Only that was a bit too risky.

Now he waited impatiently for her to come out of his bedroom. For once, she hadn't demanded that he strip naked for her. Only that he put on a shirt, tie and trousers, then she'd disappeared into his room, leaving him standing there, waiting, his cock aching inside his pants as he dwelled on the pleasures to come.

Dominique finally emerged from his bedroom. She was dressed as a school mistress in mortarboard and gown, but, beneath her gown, what she wore bore no resemblance to anything he remembered from his school-days.

She was squeezed into a black PVC basque, cut low and deep, laced right down to her navel. Then there was a strip of pale flesh and a triangle of see-through nylon for knickers. Stockings, suspenders and sharp stilettos completed her outfit along with a thin slender cane.

She stood, legs astride, looking at him with eyes that smouldered. His cock twitched and his hands went down to his fly, eager to unzip himself.

'Bad boy!' Dominique scolded him. 'Stop touching yourself; that's disgusting!'

Paul withdrew his hand immediately, and she strutted towards him, her nipples almost peeping out above the edge of the black shiny PVC. Paul's mouth went dry.

Standing directly in front of him so that he could smell the exotic scent of her, she suddenly grasped his cock and balls through his trousers, squeezing him just hard enough to make him gasp.

'Naughty boys who play with themselves deserve to be punished.'

The grip she had on him was almost punishment enough. A mixture of agony and ecstasy. Breathing hard, he murmured, 'Yes, miss.'

'You need to be taught a lesson.'

'Yes, miss,' he uttered again, writhing as her hand around his tackle squeezed a little harder.

She released him as swiftly as she had grabbed him and the relief made him gasp once more. She took a step back. 'I think we should have a look at your cock, young man. Let's see what all the fuss is about. Shall we?'

'You want me to get it out?' Paul asked, knowing he wouldn't dare unzip himself without her permission.

'I said so, didn't I?' Dominique murmured huskily. 'Let's see this thing you boys constantly need to play with. Trousers off now!'

He didn't need telling twice. They were around his

ankles in seconds. His underpants followed and his semi-erect cock bounced eagerly upwards.

Dominique looked at it, unimpressed. With her hands behind her back, slapping the cane softly on her palm, she walked slowly around him.

Standing there in just his shirt, with his bum and cock on show with her examining him, he stiffened. He wanted to touch himself again, just a little tweak, but he knew he didn't dare.

She finally stopped directly in front of him and taking her cane she slid it beneath his shaft, lifting his dick higher. He hardened instantly as the cool, smooth wood scratched against his rampant length.

Slowly, she slid the tip of the cane to the very head of his cock, then moved it in circles. Lightly scratching the bulbous purple head of his dick, she was watching his face, watching the changing expressions. Then with a knowing gleam in her eyes she slid the cane along the under-side of his penis, scratching at his balls, and then sliding it beneath him, between his legs, just tickling his anus.

He caught his breath but didn't flinch. He remained, standing there rigid, every nerve-ending focused on the movement of the cane as Dominique continued to draw imaginary patterns all around his loins.

'You're not touching yourself now, are you Paul?'

'No, miss,' he breathed, his cock twitching as the cane travelled the length of his shaft to the very eye, where a gem of moisture had already spurted. She dabbed it up with the end of her cane and raised it to his mouth.

'Suck it,' she demanded.

He sucked, tasting wood and the salty drop of moisture which was alien to his lips. Funny how strange it tasted to him. Whereas women like Dominique and Charlotte were probably pretty used to his taste by now.

'Does it taste good?' Dominique purred.

He gave a half-hearted laugh. 'I'd rather be licking your cunt, miss.'

Dominique's eyes narrowed. 'How disgusting! You bad, bad boy. I can see you need a severe spanking, talking dirty like that. Fetch a chair.'

With his cock waggling back and forth, Paul did as he was told, placing the dining chair where she directed.

'Now bend over the back, and prepare yourself for a damn good hard thrashing across your bare arse.'

He couldn't wait. Eagerly he bent over the chair back, resting his hands on the seat. His rampant cock was crushed up against the wooden slats so manoeuvring himself, he stuck his dick between two slats of polished wood. That felt pretty good too, and he congratulated himself on the extra bit of pleasure that Dominique didn't know about.

'Right m'lad,' Dominique said, standing at the side of him. 'Your arse is going to get such a caning. You are a very bad boy.' And with a swish, the thin cane came down hard across his buttocks.

He yelped, not expecting it to hurt quite that much. But then came another swish and another stinging red mark across his bum cheeks.

'Dominique!' he protested, about to straighten up. But her hand on his back told him to stay exactly where he was.

'What's the matter, Paul? If you can't take the punishment, you shouldn't commit the crime. Now are you going to be a good boy from now on?'

'Yes, miss,' he said.

'Did I hurt your bottom?'

'You did.'

'Shall I rub it better?' she asked, already stroking his buttocks with the palm of her hand.

Knowing she was right behind him and not being able to see exactly what he was doing with his hands, he gave himself a wank as she continued stroking. But another smack across his backside made him jump.

'What are you doing?' she exclaimed angrily. So angry that for a second Paul honestly felt like a naughty school-boy found playing with himself under the blankets. 'You're still touching yourself. Well, obviously spanking isn't going to cure you of your filthy habits. So there's only one thing I can do. Take the chair and place it facing your sofa.'

Extracting himself from between the wooden slats of the chair proved a bit more difficult as he'd enlarged more than he realised. But he managed, and placed the chair facing the sofa as she'd instructed.

'Now sit down and put your hands behind your head.' A little puzzled, Paul did as he was told.

'And if you dare to touch your dick there will be no fun for you later.' She eyed him steely. 'And I mean it.'

He sat, legs astride, a yard or so from the edge of the sofa while Dominique put some music on the stereo. Returning to him, she undid her headmistress's gown and dropped it to the floor. In just her tight PVC outfit, she began to gyrate in time to the music. Legs apart, she swayed in front of him, then turning her back, so that he had a close-up view of her G-string knickers and full rounded bum cheeks, she swivelled her hips directly above his twitching cock.

He felt the silky warm nylon of her panties brush the head of his knob and he longed to pull her down on to him. Turning around again, she eased her tits out of the top of her basque and brushed them in front of his face, allowing her hard little nipples to stroke across his parted lips.

Straightening again, and still swaying in time with the music, she slipped her panties down over her hips. Stepping out of them, she crushed the warm fabric against his nose and mouth. He groaned at the musky scent of her sex and perfume mingled together in a heady mixture. But still his hands clasped each other at the back of his head. He wasn't going to break the rules. Once before he'd disobeyed her and she had carried out her threat, turfing him out without him getting his end away. God, that had been frustrating – and a waste of money.

Well, he wouldn't risk that again. Domination was wonderful, and even more so since he got to shag her at the end of it. No, he'd stick to the rules. Even though he needed every scrap of willpower now not to shove his dick up her cunt and fuck her stupid.

She looked utterly gorgeous, with her mortarboard still on her head, her tits out and her delicious bald fanny swaying around in front of him. She turned her back on him then, and kneeled up on the sofa, knees apart and bum cheeks parted, giving him a perfect view of her open fanny lips and arsehole. God, how he wanted to stick his cock up her arse. But even more, he wanted the discipline that only she could give him.

He was aching now. His cock throbbing with the need to be touched, to be sucked dry. 'Miss . . .' he begged.

She turned around on the sofa and sat, legs spread wide open in front of him. With her knees bent upwards and apart, she sucked her middle finger and then coyly slid it down to her clit, rubbing it lightly before inserting it up her fanny.

Paul stretched his legs wider, his cock standing to attention and crying out for release. 'Oh, miss . . . you are so hot.'

She smiled a little and fingered herself deeper, groaning in self-satisfaction as she started to arouse herself. Rubbing harder down the side of her clit she arched her back, moaning and groaning as her orgasm reached a climax. Then squeezing her legs together, trapping her hand as she brought herself off, her body jerked uncontrollably.

When she had satisfied herself fully, she slowly stretched her legs out. 'My, what a good boy, you didn't touch your cock at all, and I bet he's just aching to be fondled, isn't he?'

Paul was sweating. 'God, yes, miss . . . please.'

'All in good time,' she murmured, uncoiling herself like a cat from the sofa, and bringing her lips within a breath of his shiny purple knob. But the hope that she would give him a suck was dashed. She simply got to her feet and wandered off into the bedroom. 'Don't move. I'll be watching.'

Paul groaned. This was getting a bit much now.

She returned a few moments later, holding a massive pink dildo. Paul's mouth became parched.

'So, Paul, you like touching your cock. Well now I have a cock too. I wonder what I should do with it.'

He stared at it, not sure whether it was for him to use on her, or whether she was going to fuck him up the arse like last time.

She soon made it clear, when she strapped it on.

'Stand up, Paul. Now, bend over that chair again. I've something else for you now.'

Paul did as he was told and once again he bent over the back of the chair, quivering in anticipation of what was to come.

Charlotte paid the taxi driver and trudged exhausted up the steps into her flat. It was cold and dark and empty. She switched on the lights, closed the curtains and turned the radio on. She dropped her bags in the hallway and put the kettle on for coffee.

As she waited for it to boil she checked her answerphone for messages. There were two. One from her mum, and one from her editor asking if she was back yet. She knew there wouldn't be any from Paul. And certainly nothing from Andrew. He didn't even know her number.

The kettle clicked off and she made herself a cup of strong coffee. She supposed she ought to ring Paul and tell him she was back. And, if the opportunity arose, she would tell him their relationship was over. Better sooner than later.

Taking her coffee across to the phone, she picked up the receiver and pressed the redial button. It was what she always did, Paul invariably being the last person she'd called. This was the easiest way of redialling.

The phone rang and rang. She was on the verge of hanging up when an answerphone clicked in. She instantly thought she'd dialled the wrong number, as Paul didn't own an answerphone. Then she remembered she'd used the redial button, so couldn't have got it wrong. Obviously Paul must have used the phone after her.

She listened, curious as to who he'd phoned. A woman's voice came over the line. A husky-voiced female who clearly intended to sound sexy and seductive. Charlotte felt her skin crawl.

'Dominique speaking. I'm probably tied up at the moment, or tying someone else up. Leave a message and if you're good, I'll call you back.'

Bile rose in her throat and she slammed the receiver back on the hook. Shaking, she stared at it, then with trembling hands picked it up and pressed redial again.

Once more, there was the long ringing tone and finally the woman's message. Wretchedly, Charlotte hung the phone on to the hook and sank down on to the sofa. At least now she knew for certain.

It took only ten minutes to walk around to Paul's flat. The lights were on and the curtains drawn. Moving softly, Charlotte went up to his floor and turned her key in his lock silently, scarcely breathing.

The hall was in darkness, but his lounge door was ajar and from behind it she heard the distinct sound of voices.

She inched towards the door and peered through the crack. What she saw sent her reeling. Two bare backsides. One was a woman, wearing a headmistress's mortarboard and little else, and Paul's bare arse bent over the back of a chair while the woman slid a vibrator up his back passage.

'Don't move,' the woman said, taking the vibrator out of him and laying it down on an armchair. 'I'll be back in a moment, and if you've moved one muscle it's another spanking for you.'

The moment the woman disappeared into Paul's bedroom, Charlotte nipped in and snatched the vibrator up from where she'd left it. Without any preamble, she angrily shoved it up straight up Paul's backside, making him yelp.

'Please, miss, don't be so rough!'

'No talking!' The woman's authoritive voice echoed out from the bedroom.

'Huh?' Paul grunted, shooting up and swinging round to find Charlotte standing there. 'Shit!'

'Only a little bit,' Charlotte said glancing at the tip of the vibrator.

He had turned the colour of beetroot. 'Charlotte, babe,' he floundered. 'I can explain . . .'

Charlotte smiled coldly at him. 'Paul, let me tell you what you can do with your explanations. You can stick them where I've just stuck this dildo.' And turning, she strode towards the door. 'Bye, *babe*,' she called, not glancing back.

Only after she'd slammed the door behind her, and dashed out into the cool night air did she crumble. She had nothing left. No boyfriend, no Andrew. A little voice in her head reminded her she still had a job, which was something. After all it was a job she had always loved – until now.

She clung on to the thought of going into work in the morning. It was the only thing that got her through the night.

# Chapter Fifteen

'Charlotte these photos are fantastic!' her editor, Georgina Grey enthused as Charlotte laid out the photos she had selected from her developed films. The nude ones of Jamie were tucked away in her briefcase. The one of herself, which Andrew had taken, was in the top drawer of her desk.

It was the shot Andrew had taken just after they'd had anal sex that first time, and the look in her eyes reflected not only her satisfaction, but something else too. Something she could only describe as a look of love.

She could hardly send him that photo. There was no point now in him knowing she'd fallen in love with him. Let him put it all down to lust or whatever.

For now, she concentrated on the shots for her article. She was quite pleased with them all, particularly the ones of the Highland Ruby with the water cascading over it.

She smiled at the shot of the Highland cow.

'What's this?' Georgina smiled, looking at the impressive beast.

'A Highland cow,' Charlotte told her.

'My God, look at its horns!'

254

Charlotte had to smile to herself. 'Yes, I saw quite a lot of large horns in those Scottish Isles.'

Georgina raised her eyebrows speculatively but Charlotte was spared any inquisition when the telephone rang. Georgina picked it up.

'Georgina Grey.'

She listened, her eyes settling on Charlotte. 'Yes. Yes she is. I see, yes.' Her gaze flicked down to the photos then back to Charlotte. 'Well, it's very kind of you to let us invade your home, Mr Alexander . . .'

Charlotte's knees buckled. 'Andrew Alexander?' she hissed.

Her boss nodded, continuing to listen to what he had to say. 'Hopefully it will be out in the Christmas edition of the magazine. Yes, of course we'll send you a copy. My pleasure, and thank you once again. Goodbye, Mr Alexander.'

Charlotte reached out for the phone, her heart pounding, but Georgina had already replaced it.

'Oh sorry, did you want to speak to him?'

'No, no, I didn't.' There was a lump in her throat. Any second she knew the tears would start. She made her excuses swiftly. 'Runny nose, Georgina, must get a tissue.'

She fled from the office, squeezing her eyelids shut. She wouldn't cry, she wouldn't.

Back in the seclusion of her own little office, she closed the door behind her. Only then did she give way to an agonised sob. 'Oh Andrew,' she wailed softly, wishing with all her heart he was there.

'Yes?' came a familiar voice.

Her eyes flew open. He was seated at her desk, the photo of her topless wearing the Highland Ruby in his hands.

'The picture came out well,' he remarked glancing at it. 'Perhaps I could get a job as a photographer here.'

'Andrew!'

He got out of her chair and crossed the room. Charlotte

could only stand there, aware that she was shaking with disbelief and a million other emotions. Not least was that old familiar tingle between her thighs.

'Andrew!'

He smiled. 'So you keep saying.'

'You're here!'

'Where else should I be?' he asked, taking her into his arms and crushing her to him. 'Forgive me. I'm a fool. I overreacted when I saw those cuttings. I should never have behaved as I did. I'm so, so sorry.'

'It's all right,' she croaked, half-laughing, half-crying. 'As long as you know now I wasn't trying to write anything hurtful about you. I wouldn't. I love you too much.' As soon as the words were out she regretted them. Love was such a powerful admittance. The last thing she wanted was to frighten him off now.

But his smile lit up the whole of his face and he swooped her up in his arms, kissing her long and passionately. 'You don't know how good that sounds, Charlotte. I think I fell in love with you the minute I saw you with your clothes off.'

She laughed and kissed him again, aware that her tingling clit seemed to have a mind of its own, and was dearly in need of his attention just as much as her lips were.

'Talking of which,' he said, setting her back on her feet. 'Is there a lock on this door?'

Charlotte shook her head, then they both glanced at her desk and together shoved it across her office door. She'd dragged his jacket from his back before he could turn around. His shirt and tie were next.

'Oh, Andrew. I thought I'd never –'

He silenced her with a kiss. 'Enough time for talking later, just carry on with what you're doing.'

Her hands hovered around his trouser buckle, deciding to pay a little attention to his pectorals. Lovingly, her tongue began tracing a circle around each small nipple before biting them gently. Then her tongue slid right down his chest and flat stomach to the buckle on his belt. She felt his erection stiffen beneath her hands and saw the shape of his adored cock bulging.

She unfastened his buckle with a flick and unzipped him urgently. As he stepped out of his trousers, she fondled his erection through the soft fabric of his underpants, pulling his head down to kiss him. His cock hardened to her touch and began to peep over the rim of his underpants. Moaning softly, she slid them down and he stepped out of them.

Lovingly she took hold of his beautiful long hard shaft and slid her hand up and down its smooth length. Then, going down on to her knees, she took him hungrily into her mouth, swallowing him down into her throat, thrilling to the way he expanded even more inside her.

She never wanted to stop doing this. She felt this was what she was born to do. But Andrew had ideas of his own, and eventually raised her to her feet and began to undress her.

Suit-jacket first, so he could caress her breasts through her silk top. Then the top was stripped off followed by her bra. Holding her close it was his turn to bite and suck her nipples. Only his bites were more wicked, making her squeal with wanton desire.

'I'm going to strip you naked, Charlotte Harvey,' he said huskily, unbuttoning her skirt and letting it drop to the floor.

Charlotte stood there in stockings, suspender belt and panties. Andrew rolled his eyes heavenwards.

'God, you are so gorgeous, I am never going to get any work done ever again. All I'll ever want to do is make love to you.'

And to prove his point, he took her pants down, leaving her feeling utterly sexy in just her suspenders and stockings. He went down on to his knees, urging her to stand over him. Tilting back his head as she straddled him, he sucked her labia into his mouth, making her stagger.

Charlotte clung on to the top of his shiny dark head, as he brought her to a climax in a way she had never experienced before. He got to his feet then and led her by the hand to a revolving typist chair. He sat down, his magnificent cock standing to attention.

'Won't you sit down, my darling?' he smiled, his eyes darting wickedly down at his long hard shaft, then up to her.

'Thank you, I think I will,' she breathed, straddling him and feeling his hot shaft driving deep into her. She gasped, closing her eyes in ecstasy, and, throwing back her long flame-coloured hair, she rode him wildly.

Charlotte lost count of the number of times she came before he did. But eventually, they collapsed together still locked in the love embrace, her head on his shoulder his arms around her naked back, holding her so close Two hearts thudding together as one.

'I've got something in my pocket,' Andrew said when he had finally got his breath back.

'What's that?' Charlotte asked, kissing him again.

'I brought the Highland Ruby with me, just for luck.'

'You did? Why?' Charlotte puzzled, drawing her head back a little to study his handsome face.

He looked at her with such emotion that her heart flipped. 'Well,' he explained. 'I thought if I'd pushed you too far and you didn't want anything to do with me, I could slip the Highland Ruby around your neck and try to win you back with a bit of magic.'

'Oh, Andrew,' Charlotte breathed, already feeling him starting to harden against her again. 'The Highland Ruby may have brought us together to start with, but we don't need it to keep us together. The way I feel about you,' she added, gyrating her pelvis down on to his cock, 'that's magic enough.'

# Visit the *Black Lace* website at

## www.blacklace-books.co.uk

Find out the latest information and take advantage of our fantastic **free** book offer! Also visit the site for . . .

- All *Black Lace* titles currently available and how to order online
- Great new offers
- Writers' guidelines
- Author interviews
- An erotica newsletter
- Features
- Cool links

## *Black Lace* – the leading imprint of women's sexy fiction.

## Taking your erotic reading pleasure to new horizons

BLACK
lace

# BLACK LACE NEW BOOKS

*Published in October*

## ALL THE TRIMMINGS
Tesni Morgan
£6.99

Cheryl and Laura, two fast friends, have recently become divorced. When the women find out that each secretly harbours a desire to be a whorehouse madam, there's nothing to stop them. On the surface their establishment is a five-star hotel, but to a select clientele it's a bawdy fun house for both sexes, where fantasies – from the mild to the increasingly perverse – are indulged.

**Humorous and sexy, this is a fabulous yarn of women behaving badly and loving it!**

ISBN 0 352 33641 2

## WICKED WORDS 5
A Black Lace short story collection
£6.99

Black Lace short story collections are a showcase of the finest contemporary women's erotica anywhere in the world. With contributions from the UK, USA and Australia, the settings and stories are deliciously daring. Fresh, cheeky and upbeat, only the most arousing fiction makes it into a *Wicked Words* anthology.

**By popular demand, another cutting-edge Black Lace anthology.**

ISBN 0 352 33642 0

## PLEASURE'S DAUGHTER
### Sedalia Johnson
### £6.99

It's 1750. Orphaned Amelia, headstrong and voluptuous, goes to live with wealthy relatives. During the journey she meets the exciting, untrustworthy Marquis of Beechwood. She manages to escape his clutches only to find he is a good friend of her aunt and uncle. Although aroused by him, she flees his relentless pursuit, taking up residence in a Covent Garden establishment dedicated to pleasure. When the marquis catches up with her, Amelia is only too happy to demonstrate her new-found disciplinary skills.

**Find out what our naughty ancestors got up to in this
Black Lace special reprint.**

ISBN 0 352 33237 9

*Published in November*

## THE ORDER
### Dee Kelly
### £6.99

Margaret Dempsey is an Irish Catholic girl who discovers sexual freedom in London but is racked with guilt – until, with the help of Richard Darcy, a failed priest, she sets up The Compassionate Order for Relief – where sexual pleasure is seen as Heaven-sent. Through sharing their fantasies they learn to shed their inhibitions, and to dispense their alms to those in sexual need. Through the Order, Margaret learns that the only sin is self-denial, and that to err is divine!

**An unusual and highly entertaining story of forbidden lusts and
religious transgressions.**

ISBN 0 352 33652 8

## PLAYING WITH STARS
### Jan Hunter
### £6.99

Mariella, like her father before her, is an astrologer. Before she can inherit his fortune, she must fulfil the terms of his will. He wants her to write a *very* true-to-life book about the male sexual habits of the twelve star signs. Mariella's only too happy to oblige, but she has her work cut out: she has only one year to complete the book and must sleep with each sign during the month of their birth. As she sets about her task with enthusiastic abandon, which sign will she rate the highest?

**A sizzling, fun story of astrology and sexual adventure.**

ISBN 0 352 33653 6

## THE GIFT OF SHAME
### Sara Hope-Walker
### £6.99

Jeffery is no more than a stranger to Helen when he tells her to do things no other man has even hinted at. He likes to play games of master and servant. In the secrecy of a London apartment, in the debauched opulence of a Parisian retreat, they become partners in obsession, given to the pleasures of perversity and shame.

**This is a Black Lace special reprint of a sophisticated erotic novel of extreme desires and shameful secrets.**

ISBN 0 352 32935 1

*Published in December*

## GOING TOO FAR
### Laura Hamilton
### £6.99

Spirited adventurer Bliss van Bon is set for three months travelling around South America. When her travelling partner breaks her leg, she must begin her journey alone. Along the way, there's no shortage of company. From flirting on the plane to being tied up in Peru; from sex on snowy mountain peaks to finding herself out of her depth with local crooks, Bliss doesn't have time to miss her original companion one bit. And when brawny Australians Red and Robbie are happy to share their tent and their gorgeous bodies with her, she's spoilt for choice.

**An exciting, topical adventure of a young woman caught up in sexual intrigue and global politics.**

ISBN 0 352 33657 9

## COMING UP ROSES
### Crystalle Valentino
### £6.99

Rosie Cooper, landscape gardener, is fired from her job by an over-fussy client. Although it's unprofessional, she decides to visit the woman a few days later, to contest her dismissal. She arrives to find a rugged, male replacement behaving even more unprofessionally by having sex with the client in the back garden! It seems she's got competition – a rival firm of fit, good-looking men are targeting single well-off women in West London. When the competition's this unfair, Rosie will need all her sexual skills to level the playing field.

**A fun, sexy story of lust and rivalry ... and landscape gardening!**

ISBN 0 352 33658 7

# THE STALLION
Georgina Brown
£6.99

Ambitious young horse rider Penny Bennett intends to gain the sponsorship and the very personal attention of showjumping's biggest impresario, Alistair Beaumont. The prize is a thoroughbred stallion, guaranteed to bring her money and success. Beaumont's riding school is not all it seems, however. Firstly there's the weird relationship between Alistair and his cigar-smoking sister. Then the bizarre clothes they want Penny to wear. In an atmosphere of unbridled kinkiness, Penny is determined to discover the truth about Beaumont's strange hobbies.

**Sexual jealousy, bizarre hi-jinks and very unsporting behaviour in this Black Lace special reprint.**

ISBN 0 352 33005 8

# BLACK LACE BOOKLIST

**Information is correct at time of printing. To avoid disappointment check availability before ordering. Go to www.blacklace-books.co.uk**

All books are priced £5.99 unless another price is given.

**Black Lace books with a contemporary setting**

| | | |
|---|---|---|
| THE TOP OF HER GAME | Emma Holly<br>ISBN 0 352 33337 5 | ☐ |
| IN THE FLESH | Emma Holly<br>ISBN 0 352 33498 3 | ☐ |
| SHAMELESS | Stella Black<br>ISBN 0 352 33485 1 | ☐ |
| TONGUE IN CHEEK | Tabitha Flyte<br>ISBN 0 352 33484 3 | ☐ |
| SAUCE FOR THE GOOSE | Mary Rose Maxwell<br>ISBN 0 352 33492 4 | ☐ |
| INTENSE BLUE | Lyn Wood<br>ISBN 0 352 33496 7 | ☐ |
| THE NAKED TRUTH | Natasha Rostova<br>ISBN 0 352 33497 5 | ☐ |
| A SPORTING CHANCE | Susie Raymond<br>ISBN 0 352 33501 7 | ☐ |
| TAKING LIBERTIES | Susie Raymond<br>ISBN 0 352 33357 X | ☐ |
| A SCANDALOUS AFFAIR | Holly Graham<br>ISBN 0 352 33523 8 | ☐ |
| THE NAKED FLAME | Crystalle Valentino<br>ISBN 0 352 33528 9 | ☐ |
| CRASH COURSE | Juliet Hastings<br>ISBN 0 352 33018 X | ☐ |
| ON THE EDGE | Laura Hamilton<br>ISBN 0 352 33534 3 | ☐ |
| LURED BY LUST | Tania Picarda<br>ISBN 0 352 33533 5 | ☐ |
| LEARNING TO LOVE IT | Alison Tyler<br>ISBN 0 352 33535 1 | ☐ |

| | | |
|---|---|---|
| FORBIDDEN FRUIT<br>£6.99 | Susie Raymond<br>ISBN 0 352 33306 5 | ☐ |
| CHEAP TRICK<br>£6.99 | Astrid Fox<br>ISBN 0 352 33640 4 | ☐ |
| THE ORDER<br>£6.99 | Dee Kelly<br>ISBN 0 352 33652 8 | ☐ |

## Black Lace books with an historical setting

| | | |
|---|---|---|
| PRIMAL SKIN | Leona Benkt Rhys<br>ISBN 0 352 33500 9 | ☐ |
| DEVIL'S FIRE | Melissa MacNeal<br>ISBN 0 352 33527 0 | ☐ |
| WILD KINGDOM | Deanna Ashford<br>ISBN 0 352 33549 1 | ☐ |
| DARKER THAN LOVE | Kristina Lloyd<br>ISBN 0 352 33279 4 | ☐ |
| STAND AND DELIVER | Helena Ravenscroft<br>ISBN 0 352 33340 5 | ☐ |
| THE CAPTIVATION<br>£6.99 | Natasha Rostova<br>ISBN 0 352 33234 4 | ☐ |
| CIRCO EROTICA<br>£6.99 | Mercedes Kelley<br>ISBN 0 352 33257 3 | ☐ |
| MINX<br>£6.99 | Megan Blythe<br>ISBN 0 352 33638 2 | ☐ |

## Black Lace anthologies

| | | |
|---|---|---|
| CRUEL ENCHANTMENT<br>Erotic Fairy Stories | Janine Ashbless<br>ISBN 0 352 33483 5 | ☐ |
| MORE WICKED WORDS | Various<br>ISBN 0 352 33487 8 | ☐ |
| WICKED WORDS 4 | Various<br>ISBN 0 352 33603 X | ☐ |

## Black Lace non-fiction

| | | |
|---|---|---|
| THE BLACK LACE BOOK OF<br>WOMEN'S SEXUAL<br>FANTASIES | Ed. Kerri Sharp<br>ISBN 0 352 33346 4 | ☐ |

- - - - - - - ✂ - - - - - - - - - -

Please send me the books I have ticked above.

Name .............................................................

Address .............................................................

.............................................................

.............................................................

............................ Post Code

Send to: **Cash Sales, Black Lace Books, Thames Wharf Studios, Rainville Road, London W6 9HA.**

US customers: for prices and details of how to order books for delivery by mail, call 1-800-805-1083.

Please enclose a cheque or postal order, made payable to **Virgin Publishing Ltd**, to the value of the books you have ordered plus postage and packing costs as follows:

UK and BFPO – £1.00 for the first book, 50p for each subsequent book.

Overseas (including Republic of Ireland) – £2.00 for the first book, £1.00 for each subsequent book.

If you would prefer to pay by VISA, ACCESS/MASTER-CARD, DINERS CLUB, AMEX or SWITCH, please write your card number and expiry date here:

.......................................................................................

Please allow up to 28 days for delivery.

**Signature** ..........................................................................

– – – – – – ✂ – – – – – – – – – – – – – – – – – –